STUART CLARKE

DEITIES

Crystal Peake Publisher
www.crystalpeake.co.uk

First edition published in April 2019 by Crystal Peake Publisher

Print I S B N 978-0-9935582-8-3
eBook I S B N 978-0-9935582-9-0

Text copyright © Stuart Clarke 2019
Cover © Crystal Peake Publisher 2019

All rights reserved. No part of this publication may be reproduced, stored in or introduced into a retrieval system, or transmitted, in any form, or by any means (electrical, mechanical, photocopying, recording or otherwise) without the prior written permission of the publisher. Any person who does any unauthorised act in relation to this publication may be liable to criminal prosecution and civil claims for damages.

A catalogue copy of this book is available from the British Library.

Typeset by Crystal Peake Publisher
Cover designed by T K Palad

Visit www.crystalpeake.co.uk for any further information.

DEITIES

STUART CLARKE

To Nicole and Courtney,
my real life goddesses

CONTENTS

1. Somewhere between Heaven and Hell	11
2. The God of Leisure	16
3. Soul Swap Hold 'em	29
4. The Arrival	35
5. The Unexpected Visitor	44
6. The Elephant in the Room	52
7. Everybody's Talkin'	58
8. The Falcon in the Desert	66
9. Calling the Sun	71
10. Exit, Stage Left	79
11. The Lady in Blue	88
12. The Great Retreat	93
13. Your Desting is Around the Corner	97
14. The Meeting of the Minds	104
15. The Demon's Lair	110
16. The Reluctant Guest	114
17. The Fall of the House of Ra	124
18. Barter	135
19. A Future Cold Case	146
20. Hel on Earth	153
21. Following the Past	161

CONTENTS

22. This is a Good Thing, Right?	168
23. Return to Darkness	175
24. Quiet	181
25. Called to the Carpet	191
26. Wings	198
27. The Roman on the Mountain	206
28. You Can't Go Home Again	215
29. Back to the City	226
30. New Shoes	239
31. Not the Plain Old Plane	247
32. Winery Crashers	254
33. Halloween	263
34. Selection	272
35. By the Sea	281
36. Gold Futures	291
37. Berserker	298
38. Hell Reunited	307
39. Spirits of Ancient Egypt	323
40. Alley Cat	328
41. The Beast Unleashed	335
42. The Mountain Top	348

1
Somewhere between Heaven and Hell

Across the Ethereal Plane, a battle looms. Norse Frost Giants and Egyptian Demons struggle to assemble. They are unlikely allies in a war that has lasted a millennia. Still, these beings of The Darkness are aligned together, ready to strike down the forces of The Light.

The Frost Giants range in size from huge to massive and are armed with clubs and axes. They attempt to communicate with the Demons; however, the Demons speak in an ancient Egyptian tongue that makes conversing impossible. Hastily scrawled maps are drawn in the sand but they are difficult to decipher. This will not prove to be of much consequence as the plan is essentially to overpower those facing them.

Durinn, a dwarf, is a Norse general. His leadership and battle tactical abilities are superior; however, his forces are gravely outnumbered – a fact not lost on those in his charge.

One of his lieutenants, Nike, the Roman goddess of

DEITIES

Victory, stares across the Plane. 'There seem to be more of them today.'

Durinn nods. 'And fewer of us.'

It is a particularly foggy day on the Plane. The archers from The Light cannot hit their targets with regularity. This does not play to Durinn's advantage. In order to defeat the enemy, his forces need to keep them at bay. However, this battle will be fought at close quarters – further diminishing his odds in an already bleak situation.

The Frost Giants beat their chest and roar. The Demons light their spears. Within minutes, they will charge The Light.

At Durinn's command, the Roman and Greek demigods assume a defensive phalanx. His orders must be followed to the letter if they are going to survive the onslaught. Even still, the odds are stacked against them.

The Frost Giants charge directly into the clash, intent on making quick work of their enemy. The phalanx holds strong. For a while.

The Demons hurl their flaming spears into Durinn's defensives. Most of these are blocked by shields; however, many are not. A Roman demigod is pierced in the heart. He drops his bow and falls to the ground. The others leave him writhing in pain as his last seconds pass. There is nothing that can be done for him.

The Frost Giants swing their axes, beheading those on the front lines. At last, the archers can properly engage. Close range arrows pierce the mighty chests of demons and giants. But it is too little, too late. The phalanx collapses and the archers are overrun. The demigods scatter for protection, as the

STUART CLARKE

forces of The Light are routed.

An unidentifiable hero rides into the fray on horseback. This hero exhibits no fear and skillfully manoeuvres through the carnage. The Frost Giants take notice. They redirect their attention to this newcomer.

An alpha giant attacks. Wildly swinging a club, he attempts to knock the hero from the steed. His hands are met by the blade of a broadsword. The club and his hands fall to the ground. The Frost Giant wails but his agony is short-lived. The hero's blade slashes his throat and he drops to the ground. Dead. Or something like it.

The hero dismounts the horse and is soon surrounded by a pack of Demons. Flaming spears fly but they are blocked by a shield marked by a feline emblem. Soon, the cadre of Demons is reduced to nothing. Black ash fills the air.

The blunt end of a spear connects with the back of the hero's head. Now standing over the hero is a Demon with a newly lit spear. He thrusts it downward. The hero rolls away in the nick of time.

The Demon has trouble freeing the spear from the ground. Now, it is he who is in danger. Instead of fighting back, he seethes. 'Strike me down, slave to The Light. We shall meet again.'

'Perhaps. But not today.' The hero plunges the broadsword deep into the Demon's chest and he bursts into flames.

The remaining Frost Giants and Demons are intimidated. They scatter, rushing back to whence they came. They would regroup and live to fight again another day.

Satisfied, the hero sheathes the sword and removes the

DEITIES

helmet. A gush of dazzling reddish blonde hair falls to the shoulders. This is no hero – this is a heroine. Freya, the Norse goddess of Beauty stands triumphant, her exquisite looks matched only by her battle skills. She senses motion from behind and, in a single fluid motion, unsheathes her sword and holds it to the throat of her would be attacker.

'Easy.'

The voice of Durinn gives her pause. She sheathes the broadsword.

'What took you so long?' Durinn asked. 'So much for your legendary timing.'

Freya is still distracted. She watches the horizon intently. 'Maybe, I thought you'd handle this one on your own.'

Dismayed, Durinn responds. 'You do realise, O Queen of the Valkyries, how grotesquely outnumbered we are? And this isn't a recent occurrence. Our Egyptian brothers and sisters are not sending their troops as they once did.'

Freya stares him down. 'Of course, I am aware. But we must fight on. Our very existence depends upon it.'

Durinn nods. 'The Spheri Eternus. It is the last known portal between Heaven, Hell, earth and all other realms.'

'And need I remind you what will happen if The Darkness were to gain its control?'

'No. The Darkness would have carte blanche over the fate of all worlds. Life, as we know it, would end.'

The slightest glimmer of a smile creeps across Freya's face. At least, Durinn understands what is at stake.

Durinn, however, has not finished complaining. 'We are overrun on a daily basis. We are losing ground. Slowly, naturally but still. Our forces are no match for theirs. We need help from the Egyptians, or all will be lost.'

Freya's smile disappears. Instead, fury flashes in her eyes. 'You will follow my instructions. Now is a time to rise to greatness. I trust that is something you would like.'

Durinn stammers. 'Of course, it is, my queen. But reinforcements are needed.'

'And reinforcements you shall have. Athena is on a special mission to bring a major god back into the war.'

Durinn perks up. 'That is wonderful news! Could it be Horus, the Egyptian god of War? We need him! Or perhaps, Mars? Or Ares? Or even a trusted Greek Titan?'

Freya doesn't respond.

'Someone else, then?' Durinn asks. 'Can you give me a hint?'

Freya frowns. 'Word is, he was once quite the archer.'

Durinn puts his head in his hands. Apollo was not the god he was hoping for.

2
The God of Leisure

This little love nest has everything lovers could want. Canopied bed. Soft white linens. Room service. And a beautiful goddess.

Venus, the Roman goddess of Love and Beauty, lies naked across the bed. She has brought her hair down, so it covers the nipples on her exposed breasts. Just leaving a little to the imagination but not too much.

Venus is a sight to behold. Long blonde hair and a perfect hourglass figure. Her light skin and ruby lips are enough to make her an otherworldly pinup model but there is much more to her than that. Describing her sexual appetite as voracious does not do it justice – it is without bounds. She overwhelms every lover she's ever been with. All except Apollo.

She loves Apollo's suite in Heaven's hotel. It is a utopia for carnal delight. Dozens of candles flicker throughout the room. The walls, the ceiling and even the floor are mirrored – which makes every lovemaking session appear as an orgy. Except for the actual orgies; they appear as a carnal house of sexual depravity. Sofas and chairs aplenty are scattered throughout the room. And she's tried them all on for size.

****

The Hotel Bar in Heaven is a wondrous place. Gods and goddesses from a myriad of mythologies make reservations years in advance to taste the fine wines and nectars, to dine on the scrumptious ambrosias and just to be seen. It's an experience worth waiting several lifetimes to enjoy. And the waitlist is frequently that long.

The bar's colours are white and cerulean, the colour of the sky. Exotic flora decorates every nook and portico. Waterfalls emerge from thin air. And actual fluffy, white clouds float majestically in the air amongst the tables.

Most gods wait impatiently for their tables. The Atrium remains packed as no one seated ever wants to leave. However, most gods are not Apollo. Apollo doesn't just have a table – he has his own table. It remains empty just in case he decides to make an appearance. The sight of Apollo entering the bar makes the goddesses swoon and draws the ire of the male gods. They cannot help but like him, as arrogant as he may be.

Lesser Enochian angels escort Apollo past the velvet rope to his table, which offers a panoramic view of the Heavens. Already seated at his table is his best friend, Bacchus, the Roman god of Wine.

Bacchus rises to hug his pal. 'Running a little late there, Apollo. Was beginning to think you weren't coming.'

Apollo chuckles. 'I was with Venus, so I can assure you, I was coming.' Apollo takes a sip of the nectar that had been brought without a request. If there's one thing to love about Heaven, it's the service. 'She was insatiable today. Every time I tried to leave, she'd cling on tighter. I swear I was watching the sands fall through the hourglass, wondering when, or even if, I'd be allowed to make my escape.'

'Oh, to have such problems.' Bacchus grins. 'You know, I would expect Venus to have more self-respect. She is the Roman goddess of Beauty, after all.'

'I think you've solved the riddle, dear friend. She's Roman. Aphrodite would never sink to such levels.'

This angers Bacchus slightly. He is, of course, used to being treated like a knock-off god. A poor man's Dionysus. Still, his Italian vintages far exceed those of his Greek counterpart.

Bacchus' takes the last swallow of his wine and an angel immediately refills it. She pours slowly, trying to simultaneously be careful and catch Apollo's eye. However, she overfills Bacchus' glass, spilling drops of his precious wine on the table. In a flash, another angel is there to clean the mess.

Apollo cannot help but laugh at Bacchus' despair. He knows how much Bacchus values his wines – he brings his own bottles to supplement Heaven's vast wine list. To Apollo, it was particularly humourous that he was the cause of the mishap. Had he have looked her in the eye and winked, the angel might have emptied the entire bottle in Bacchus' lap.

Almost certainly the most handsome of the male gods, Apollo lived the life of a rock star in Heaven. The son of Zeus had it all – perfect looks, perfect charm all wrapped up in a perfect body. And his hair. Oh, how he loved his flowing sandy blonde curls.

Across the table was Bacchus. Bacchus was not as blessed with the physical beauty as his friend. He was slightly portly and his lips and teeth were permanently stained with red wine. However, Bacchus' quick wit and humourous observations still made him quite the hit with the goddesses.

'So, what shall we do today?' Bacchus asks.

'I thought we might eat and drink,' Apollo replies. 'But not necessarily in that order.'

Bacchus smiles. 'I was hoping you'd say that.'

They drink in silence for a few short minutes. Bacchus chugs his wine while Apollo sips nectar. Soon, they are joined by their friends – Pan and Kyrene.

Pan isn't a satyr. He is the satyr. A truly powerful wilderness god, at least in his heyday. Pan would party and frolic on earth where he was worshipped by shepherds and consorted with nymphs. Occasionally a hothead, Pan threw outrageous parties where he would panic the mortals by displaying his horns, tail and goat legs. But typically, he would entertain by playing his own invention, the pan flute.

Kyrene was a forest nymph. Petite and beautiful, she is one of the most desirable of all the nymphs. She harbours an unrequited crush on Apollo.

Sadly, Apollo doesn't show much interest. Still, he likes having her around. Eye candy that looks good on the arm. A cute sense of humour. Generally, Kyrene was a lot of fun but those occasional jealous fits make her the wildcard in this group.

Bacchus rises to greet his friends. He gives Pan a large hug. These two have three things in common – wine, goddesses and song. Kyrene is standoffish to Bacchus. She doesn't want to seem overly attentive to him, especially when Apollo is nearby.

DEITIES

Pan sits between Apollo and Bacchus. Kyrene deposits herself on Apollo's lap. Drinks for the two of them are brought immediately.

Apollo is taken aback. 'Uh, Kyrene?'

'Yes, my dear?' she responds.

'You should probably move. I can't reach my drink.'

Kyrene turns and picks up his glass. She wiggles a bit as she hands it to him. She frowns. 'Nothing going on down there?'

Bacchus laughs. 'He'd be a fertility god if there were. Apparently, he spent all day with Venus.'

Kyrene cheeks turn a shade of green. She gets up in a huff and sits in the chair furthest from Apollo.

Pan looks her way. 'I'm a fertility god,' he offers.

Kyrene snaps back. 'Not interested.'

This brings a hearty round of laughter from the table. All join in except Kyrene, who is still pouting.

'You know, all things considered, Heaven is a pretty wonderful place. Here, we sit back and relax. Nothing like the olden days, when we had mortals to worry with,' Bacchus muses.

'Ha! Mortals!' Apollo can barely contain himself. 'A fickle creature to be sure. Now, they worship different gods and some worship none at all.'

'I sometimes miss humanity, though,' Bacchus says. 'The offerings, especially. There was this one instance where a goat was sacrificed to me. A goat! Can you imagine?'

Pan is peeved. 'You got something against goats?'

'Of course not. It just seemed like they had the wrong god in mind.'

STUART CLARKE

Pan is still peeved. 'You know, there were plenty of goats sacrificed to me.'

'Of course, there were. I just didn't have any wine to go with such a scrumptious feast. I mean, what wine pairs well with stringy meat?'

Pan is about half a second from making a huge mistake. Rolling through his satyr mind is a question. Can he punch Bacchus and still be invited back into the VIP section in Heaven's atrium bar? Probably not. So, Pan thinks better of getting physical with Bacchus and instead lets loose a fiery insult. 'I'm sure Dionysus would have something appropriate. He certainly makes a lot more wine than you ever could.'

Bacchus is speechless. Fortunately, Apollo intervenes. 'Appropriate or not, I've always preferred Bacchus' vineyard to those of my half-brother's. So, you two relax and enjoy the sunset.'

Pan's glare eases. 'You were once the Sun God, I'm sure you received some of the most finest offerings.'

Apollo thinks backward in time. 'You know, the gifts would pile up at Delphi. And I'm speaking of real gifts – gold, silver and the like. There were so many, I took to distributing them among my followers. Nymphs, mostly.'

Kyrene's eyes shoot daggers across the table. 'I don't believe you ever gave any to me.'

'Well,' Apollo replies, 'I'm sure that was unintentional. I mean, I thought I serviced all the nymphs quite nicely.'

The green hue returns to Kyrene's face. She sits with her arms crossed and glares at Apollo.

Pan notices this and pretends to comfort her. 'Apollo

DEITIES

never gave me any gold either. But then, I assume he had no romantic intentions with me either.'

'That's enough, Pan,' Apollo said. 'She's angry enough as it is. No sense in making it worse.'

Kyrene is, for the moment, mollified.

Bacchus moves to change the subject. 'Here's something odd, Apollo. I was visiting Olympus and you will never guess who wasn't there.'

Apollo thinks. 'I don't know. My dad?'

'Exactly,' Bacchus verified. 'I mean, isn't he always there?'

'Pretty much. Unless he was out creating more half-siblings for me.'

Bacchus rubs his beard. 'Perhaps. But I got the impression he hadn't been there in some time.'

Apollo shakes his head. 'I'm the wrong one to ask about Zeus' whereabouts. I've been avoiding him for centuries.'

'Why is that?'

'Because Dad doesn't agree with his lifestyle,' a voice behind Apollo said.

Apollo turns around and is surprised to see his half-sister, Athena, the Greek goddess of Wisdom. 'Well sis, how wonderful to see you. But it's still early. Shouldn't you be off in battle? Fighting the good fight?'

'I left early today,' Athena replied. 'I'm on another mission.'

'And what mission might that be?' Apollo asked.

Before she could answer, Bacchus interrupts. 'What was the body count like today?'

Athena cocks her head. 'You're interested in the war?'

Bacchus smiles. 'Certainly. Mostly as a spectator, of course.

Did any major gods meet their demise today?'

'Well, not particularly. We did lose a Welsh river goddess named Damona.'

Bacchus high fives Pan although Pan seems less than thrilled about the news.

Athena is ticked. 'Okay, what was that about?'

'Can't tell you. You'll just get mad.'

'I'm already mad.'

Bacchus realises he probably shouldn't have said anything. 'It's just something Pan and I keep track of.'

Athena is fuming. 'Tell me you're not wagering on the battles.'

Bacchus is trapped. 'Well…'

Athena is now fully enraged. 'Listen, god of Drunkenness, do you have any idea what we're fighting for?'

Bacchus scratches his head. 'Is it still that portal thing?'

'Yes, damn you! Do you even know what happens if we lose control of it?'

Bacchus gestures as if he has an idea but in reality, he doesn't. 'Something bad?'

Athena sits down next to Apollo and slams her shield onto the floor. As soon as she sits, an angel dashes over with a glass of nectar.

'Yes, bad things. Very bad things. Including Heaven and Olympus being reduced to rubble. I'm sure you Romans must have a place that is sacred to you. That will be gone as well.'

Bacchus shudders.

Apollo intervenes. 'Okay, sis, I think he gets your point. So, you said you were on some sort of a mission?'

DEITIES

Athena exhales. 'Yes, Apollo, I am. I am here to recruit you to join the battle.'

The table explodes with laughter.

Athena ignores them the best she can and focuses on Apollo. 'We are losing this war. The Darkness continues to gain ground. Soon, they will overrun us entirely. We need someone strong to join us. We need you. I need you.'

Apollo waves her off. 'I have no interest in fighting. You know that. This is a conversation we've had before and frankly, one I am weary of.'

'You were such a wonderful warrior. You slew beasts and Titans. Olympus would have been destroyed if you and I had not saved it.'

Bacchus feels the need to re-engage the conversation. 'That was millennia ago. Apollo is not even the same Apollo.'

Athena ignores him. She grabs her bow from her back and hurls it at Apollo. He catches it by the grip inches before it would strike him in the face.

'Remember, how you used to use this bow? Remember Python? Remember your mother?' Athena asked. 'Oh, your twin sister, Artemis, has been missing for months. Likely being tortured by Anubis and his ilk. You want that on your head?'

Apollo stares at the bow. He falls into a trance.

****

Hera, the Greek goddess of Marriage, has little patience for Zeus' infidelities. From her throne on Mount Olympus, she summons the great monster, Python, to eliminate one of her rivals. She promises to reward her handsomely if she will kill Leto, the mother to Apollo and Artemis. Python is more than happy to take her up on this.

Hera directs Python to Mount Parnassus, where Leto's home is. Though a goddess, Leto lives a simple and quiet life. She hides from Hera's wrath and picks olives from the nearby vines.

Python spies Leto near a creek. She is washing her face and her flowing robe rustles in the breeze. The slight sound of the wind gives Python the ability to move undetected. She slithers and stalks Leto, preparing to strike.

By the time Leto looks up, Python is close by. She cocks her massive head. 'I assume you know who I am.'

Leto stands stunned. 'Hera sent you. Am I right?'

'That she did. So, I assume you know why I'm here.'

Leto nods. She slowly backs away from the giant serpent but trips and falls to the rocky ground.

Python arches the muscles in her back, bringing her monstrous head high in the air. With the majority of her body on the land, she is roughly twenty feet tall. Her lengthy tongue reaches out a few feet from Leto's face.

Leto is not going down without a fight. She flings rocks at the Titan's head. This only serves to anger her.

'Oh, Leto,' she says, 'I was going to make this quick and painless. But now, I think I'll have a little fun before devouring you.'

Python swings her mighty tail at Leto's legs. She falls hard on the rocky ground. She struggles to her feet but is met once again with the tremendous force of the tail. She is flung solidly against the base of the mountain.

Python slithers closer. Her forked tongue is now fully in

DEITIES

range of Leto's face, so Python licks Leto's skin and ululates with satisfaction. 'I'm torn,' she said. 'Do I swallow you whole? Or do I squeeze the life out of you first? Either way, I will feed well today.'

Python suddenly feels a sharp pain in her back. She turns quickly to see the shaft of an arrow protruding from her skin. She simultaneously hits Leto with her tail and looks to find the perpetrator of the arrow.

It is Apollo, maybe eight years of age. The youngster has readied his golden bow to launch another missile into the serpent.

Python smiles as only a snake can. 'Ah, Apollo, how convenient of you to make an appearance. You can bear witness to your mother's undoing before I kill you as well. My reward will most certainly be increased tenfold.'

'Apollo! Run!' Leto screams.

'Sorry, mother, that I cannot do,' Apollo replies. He fires another arrow towards the great beast but it misses its mark.

Python laughs. 'You're a little out of your element, young one. Perhaps, you should listen to your mother. Not that it will do you any good now.'

Leto rises to her feet and leaps onto the serpent's back. Python shakes Leto off as if she were a gnat, sending her flying back to the base of the mountain.

But now, Apollo is ready. Python turns to look at him as Apollo's arrow connects with the serpent, piercing her eyelid and blinding her in her right eye. A second later, Apollo has reloaded. His aim is once again true and Python's left eye goes dark.

Now all Python can do is thrash about wildly. She hisses. 'Come closer, young one. This fight is not yet complete.'

'Apollo,' his mother pleads. 'Please take your leave at once. She cannot hurt us anymore.'

'I don't think that's the case,' Apollo replies.

Python's huge nostrils flare. She can smell Apollo. She slithers towards him and arches her back. She is preparing to strike.

However, Apollo does not back down. A fresh arrow lines the bow. He lets loose of the string and the arrow lodges in Python's throat. The serpent can no longer breathe. She coughs and desperately tries to remove the barb. But Apollo is on her in a flash, driving the arrow deeper into Python's neck. Python falls to the ground with a tremendous thud. She would be the first Titan Apollo slew but certainly not the last.

Leto scolds her son for not listening to her requests. 'Apollo, I told you to run. Why would you not listen to me?'

'Because only I could save you.'

*****

'Apollo! Apollo!' Athena is practically screaming in his ear. This awakens Apollo from his archery-induced trance. She is furious. 'Have you listened to a word I've said?'

'Most of it,' Apollo lies.

'I'll bet he was daydreaming about Venus,' Bacchus inserts.

Expecting the worst, Athena says, 'Please tell me you weren't.'

'No. I wasn't. But thanks for asking.' Apollo replies, copping an attitude.

'Well, what then?'

DEITIES

Almost on cue, Venus enters Heaven's atrium. Apollo notices her immediately. She looks fabulous. Her blonde hair was perfect. She oozes sensuality, wrapped in a sultry, skintight satin sheath. All the male gods and most of the goddesses leer lustily in her direction. She air-kisses all she comes in contact with but makes a beeline towards Apollo. When she arrives at his table, she plants a prolonged French kiss on his lips.

Bacchus and Pan's jaws drop to the floor. Kyrene turns a green shade of envy. Athena simply rolls her eyes.

'Not this again,' Athena mutters.

Venus extends her hand to Apollo. He rises from the table and begins to follow her.

Athena is livid. 'Please, Apollo, think about what we were talking about. We need you in this war.'

Apollo smirks. 'I will give it all the necessary consideration it is due.'

Bacchus laughs. 'Athena, I think you have your answer.'

Suddenly, Apollo begins to phase in and out of view. Literally becoming transparent. Venus drops his hand in utter fright.

Bacchus is astonished. 'Apollo, you're disappearing!'

Apollo winks. 'Of course I am. Wouldn't want to keep the goddess of love waiting.'

Athena cries, 'No, Apollo, you're really vanishing. I can see through you!'

Apollo looks at his hands and sees they are right. His hands are barely visible. 'What is happening to me?'

He barely gets the words out before he disappears completely. The patrons of Heaven's Atrium murmur in shock.

3
Soul Swap Hold 'em

The Treachery Bar and Grill lies within the Ninth Circle of Hell. Here history's villains wish they could meet their final demise. However, that is not to be. Outside, their agony is apparent. Some are buried from the waist down in deep ice; others are completely encapsulated in it. Just outside of their senses is warmth. But they will never feel it. They will never escape their curse.

On the inside, the denizens are able to move freely. Here, the Lords of the Underworld relax. Embers from the burning ceiling fall upon them but they do not mind. The Treachery Bar is a favourite place.

Hades, the Greek god of the Underworld; Pluto, the Roman god of the Underworld; and Hel, the Norse goddess of Death sit at a table fashioned of human remains. The tabletop is made of stretched skin. The table legs are constructed of bones. The chairs are a mixture of each. Skulls rest upon the backs of their seats.

The three are engaged in a never-ending game of Soul

DEITIES

Swap Hold'em. These gods do not wager money – they wager the very essence of those around them. Each chip is inlaid with souls desperately trying to escape their eternal predicament. But no relief will ever occur. Their very essence will belong to Hades. Or Hel. Or Pluto.

Hel collects the antes and deals the cards. Without even looking at his hand, Hades goes all-in. The others immediately fold.

Hel makes an observation. 'It is my understanding that these games of chance are more interesting when clairvoyance is not evoked.'

Pluto nods. 'Perhaps, we could try playing without seeing into the future.

Hel laughs. 'I'm not sure that's possible. I trust you two less than I trust Loki.' Hel is the quintessential Goth goddess. Spiked black hair, porcelain skin, piercing green eyes and a generally nasty attitude. The war is her favourite pastime. Occasionally, she will lead her beloved Frost Giants across the Ethereal Plane. They tend to fare better when she is by their side. Her beauty lies on the right side of her face. The left side, not so much. It is like a skull, an astounding dissimilarity from the right. She's delectable on one segment but equally frightening on the other.

Hades tosses his chips into the center of the table. 'Well then, I'm bored. Surely someone must have a devious plan. It's not like we have mortals to torment any longer.'

There is a silence at the table. Hel lights a cigar off of the burning chair behind her. 'I understand there is a woodland festival hosted by Pan,' she says, 'Perhaps, we could terrorise some fauns and nymphs. I particularly dislike the nymphs.'

Hades shrugs. 'Seems like we do that a lot. Never really accomplishes anything except for minor amusement. Pluto? You have any ideas?'

Pluto doesn't speak very often. At a whopping six-foot-six and two hundred eighty pounds, he's essentially the muscle of the group. But he's as slow as he is big. 'How about this?' Pluto said. 'We could invade Jotenheim. I've never killed a Frost Giant before.'

Hades winces. He knows what to expect.

Hel's eyes flash from green to red. 'You do know that the Frost Giants are in my charge, right? Or are you really that dense?'

Pluto doesn't understand. 'I thought we were fighting the Frost Giants. Do I have that wrong?'

Hel backhands Pluto across the face.

Hades laughs. 'Be careful, Hel hath fury.'

This draws the ire of the god sitting alone at the neighbouring table. Anubis, the Egyptian god of the Underworld, has casually watched the exchanges between the three but now he is annoyed. Nobody, including Hel, can lay a hand on Pluto. Especially, when he figures so deeply in Anubis' plan.

Anubis walks to the table and violently lifts Hel from her seat. He twists her arm behind her back. Hel moans in pain. Hades rises to confront Anubis. Anubis lets go of Hel and reaches for a red-hot poker stick from one of the Treachery's many fireplaces. He holds it to Hades' face. 'Do you remember who the leader is here? Or would this flaming stick lodged into

DEITIES

one of your eye sockets help remind you?'

Hades relents. 'You, my Lord, are the leader.'

'Yes. And you will not question my actions again.' Anubis points to Hel, who is still rubbing her elbow. 'You two should get out of my sight. I have important matters to discuss with Pluto.'

Hades takes Hel by the hand and leads her away. She glares daggers as she takes her leave.

Anubis invites Pluto to his private table. There, his jackal-headed helmet rests. Anubis lays it aside. He wants to talk to Pluto god-to-god.

'Pluto, do you believe in fate?'

'Well, yes. Of course.'

'You are wrong. There is no such thing as fate. Not for immortals, anyway.'

Pluto nods as if he understands.

Anubis continues. 'We are gods. Gods make their own choices, take their own risks and reap their own rewards.'

The beautiful demon goddess Inanna slinks behind Anubis as he speaks. Her forked tongue licks him on the neck and earlobe. But Anubis is far too focused on Pluto to pay her any attention.

'Pluto, let me tell you a story. I was once a minor deity. Set, the Desert god, pushed me from my station. He trampled upon my ambitions and left me to survive on my own. But you see, Set had an enemy, Osiris. They waged war of epic proportions until Set ultimately defeated him. However, Osiris had a son. You know him as Horus. And what Set wasn't counting on was what a worthy adversary Horus would be.'

STUART CLARKE

Anubis shrugs Inanna off and rises from the table. Pluto joins him and they walk and talk.

'All of Set's time was spent battling Horus. And that's when I made my play to recapture the Underworld. Set's armies were depleted and no match for mine. I regained my place and have held it for thousands of years. Do you understand what I am telling you?'

Pluto is slow to answer. 'I think so.'

'Then, let me spell it out for you. I made my own choices, took my own risks and reaped my own rewards. I have no use for fate. And neither should you.'

Pluto still does not understand.

'And don't think that The Light doesn't engage in similar atrocities. All of those Titans were not evil, yet they still suffered. Prometheus gave fire to the mortals. Zeus murdered Kronos, his own father. And then, there's the story of Helios, the Greek Sun god. His son was tragically killed and during his period of mourning, Zeus replaced him with his own offspring.'

Pluto connects the dots. 'Apollo.'

Anubis smiles. 'The very same.'

'I did not know the true history.'

'So now I look to you, my new general. This is your time. This is your chance. This is time to reap your rewards.'

Pluto looks confused. 'My liege, I do not understand.'

'I am offering you the opportunity to erase this son of Zeus with impunity. You will deal a harsh blow to The Light and be celebrated like never before. Hades would kill for a mission such as this. I trust you will too.'

'But how?' Pluto asks. 'I cannot breach Heaven's gates or Mount Olympus. And he is immortal. He cannot die.'

'Ah but you will not be going to Heaven nor Mount Olympus.'

'Where, then?'

Anubis smiles an evil grin. 'Oh, I'll think you'll like my plan.'

4
The Arrival

Seated alone at an isolated table, Apollo materialises in both an unlikely and convenient location. A fraternity toga party. Good thing he was dressed for the occasion.

He stares at his hands, running one over the other to make sure they are real. He gently touches his face and hair, making sure they were also intact. Satisfied, he observes his surroundings.

The strobe lights confuse him, especially the way they bounce off the mirrored ball attached to the ceiling. He is confused by the décor – cheap furnishings, man chairs and grimy tables. But what challenges him most are the Greek letters attached to the largest wall. They didn't spell anything. Just letters. An Alpha, a Tau, an Omega. Other than being in the correct order, Apollo couldn't make sense of the word. Maybe a new dialect sprung up while he wasn't paying attention.

Music blares through the house speakers. Well, not any type of music Apollo was familiar with. It was a mixture of

DEITIES

Hip-Hop, 80's New Wave and current dance music. Basically, it was just noise at an earsplitting volume. He rises from the table, intent on seeking out its source. He could show them what real music sounded like.

He manoeuvred through the crowd of frat boys and college coeds. They were dancing and grinding upon each other as if sex was in the making. Apollo could not help but smile. The mating calls of mortals never failed to amuse him.

Apollo searches the room, trying to find the source of the noise but a young coed intercepts him. 'Hey there, hottie,' she slurs. 'What's going on under the toga?'

Apollo is baffled by the question. 'Whatever do you mean?'

She whispers in his ear loudly, 'You can tell me. I won't tell. Promise.'

'I'm not sure I understand your query.'

She flicks ash onto the floor. 'Come on. Boxers or tighty-whiteys? What are you wearing beneath the sheet?'

Apollo is still confused. 'What one usually wears beneath a toga.'

'Ah, so you're going commando. Very sexy. I'm Jinna, by the way. And you are?'

He is surprised not to be recognised. 'Apollo, god of Music and Light,' he replies.

Jinna flashes a Mona Lisa smile. 'I do like how seriously you are taking this party. Are you an actor? A musician?'

'Both.'

Another song plays – this one worse than the last. Apollo's head throbs. 'Could you please direct me to the musicians? I'd like to discuss their questionable talent.'

STUART CLARKE

She takes the final drag of her cigarette and discards it to the floor. 'There is no band here tonight. Just a deejay,' she responds and gestures. 'Just a deejay. He's over there.'

At last, Apollo spies the source of the noise. A man wearing a baseball cap backward with a t-shirt that read 'Shirt With Words On It' stands behind a table surrounded by foreign technology. 'I need to talk to that man. Something isn't right.'

Jinna lights another cigarette. 'Well, don't go too far. I'll be watching for you.'

Apollo approaches the deejay. True to Jinna's words, this is from where the noise was emanating. Cautiously, Apollo runs his hands over the equipment. He feels the bass and can barely distinguish it from the treble. This is not music. It is little more than clamour. He reaches past the woofer and places his hands on the glowing machine – the deejay's laptop.

The deejay reacts gruffly. 'Don't touch that, frat boy. This shit's expensive. Break it and your daddy will have to buy me a new one.'

Apollo removes his hand from the device. 'What is it?'

'This is how music is made, dude. I have over one hundred thousand songs on this puppy. Got anything you'd like to hear?'

Apollo thinks. 'I did enjoy the Classical period. I had a reemergence then.'

The deejay shakes his head. 'You and me both. But this isn't exactly the Classic Rock sort of crowd. I can probably sneak a Cars song in though. That work for you?'

Apollo doesn't know how to respond. He's never heard of anything called Classic Rock, much less, The Cars. But still, he nods. Anything would be better than the aural assault he was

DEITIES

experiencing.

He backs away from the deejay and knocks over a vacant table near the back of the room. He stands over it and waits.

A voice from the next table calls to him. 'Hey, idiot. Whatcha standing around for?'

Apollo turns. He sees a black-haired man with sun-worn skin sitting alone at a table near the exit. 'This table has been upended. I assume someone will tend to it, so I might sit.'

'Might be waiting a while.' The man rises and turns the table upright. He motions for Apollo to join him.

'Thirsty?' the man asks. He offers his bottle of Budweiser to Apollo.

'Parched.' Apollo takes a swig of the man's beer and promptly spits it to the floor.

'Not a beer man, I take it. Not to worry, it was mostly backwash.'

'I don't suppose there is any nectar in this dingy abode?'

The man laughed. 'The closest thing to nectar you'll find is the hunch punch. And I don't recommend it. It's a little stronger than what you're used to in your realm.'

Apollo looks a tad confused. 'My realm? Which realm am I in now?'

'You're on earth. idiot.'

Apollo shakes his head. 'No, this is not earth. I've been to earth. It was never this filthy.'

'But it's been a while, hasn't it? A lot has changed. Besides, this is not Greece. It is an area the locals refer to as California.'

'Never heard of it.'

'It's new. They didn't have it in your heyday. And sitting up on a Heavenly barstool has caused you to lose touch with the mortals.'

'How do you know how I pass my time?'

'Just a guess. How else would you be so naïve?'

Apollo becomes angry and raises his voice. 'I will listen to your insults no longer. Do you not know you sit before the great Phoebus Apollo, god of Music and Light?'

'Cool your jets,' the man replies. 'I know damn well who you are. It's just the great Phoebus Apollo, god of Music and Light is such a mouthful.'

'And who might you be?'

'You should call me Coyote.'

'Coyote? Strange name. But tell me, how do I get out of this godforsaken place? Surely, there is a portal nearby.'

Coyote grins. 'Afraid not. I think you'll like earth though. I'd like to show you around. But first thing's first. We gotta get you in some regular clothes. I can't be seen with you dressed in a bedsheet.'

Apollo looks at his toga. It was one of his finest and he was reluctant to part with it. But he was always keen to add to his wardrobe. 'How do we do that?'

Coyote rises. 'Follow me.'

Coyote leads Apollo up a flight of a dimly lit staircase. There he finds the fraternity bedrooms. Coyote opens the first door he sees. Inside they find a couple having sex. The girl rides the fraternity boy. They are surprised to see Coyote.

'Hey, close that door!' the fraternity boy demands.

Coyote makes a half-assed attempt at an apology. 'Sorry, wrong room.'

DEITIES

Coyote and Apollo make their way down the hall. Coyote reaches for the doorknob. It is locked. Coyote reaches into his jacket pocket and produces a lock pick set. 'Apollo, you're on lookout duty,' he says as he inserts the pick into the lock.

Apollo isn't exactly sure what 'lookout duty' is. But fortunately, no one happens to walk by in the short amount of time it takes Coyote to open the door. Coyote invites Apollo to step inside.

The room looks like a Federal Disaster Area. Clothes are scattered everywhere. The odour of dirty underwear and socks fill the cramped quarters. Apollo winces at the stench. Coyote laughs. 'Doesn't look like he does much laundry, does he?'

Coyote begins rifling through the desk of a fraternity boy until he finds what he wants – the wallet. He pulls out forty dollars in crumpled bills before tossing the wallet over his shoulder. Then, he turns his attention to the closet. He swings open the door and is satisfied with what he sees. 'Jackpot.'

Coyote motions for Apollo to join him. Coyote passes Apollo a button-up blue and white shirt. 'What do you think of this shirt?'

'It looks like a tunic worn by a Greek peasant woman,' Apollo replies.

Coyote cocks his head. It kind of did look like that. 'Well, it's all the rage now. Put it on you'll look great.'

Coyote looks back inside the closet, hoping to find a pair of jeans that are relatively clean. He finds a pair that are grey-black. He turns to see Apollo standing naked before him, struggling with the buttons. Coyote is astonished at Apollo's penis. He throws the jeans to Apollo. 'Good god, cover that monster up before I get a complex.'

It takes Apollo quite a while to get the buttons worked out. Then, he attempts the jeans. His sandal gets caught in the pants leg.

'You are hopeless! Sandals off!'

Eventually, Apollo figures it out. Coyote smells a pair of socks. Clean enough. He tosses them to Apollo. 'These go on your feet.' Coyote pulls out a pair of boots and a black leather jacket. Apollo's makeover is complete.

'How do I look?' Apollo asks.

'Like every pussy hound in the city. You'll fit right in.'

****

Coyote and Apollo make a hasty retreat down the back stairs. Once outside, they hear the muffled screams of a girl. It is Jinna and she obviously doesn't want to have anything to do with the frat boy who's trying to stick his tongue down her throat.

'Stop!' she demands. But her protests are falling on deaf ears. This boy isn't taking 'no' for an answer.

'We need to do something,' Apollo whispers to Coyote.

'No, we don't. I keep a strict no interference policy. This does not concern us.'

Despite Coyote's disapproval, Apollo walks to the scene. 'Let her go.'

The frat boy does not release his grip on Jinna. 'What's it to you?'

'Where I come from, true men do not force themselves upon unwilling females. They use their wit, charm and good looks. All of which, you lack.'

DEITIES

The frat boy pushes Jinna to the ground. 'It seems only fair to warn you, I am a black belt.'

Apollo whispers to Coyote. 'What's a black belt?'

'Oh, I have a feeling you're about to find out.'

The frat boy is inches away from Apollo's face. He pushes Apollo in the chest. Apollo does not push back. The frat boy repeats his assault. Again, Apollo does not respond.

'What is the matter, tough guy? Don't want to fight? Fine by me. You and your little friend should run.'

'I think it's only fair to warn you that I am a god.'

The frat boy laughs. 'Well, I shouldn't be any challenge for you then. Go ahead, take a swing at me.'

'I do not fight with mortals.'

The frat boy shoves Apollo in the chest again. Now, Apollo is angry. He throws a punch that the frat boy easily blocks. The frat boy follows the block with a punch in the ribs. Apollo doubles over. The frat boy prepares to hit Apollo in the face, when…

SMACK!

Coyote hits the frat boy with a cinderblock.

Jinna is most grateful. She hugs Apollo. 'Thank you for standing up for me. Most people wouldn't have done that.' She gently touches Apollo's ribs. 'I'm sorry you got hurt.'

She turns to Coyote. 'Thank you for your help as well.'

Coyote grimaces. 'As well.' He looks at Apollo. 'We should really get moving.'

'Shouldn't we escort the lady home?' Apollo asks.

Coyote shakes his head. 'She'll be fine as long as she stays away from frat boys.'

Apollo looks apologetically at Jinna. 'Be careful. Apparently, there are some gods less benevolent than me.'

Jinna leaves; Coyote seems energised. 'Come Apollo. We have a city to explore.'

5
The Unexpected Visitor

A grey-bearded god atop a white stallion crests a hill and Valhalla comes into view. He rides alone yet requires no protection. As he gallops towards the Great Hall, plants bend in their stems as a show of reverence.

He is not a native here but all know who he is upon sight and sound. His very presence creates a vibration in the air. It is Poseidon, the Greek god of the Sea. He sports a thick, greying beard.

He approaches the gates of Valhalla. As his stallion comes to a stop, the gates have already begun to open for him. He dismounts his steed and approaches the entrance. He passes his trident to a high-ranking Norse guard. He will not need it here.

Poseidon enters the legendary hall of the slain. A clear pathway has been left unobstructed through the middle of the mass of dead warriors. Poseidon makes his way to the center of the hall to an awaiting Odin, the chief Norse God.

However, as the warriors bow, there are whispers amongst

them. Was Poseidon expected? The legendary fanfare preceding this meeting could have only meant one Greek god and that was Zeus.

Odin notices his warriors peeking up to look upon the face of Poseidon. He taps his cane on the ground, creating a small quake. The warriors now keep their eyes to the ground and their lips sealed.

Odin and Poseidon are now face-to-face. They smile and share a long embrace.

'My friend, it has been far too long,' Odin says. 'Thank you for coming on such short notice.'

Poseidon nods. 'It must be centuries. We should make an effort to visit more frequently.'

'I'm afraid that this cannot be a social call. I am certain that Zeus has explained what has transpired.'

Poseidon hesitates. He doesn't know. 'Perhaps, I could hear it from you. My brother was somewhat vague on the matter.'

'I am certain he is most concerned. I have sent messengers to Olympus but they have not returned.'

'When I return to Olympus, I will ask Hermes to seek for answers. Surely, there must be an explanation. It is possible that he is on one of his self-imposed sabbaticals. Zeus is very difficult to reach when he breaks from us. That is why I came in his stead.'

Odin scratches his long, grey beard. 'I see. Well, I hope you are able to compensate for his absence. The days are dwindling, Poseidon. I fear that the final battle, Ragnarok, may be coming upon on us. I have spent my entire life in an attempt to quell the Prophecy.'

DEITIES

'And don't think for one second that your efforts are underappreciated. No one wants to see the Prophecy come to its fruition. The final war between good and evil translates to tremendous casualties for both sides.'

'That it will.' Odin looks thoughtful. 'But these casualties will be different. We, as gods, may die but regenerate in a matter of days. Once Ragnarok begins, the death becomes permanent.'

Poseidon's eyes widen. 'You are certain of this?'

'It is written and so I believe.'

Poseidon follows Odin down a long hall to an empty table set for two. The view is amazing. Poseidon cannot help but gaze through the windows at the majestic glory just outside the glass. A large stag comes into view. It eyes Poseidon as it chews grass.

A tray of drinks is brought to the gods by a gorgeous Norwegian warrior. Like the others in Valhalla, she died on the battlefield. She is honoured to be serving Odin.

'There are three glasses on the table, Odin. Are we expecting a third?'

'No. I must insist you try our mead. I assure you it is quite delicious.'

Poseidon lifts the mug and smells it. It seems okay. 'Would you like to propose a toast?'

Odin smiles. 'To Zeus. May he return soon.'

Odin takes a healthy swig of mead. Poseidon tries to drink it but it is sticky sweet. He has a hard time swallowing it.

Odin laughs. 'You were wondering what the third glass was for?' He reaches under the table and reveals a bottle of wine. 'Imported from Bacchus himself.' Odin summons the Norwegian warrior to open the jug.

Poseidon is gracious. 'Thank you. This is much more in my palate.'

'I thought it might be. But I do hope you're not going to give up on mead entirely. It is quite the delicacy here.'

'Perhaps, I shall brave it another time. But for now, I'll stick with the wine.'

Odin suddenly changes the subject. 'It is my understanding that the battles are being lost due to a lack of forces. I've heard from my generals that the Egyptians are not defending the portal.'

'I have heard rumours to that effect.'

'It is Athena's summation that I would value most. Could you get verification from her?'

Poseidon sits very still. 'You know Athena is not in my graces.'

Odin stares down the Greek god. 'Now is not the time to allow petty quarrels interfere with the larger landscape. We do not have that luxury.'

Poseidon relents. 'Of course. I value her opinion as do you.'

'If this is true about the Egyptians, Ra will need to be reminded that the portal affects all planes. His included.'

Poseidon considers this. 'Yes. But we must be careful not to offend him. He can become quite pompous and defensive.'

'Harsh words, Poseidon. Harsh but accurate.' Odin is satisfied, yet troubled. 'There is one other item I want to discuss. This has more relevance to Zeus but it affects you as well.'

'What is that?'

'This game. This new game. The rules are not yet set but the first pawn has moved.'

Poseidon is confused by this statement. He is beginning to think he is listening to the ramblings of an old man. 'I do not understand.'

'There is a wild tale circulating that one of your nephews has disappeared.'

'Which of my nephews? Like you, I have many. Zeus sees to that.'

'It is Apollo. He vanished from Heaven without a trace. Multiple gods claimed to have witnessed the event.'

Poseidon looks relieved. 'Apollo is most likely on a love tryst amongst the forest nymphs. Or the Roman demigods. Or perhaps an Egyptian deity. I wouldn't put much faith in such speculation.'

Odin stands his ground. 'I dreamt he had fallen to earth and the very next day this 'speculations' began in earnest.'

'Earth? Why earth? None of us have been there in centuries.'

'This is true and is what worries me most.'

Poseidon counters, 'With all due respect, I feel your worries are unnecessary.'

'That is my sincerest hope. But as a precaution, I have dispatched a reliable escort to see to his safe return. He is in good hands.'

Poseidon exhales. 'That is a relief. No being of The Light, particularly an Olympian, should be in danger.'

Odin lets Poseidon's statement of superiority pass. 'Gather the wisest among you so that we can reconvene. Take note, I do expect to see Athena amid our presence. Put your feud on hold for now. The Light must come together as one.'

'What of earth? Will they be spared from this game of gods?'

Odin is silent for a moment. 'I fear not. In our absence, humanity has lost its way. Many mortals may fight with us but others share parallels to The Darkness. Their losses will be great in number.'

Poseidon has an idea. 'I shall contact Thoth before attempting to reason with Ra.'

'My memory is sometimes like that of an old man. Which god is Thoth?'

'He's a counsellor of Ra. He's the Egyptian god of Wisdom and Jurisprudence. He's the god we need on our side as he has the Sun God's ear.'

Odin is impressed. 'It is time for us to get to work. If you like, I can come to Olympus for our next meeting.'

'I think I'd prefer to come to you. Maybe, I'll even sample your mead again.'

Odin laughs. 'I'll keep plenty of wine on hand, just in case.'

'Well, my lord. We have much to accomplish. I'd best take my leave.'

Poseidon rises and walks the hall alone. The massive

DEITIES

doors are opened for him and his stallion awaits him. He relieves the guard of his trident and mounts the horse to journey back to the sea.

****

The Norwegian warrior refills Odin's mead and he is soon joined by Njord.

'Sit,' Odin offers.

Njord takes the seat across from Odin where Poseidon had been sitting. He winks at the warrior. She blushes.

'I suppose you know why I asked for you,' Odin says.

'Could be one of two reasons. Could be because I'm part of the Vanir and you need a seer. Or it could be because I'm the god of the Sea and you just met with my rival.'

Odin smiles. 'Could be both. As a member of the Vanir, you have great wisdom and can predict the future. And thus, I need your advice.'

'Yes, I would be honoured to provide you with all that I know.'

Odin scratches his beard. 'What do you see happening in the coming months?'

'Many things. However, most are hazy. The fight will continue and we are not likely to win. But that is not yet carved in stone. A hero could still emerge to save us.'

'I will hope for that,' Odin says. 'Njord, did I do the right thing by requesting for Apollo's safe return?'

Njord looks Odin straight in the eyes. 'Not the right thing but the only thing. It surprises me that the Olympians have not taken it upon themselves to rescue him.'

'Yes. That is rather odd.'

'Is that the extent of your queries?' Njord asks.

'No. There is something else.'

Njord grins. 'Should I smoke you a slice of salmon?'

Odin remains serious. 'Tell me what you thought of Poseidon.'

Njord lifts the glass that Poseidon once held, albeit briefly. 'I say never trust a god who doesn't drink mead.'

6
The Elephant in the Room

Bacchus sips from a goblet of wine while minding his fields. It is harvest time and the grapes are ripe for the picking. He employs a variety of satyrs, fauns and nymphs this time of year. Sort of celestial migrant workers.

There are rows upon rows of vines. A barefoot Kyrene dances playfully through them. She spins and twirls and leaps and, occasionally, falls. But she jumps straight up and continues to dance.

Bacchus carefully removes a red grape from a nearby vine and bites into its skin. He tilts his head and then drops the grape to the soil.

He picks another grape and tosses it to Pan. Pan catches the grape.

'Tell me what you think,' Bacchus asks.

Pan pops the grape into his mouth. He chews and swallows it, seed and all. 'Tastes great. Bacchus, you have outdone yourself again.'

'Pan, you give me too much credit. This vintage will not be as good as my last.'

Pan shrugs. 'Well, I suppose when you drink the copious amounts that I do, quality is secondary to quantity. And, I might say, this looks like a bountiful harvest.'

'Pan, you fool, quality always comes first. If drunkenness is all you aspire to, you might as well drink beer with our Egyptian friends.'

'Hey. Don't knock beer. Some of those gods are a lot of fun. And Nephthys, the goddess of beer, is very beautiful and sexually-attainable. And I do like sexually-attainable.'

Kyrene bounces back into the scene long enough to shout at Pan. 'Swine!' And, with that, she bounds back along the rows of vines.

Bacchus laughs at Pan. 'It had to be said.'

There is a prolonged silence between the two of them. They both know what the other is thinking but neither wants to be the first to bring up the unpleasantness. Finally, Pan relents. 'Bacchus, what do you think happened to Apollo?'

'I really don't know. Perhaps he was summoned to another realm.'

'Yes, maybe.'

Kyrene darts between them. 'Apollo is going to be just fine! Back before you know it!'

Bacchus opens his mouth to question her but she has already twirled down the vineyard.

Pan answers the question Bacchus was unable to ask. 'She claims to have had a vision. That Apollo is safe and in good hands.'

DEITIES

'A vision? Where exactly does she visualise him?'

Pan smirks. 'You know where she visualises him. Right between her legs.'

Kyrene bounces between them. 'Earth! Apollo is on earth!' She pirouettes around Bacchus. 'And, Pan?'

'Yes?'

'You're a swine!' She leaps back through the vines.

Bacchus thinks out loud. 'Earth? I guess that wouldn't be too terrible. But I would have expected him back by now.'

Pan sees something coming over the hill that he wished he hadn't seen. 'Uh, Bacchus. Looks like we have company.'

A chariot led by four winged horses has made its way along the unpaved path leading to the vineyard. Watching the chariot rocking from side to side makes it painfully obvious that the driver is inebriated.

It is Helios, once a great Sun god and now a great lush. And he appears to be on one hell of a bender. Venus rides at his side, holding on tightly to the chariot.

Bacchus rolls his eyes and waves them over. Helios is barely able to control his horses. He finally gets them to a stop before they run over the oblivious Kyrene.

Helios stumbles from his chariot, extending his hand in Bacchus' direction. Reluctantly, Bacchus shakes it. He goes to kiss Venus' hand but she quickly pulls it away.

Bacchus laughs at this. 'Venus, I thought you would have wanted a private tour of the vineyards. Instead, you bring Helios? I don't understand.'

Venus scoffs. 'I'm just here to gather information.'

'Happy to oblige. But tell me you didn't just pounce on the

first Sun god who showed interest. I mean, seriously, you could do better.'

Venus snarls. 'I want to find Apollo just as badly as you do. But Helios insisted we come here before he'd tell me.'

Feeling resigned, Bacchus engages Helios. 'Helios, to what do I owe the dubious pleasure of your visit?'

Helios slurs as he speaks. 'I just thought you'd want to congratulate the one true Sun god.'

'In this scenario, I assume you're laying claim to the mantle?'

'Damned right!'

'Listen, Helios. I'd love to have a nice long chat but we're kind of busy here,' Bacchus says.

Helios looks around. Pan is pouring himself yet another goblet of wine while Kyrene continues to flit through the fields.

'I can see that,' Helios says. 'But I have such wonderful news to share.'

Bacchus figures if Helios has his chance to make his speech, he might leave sooner. 'Fine. By all means.'

Helios shouts and waves his arms wildly. 'Apollo is gone!!!'

This brings a smirk to Bacchus' lips but the words enrage Kyrene. She bounces into Helios' face. 'Ha! He's coming back! Back before you know it! We'll be seeing him soon!'

Bacchus really admires Kyrene's exuberance as she twirls away. He looks at Helios. 'I'll be sure to give Apollo your regards.'

'Wait! What does your little twit know about Apollo's whereabouts?' Venus interjects.

DEITIES

Bacchus shrugs. 'Don't know. You'd have to ask her.'

Kyrene hears Venus' remark and dashes to confront her. 'Twit? Aren't you like the goddess of sleeping with other gods or something?'

Venus' smile is not a kind one. 'That's right. You've had but a small taste of Apollo. Let me assure you that the second, third and fourth helpings are equally as delicious.'

Kyrene glares but tears well up in her eyes.

Venus continues her assault. 'There, there. At least you have your little drunken tryst to look back upon. Does it make you wet when you think about it?'

Kyrene charges at Venus but is restrained by Bacchus and Pan. Still, she kicks and screams insults. 'Whore goddess! Whore goddess!' Then, she breaks into a woodland dialect that no one but Pan understands. He quickly covers her mouth.

Venus, though thoroughly amused, is still focused. 'Bacchus, where is Apollo?'

Before Bacchus can answer, Helios screams, 'He's gone! He's gone forever!'

Kyrene escapes Pan's grip on her mouth. 'No! He's safe! He's safe, I can sense it! My visions are never wrong!'

Bacchus intervenes, 'Helios, listen to the lady.'

Helios suddenly becomes sullen. 'Bacchus, do you remember when I was the Sun god?'

Bacchus feels sympathetic. 'Yes, Helios. I do.'

'I was a fine Sun god.'

'You were. You had your day.'

Helios becomes angry. 'But then, Zeus stole it from me. He stole it and gave it to his spoiled, bastard son. Oh, Apollo, you're already the god of Music. Why did you have to take Light as well?'

'Being a god can be tough. It seems we've all been replaced now.'

'But this was different. I was called to Olympus and relieved of my station. The anointed one received his prize in my very presence. In front of all the Olympians. You were there!'

'Actually, no. Olympus is not my home.'

'Must have been Dionysus, then. Can't tell you wine gods apart, anyhow.'

Pan detects that Bacchus is rapidly tiring of the conversation. 'What do you say you go on and leave?'

Helios looks down his nose at Pan. 'Who do you think you are to speak to me that way?'

Pan grins. He likes this. 'It's an awfully nice chariot. Would be a shame if someone butted it over.'

'Shut up, Goat Boy!' Venus snaps.

Helios surveys the expressions of the others and determines that leaving is the better part of valour. But not before dropping a few last words. 'Apollo is gone! Apollo is gone forever! And I could not be happier!'

Helios stumbles back to the chariot and manages to lead his winged horses through the vineyard. Venus accompanies him but she clearly is unhappy about it.

Bacchus raises his goblet in a mock cheer. But Helios' words are of concern. Bacchus speaks to himself beneath his breath. 'Apollo, my friend, I do so hope you are safe.'

7
Everybody's Talkin'

San Francisco is known for many things. The Golden Gate Bridge. Trolley cars. Seals in the San Francisco Bay. A restaurant that serves garlic ice cream. And hills. Oh, the hills.

At the moment, the latter confounds Apollo. He struggles to keep up with Coyote along the dingy, cigarette butt-laden sidewalks. He is winded. He is out of breath. His side hurts. He stops dead in his tracks.

Coyote laughs. 'What's the matter, Greek god? Not quite in the same shape you were on Olympus?'

Apollo pants. 'I think I'm all right. It's these shoes. They are not comfortable like my sandals.

'Perhaps those boots aren't made for walking.'

'We should rest.'

If Coyote owned a watch, he'd be looking at it. 'I suppose.'

Apollo leans against a building. Across the street stands an electronics store. He can see the televisions in the window. Curious, he walks to the store. Horns honk at him as he obliviously crosses the street.

STUART CLARKE

Coyote rushes to keep up with him. 'Where are you going?'

Apollo doesn't answer. He focuses intently on what lies ahead. Once he reaches the sidewalk outside the store, he stops. He is mesmerised.

On the screen, there is an old video of Jimi Hendrix playing. Jimi is strumming 'Voodoo Child' and shredding the guitar. The sound is turned down, so Apollo cannot hear the notes but the sheer visual of Jimi's fingers on the neck of the instrument is more than enough to hold Apollo's attention. He studies the movements as Jimi slithers his hands along the neck of the guitar and is astonished.

Coyote touches Apollo on the shoulder. 'Music has changed a bit, hasn't it?'

Apollo doesn't take his eyes off the screen. 'What is that he's playing? It doesn't look like any lute I've seen before.'

Coyote grins. 'That, my friend, is an electric guitar.'

'Where does one obtain such an instrument? Does the little man in the box have them?'

Coyote bursts into laughter. 'That little man has been dead for forty years. You're watching a recording.'

Apollo nods as if he understands.

Coyote grabs Apollo by the wrist and pulls him away from the storefront. Apollo watches the screen until it disappears from view.

They walk a few blocks and Apollo stops again. He looks impatient.

'Please tell me you're not waiting for someone to bring you food,' Coyote says.

'That I am. I must say the service on this planet leaves much

DEITIES

to be desired. In the Heavens, I would be served immediately,' Apollo replies.

Coyote sighs. He is annoyed. 'It doesn't work that way here. Here you must take your food. That, or trade for it.'

'What do we trade?'

Coyote reaches into his pocket and retrieves the frat boy's crumpled bills. 'We trade this.'

Apollo examines the paper in Coyote's hand. 'I should think not. It is nothing but simple parchment.'

'It's lighter to carry than the coins you are accustomed to. It is the new gold.'

'You'll forgive me if I still have my doubts.'

Coyote finds this funny. 'Watch and learn.'

The two round the corner and see Totec's taco truck. Coyote steps up to the counter. 'This is what I'm talking about.'

Apollo sniffs the air. It's an interesting scent, not one that he's familiar with. 'I'd prefer ambrosia and nectar.'

''Fraid that's not going to happen. All he has are tacos.'

'What's a taco?'

'They're kind of a local delicacy,' Coyote answers.

Totec looks down at Apollo and Coyote. 'You boys hungry? Beef or chicken. Two bucks each. How many you want?'

Apollo responds, 'All of them.'

Reluctantly, Coyote hands the bills over to Totec. Now he is the proud owner of fourteen tacos. Totec offers to make more but Coyote waves him off. 'No. Really, I think we're fine now.'

Apollo and Coyote sit on a park bench. Coyote passes Apollo a taco and waits to see his reaction to street food.

Apollo bites into the aluminum foil-covered taco. He

immediately spits it to the ground. 'These disgust me! You shall pay for your insolence!'

'No idiot, you eat the inside.' Coyote peels back the foil and takes a bite. 'See? Delicious.'

Apollo peels back the metallic outer layer and bites into the flour tortilla. Coyote was right. Tacos are delicious. 'So, let me get this straight,' Apollo says. 'If you give someone parchment, they give you tacos?'

'That's basically the way it works.'

'What if you have no parchment?' Apollo asks.

'No money, no tacos.'

Apollo and Coyote eat 'til they've had their fill. It is quite apparent that Apollo ordered too many tacos. Several are left untouched.

A homeless woman with a six-year-old boy in tow happens by. 'Excuse me,' she says, 'would you have any extra food? My son and I haven't eaten for two days.'

'Two days? Why that is terrible,' Apollo says. 'Here. We are not going to eat these.'

Coyote protests. 'We paid for those with hard earned cash.'

Apollo corrects. 'He stole it.'

Coyote glares at Apollo.

The homeless woman laughs. 'It's okay. We won't tell.' She makes eye contact with Apollo. 'About those tacos?'

'Of course.' Apollo gathers them together and hands them to the woman.

She smiles, 'God bless you.' She looks to her son who is hiding behind her legs. 'Tell the nice man, thank you.'

The boy rushes into Apollo's arms out of gratitude. This

DEITIES

surprises Apollo. While he sired many children himself, he never really spent any time with them. The feeling of the boy's embrace is an unexpectedly pleasant sensation.

Coyote chastises Apollo. 'You must never, ever give anything away without getting something in return. It's the way of the system now.'

'But why? They had nothing and we had plenty,' Apollo counters.

'Let me put it in a language you'll understand – quid pro quo.'

Apollo nods. He understands. He doesn't agree but he understands.

****

The two walk side-by-side for several blocks. Coyote points out the sights.

'These are office buildings. People work there,' Coyote says.

'What do they do?' Apollo asks.

'I don't know. Officey-type stuff, I guess.' Coyote really has no idea. He's never held a job before. 'And those are restaurants. Some are expensive and fancy like that one.' Then, he gestures towards a nasty looking dive. 'Some, not so much. That's my kind of place.'

Apollo stares at the neon Budweiser sign that is flickering to stay lit. He is confused. 'Why would you prefer it there? The other seems much more elegant.'

'Those who frequent it are the salt of the earth. Real people. Not phonies.'

'If you say so.' Apollo thinks of Bacchus. 'But I doubt that place has an extensive wine list.'

STUART CLARKE

Coyote laughs. 'I doubt they have wine. But let's go inside for a spell. We'll see if you like it any better than the fraternity houses. Besides, I have some business to take care of.'

They enter the Joe's Dive Bar. It is filthy – one Health Department visit away from ceasing to exist. Despite California's statewide indoor smoking ban, the place is a chimney. The smoke hurts Apollo's eyes and the thickness of it makes it hard to see. But Coyote knows exactly where he's going, so Apollo trails behind him.

Coyote grabs a seat at the bar. Immediately, the person sitting next to him gets up and moves across the bar. It appears he doesn't want to have anything to do with Coyote. Then again, neither does Joe.

'You gotta a lot of nerve coming in here, Coyote,' Joe says, 'You better have my money.'

Coyote scoffs. 'Joe, where are your manners? We simply engaged in a transaction that didn't quite reach fruition. There is always some risk involved. You know that.'

'Seems like I always come out on the short end of the stick. And look at you. Is that a new jacket?'

'It is. And thank you for noticing. You'll get your money back soon enough. I've got a new deal I'm in on. All goes well, I'll even cut you in.'

Joe's anger doesn't exactly soften but he's a little more civil. He reaches into the well and pulls out a cheap bottle of whiskey and a rocks glass. 'Firewater for the Indian?'

Coyote nods.

Joe motions at Apollo. 'Who's the stiff?'

'That's Apollo. He only drinks nectar. Make him something

DEITIES

sweet, would ya?'

Joe pours for Apollo. 'Fuck that. He can drink the rot-gut, same as you.'

Apollo picks up the glass and examines it. The fragrance is terrible. 'What is it?' he asks Coyote.

'It's whiskey. Try not to think about it too much, okay? Down the hatch.' Coyote finishes his drink in a single chug.

Apollo mimics Coyote and tilts his head back. He ends up with watery eyes and having a coughing fit.

Coyote laughs. 'Atta, boy. Now, you're drinking like a man.' Coyote gets up from the barstool. 'I gotta speak with that man in the corner. I'll be back.' Almost as an afterthought, he says, 'Joe, set him up with another one.'

Joe shakes his head. 'Anything you say.' Joe pours another glass.

Coyote leaves and heads to the back of the bar, leaving Apollo alone with Joe.

'What are you doing with a lowlife like Coyote?' Joe asks.

'I don't know,' Apollo replies. 'I guess he's my friend.'

This brings a huge grin to Joe's face. 'Let me tell you something. Coyote is no one's friend. He's just some punk. Story is his dad used to be some big shot over on the reservation. Like a chief or something. I don't know. But Coyote got himself kicked out. What you gotta do to get booted from the Indian reservation, I don't know. But he's trouble. Watch yourself.'

'He's been very pleasant. He's helping me get acclimated. He even chose these clothes for me,' Apollo says.

'He must be playing some long con, then. Your family got

money or something.'

Apollo thinks about the answer. 'Yes. But that's a long way from here.'

Joe looks over his shoulder and sees Coyote talking to a hooded figure. 'Look at that. They're talking about you.'

Apollo looks. Coyote is pointing in his direction as he speaks. Coyote looks over and sees that Apollo has noticed him.

A few moments later, Coyote returns to the bar. 'Okay, we're out of here,' he says.

'Who was that gentleman you were conversing with?' Apollo asks.

'Nobody you need be concerned with.' Coyote looks at Joe. 'I trust you were spewing niceties about me.'

'I gave him the short version,' Joe responds. 'Except with you, it's the only version.'

Coyote grabs his coat and ushers Apollo towards the door.

'Hey!' Joe yells. 'You paying for these drinks or what?'

'Just add it to my tab. You know I'm good for it.'

8
The Falcon in the Desert

The winds are ferocious as the army marches forward. Sand, as hot as the sun itself, blows into their faces. But these troops are not discouraged. This is the furthest into enemy territory they have been. It is a time for war but also one for celebration.

Horus, the Egyptian god of War, instructs them to form a camp on an embankment atop a hill. There, they can watch for enemy movements while the reconnaissance raptors fly over the upcoming sandy cliff. These winged gods will provide assurances that Horus can move his men onward.

One of the birds of prey returns on schedule. He lands on Horus' shoulder and squawks. 'There is no one in the immediate vicinity, your Highness.'

'And what of the other two falcons? Why have they not returned as well?'

'I cannot be certain. I do know it is rather flat in those directions. They could still be flying.'

Horus is satisfied by this assessment. He gathers his

lieutenants and barks his orders. They would continue south deep inside the red land.

As the march progresses across deeper into the heartless heat, another raptor returns. She has news as well, although hers is of concern. 'A small base camp exists,' she informs. 'Strangely, near the bottom of the upcoming hill.'

Horus considers this. That would be an indefensible position. He wants to act cautiously but some of his troops have already crested the summit. Already, they have begun their charge down the embankment. Each soldier knows that he with the most kills earns Horus' favour and each wants to be held in that high regard.

The lieutenants are unable to stop them as the army rushes to engage the camp. As the first wave of men arrive, they see that no encampment exists - it was all a mirage. Or, more accurately, a ploy. Suddenly, walking warriors and chariots emerge from all directions and a wholesale slaughter of Horus' now disorganised army ensues. They attempt to flee back up the peak but are met by a pack of winged, carnivorous lizards spewing fire from their great mouths.

Horus' army is routed. The only thing to do is to attempt a truce. 'Take me,' he calls to a general on a chariot. 'Take me to Set.'

The Egyptian general smiles. He knows what Horus' capture would mean to Set as well as The Darkness as a whole. 'Get in,' he orders.

Horus does as instructed. His hope was that his surrender would ease the butchery his troops were receiving. But this is not the case. The general slows his horse to a trot, so Horus

DEITIES

can witness demigod after demigod suffer atrocities like he has never seen. Arms and legs are severed. Spears enter eye sockets. Genitals are mutilated. It was more like a torture chamber than a battle scenario.

Finally, Horus arrives in front of Set. Horus removes his falcon helmet as a sign of respect and defeat. He lays down his weapons at Set's feet. 'What would it take to end this senseless massacre?'

Set does not respond immediately.

'Set? I beseech you. What may I do to appease you?'

'Horus, you shall bend to your knees before me.'

Reluctantly, Horus kneels.

Set circles the god of War. 'You know, as long as we've fought, I expected a better showing of your troops. They are inferior to mine, of course, and it was highly foolish for you to venture onto the Red Land like you did. You are far more suited for the Black Soil. Wouldn't you agree?'

Horus has no choice. 'Yes, I agree.'

Set has been waiting for this moment for so many millennia. He intends to savour every rich second of it. 'You and your forces are going to join me.'

Horus cannot fathom such a request. 'No. I'd sooner die.'

'And sacrifice the rest of your army as well? In reality, I care little for you and those in your charge. I really want the city of Heliopolis. And I want you to deliver it to me.'

Horus shakes his head. 'Ra would never allow that.'

'Ra is fickle and weak. How he has remained in favour is a mystery to me. But you, my dear nephew, will do as instructed. We shall rule all of Egypt together, you and me. As it was written.'

'I'm afraid I don't remember that book.'

Set smiles. 'Perhaps, I should enlighten you. Or perhaps, someone else should.'

Isis, the Egyptian goddess of Magic, emerges from the tent of Set.

This stuns Horus. 'Mother?'

'Listen to your uncle, Horus. We have devised the most devious of plans. Together, you will conquer Alexandria and topple Ra from his throne. You and Hathor shall reign supreme.'

'Of the day,' Set reminds. 'The night belongs to me.'

Horus is adamant. 'Hathor shall have nothing to do with Ra's wrath. She is my wife, not a warrior. She is the goddess of Beauty, not one of conflict. She shall be spared from any part of your plans.'

Set loves this. 'Horus, she is my final bargaining chip.' He nods to his bodyguards and they disappear behind the tent. When they return, the magnificent Hathor is chained and blindfolded. She does not struggle. It seems she has accepted her fate.

Enraged, Horus scrambles to his feet and is met with a boot to the chest. Set puts his hand on the guard's shoulder and indicates that Horus can approach his wife.

Horus is in utter shock. 'Hathor! What have they done to you? How long have you been here?'

She is still a little hazy. 'I do not know. I was with your mother and the rest is foggy.'

'I drugged her,' Isis admits. 'It was the only way to get you to negotiate with Set. But trust me; our plan is for the best. Ra's time is bygone; it is time for him to be dethroned. And together with Set, you shall take your rightful place.'

Set orders Hathor unchained. Finally, she is finally free to embrace Horus. The two hold each other for a long time.

'That's enough,' Isis says. 'We have a Sun god to defeat.'

Horus wonders aloud. 'What of The Light? The portal will now surely fall into the hands of The Darkness.'

'No,' Set says, grinning. 'Together, we shall ensure it falls into the hands of the Egyptians. Let the Greeks, Norse and the rest kneel before us as they once did.'

Isis holds the hands of her brother and her son. 'My lineage will be the most powerful the world has ever seen.'

9
Calling the Sun

Thoth knows what is expected of him. The Egyptian god of Wisdom knows his place in the pantheon hierarchy. When he should stay silent, he stays silent. But when he speaks, he speaks his mind. This is one of those times.

Two horses ride side-by-side. As they come into view, Thoth worries. Never before has he encountered Greeks this close to Ra's home. They would be requesting an audience with the Egyptian Sun god. It is Thoth's duty to prevent such interactions. Ra, his superior in every aspect, has little patience for outsiders. However there they are, intent on an audience. Thoth feels impotent to stand in their way.

The horses kick up sand as they approach. They are thirsty horses; they are not accustomed to the inhospitable heat the Egypt offers. Thoth arranges his subordinates to supply cool water so that they may drink and be washed, so that their sweat may be soothed.

He is familiar with both riders. Athena, he knows well. She is his Greek counterpart; however, she is held in higher esteem

DEITIES

than he. When she is not fighting, the two of them often engage in friendly philosophical debates. She is, more often than not, the victor in these wars of words. The second rider, he knows more from reputation. Poseidon is generally considered to be the chief god of the Sea, eclipsing the Egyptian god, Sobek and the goddess, Nephthys.

Thoth rushes out to greet them. 'Friends,' he says, 'it is good to see you.'

Athena dismounts her horse and embraces Thoth. Poseidon extends his hand. Thoth smiles through the handshake, even though the Sea god's grip is crushingly firm.

'I trust you received word of our arrival from Hermes,' Athena says.

'That I did,' Thoth replies. 'However, I am a bit confused. An audience with Ra is difficult to arrange. I fear he will be most circumspect, considering that Zeus will not be present.'

'Zeus is unable to travel,' Poseidon explains. 'But we can assure you, it is of the utmost importance that we speak with Ra immediately. There are grave matters at hand. Zeus has entrusted me to speak on his behalf.'

Thoth nods. 'Very well. Follow me.'

They follow Thoth down a flight of stone-carved steps, entering Ra's pyramid. They arrive in a large room with thrones along the wall. Poseidon is ready to take a seat but is warned by Thoth. 'Do not sit upon any of those thrones. They belong to our gods.'

'And not your guests?' Poseidon asks.

'I am sorry but neither of you are considered true divinities in Egypt.'

Poseidon is offended and it shows. 'I can assure you that your pantheon is held in the highest regards on Olympus.'

Thoth backtracks. 'The same feeling exists here; however, it is the Egyptian gods that are the most revered.'

Athena intervenes before Poseidon can create a scene. 'We understand. We can stand while we wait.'

Thoth is relieved. 'Thank you. Now I will ask for Ra's presence.' Thoth disappears down a corridor.

Poseidon is angry. 'Do not interrupt me again, Pallas Athena.'

'I am trying to help. Do you think Ra would be pleased with Greek gods arguing in his vestibule?'

Poseidon relents. 'I suppose you are correct in your assumption.'

'Good. Now explain something to me. You claim to have had contact with Zeus. I have not been able to contact him for some time. And yet, you have his trust. Surely, you must know where he can be found.'

Poseidon lowers his voice to a whisper. 'I do not. No one can find Zeus. I suspect he is fathering more siblings for you, Athena. But for us Greeks to remain strong, we must keep up appearances. If that means I must lead in his stead, then so be it.'

'I wish you had informed me of this before we made this trek. I may have been less likely to follow your plan.'

'You have little choice now.'

Athena considers this. 'I'm afraid you are correct in your assumption. I shall help you. But remember, if this turns sour, you are on your own.'

DEITIES

Poseidon reassures her. 'Trust me. Our differences aside, we both have the same goal – to encourage the Egyptians to send their forces to help defend the portal. You could use their support on the front lines, so I am told.'

Athena nods. 'You could have mentioned that far sooner. I would have come along most willingly.'

'I need you to engage Thoth, as you have a kinship. He will aid our ability to talk sense to Ra.'

'I can do that. I will regale tales of the war and explain how badly we need their support.'

'Excellent.'

A few minutes later, Thoth emerges from the corridor. 'May I present to you Ra, the one true Sun god.'

Ra walks slowly into the room without making eye contact with Poseidon or Athena. He takes his seat on the largest of the thrones. Ra appears as an eighteen-year-old boy but a very surly one. He seems distracted as he was disturbed from slumber. He peers down upon Poseidon and Athena with distaste. 'Thoth, why have you allowed these demigods into my chamber?'

Athena kneels before him. She instructs a reluctant Poseidon to do so as well. Grudgingly, he follows suit.

Thoth explains, 'They have come from many miles away for an audience with you, my king. They expressed that it was of paramount importance that they meet with you.'

Ra addresses Poseidon and Athena. 'Rise. Tell me why you have sought me. Tell me why you would disturb the great Ra.'

Athena answers. 'It is because of the war over the portal. We are losing traction and need reinforcements on the battlefield. We are hoping that you could…'

'Silence!' Ra orders. 'When I wish to speak to a female, I shall make that clear. And, as for you, Poseidon, why have you come instead of your brother? I suspect I would have more patience with him.'

'If I may,' Poseidon answers, 'Zeus is unable to attend. I will be negotiating on his behalf.'

Ra growls. 'There are few negotiations I will entertain with you, minor god. But speak. Speak if you must.'

Poseidon readies himself. 'We need a stronger show of armies from you. There must be a heightened commitment from the Egyptian soldiers. The battle for control of Spheri Eternus depends upon it. Ra, it depends upon you.'

Thoth interjects. 'Our forces of The Light are engaged at the moment. There is an ongoing civil war between the gods of the Black Soil and the Red Desert. This must be resolved before we can bind our forces on outside battles.'

Athena cannot control herself. 'Ra, I am certain you are aware that the Spheri Eternus controls all planes. If it falls into the hands of The Darkness, the entire universe will fall under their domination. Do you really want to see Egypt beneath the reign of Anubis?'

'Enough!' Ra exclaims. 'I do not wish to hear another syllable. I control Egypt. Not you nor Anubis nor Set. Egypt has been safe under my rule for thousands upon thousands of years. It will continue to be so, regardless of your power struggle.'

Athena gets her final licks in. 'With all due respect, why can the demons from The Darkness continue to wage war upon

DEITIES

us while your armies simply fight amongst themselves?'

Ra's eyes beam red. 'Thoth, please show these putrid gods out. My tolerance has worn thin.'

Poseidon becomes infuriated. 'I never thought that dealing with someone of your purported character would be so difficult. If you do care not for your brothers and sisters of The Light, then Odin and I have no use for you.'

'Nor I for you. Now exit at once!'

Thoth leads the two back through the hallways and outside the pyramid. 'I am sorry. Ra can be challenging. He was already having a trying day.'

Athena warns. 'You know what the portal means. We will all be helpless to defend against The Darkness if it is captured.'

'I am certain that I can reason with him. Perhaps, it will come better from me and not two outsiders.'

'Very well,' Athena says. 'Contact me when you gain traction with him.'

Athena and Thoth embrace. Thoth extends his hand to Poseidon but Poseidon refuses it. 'If we are to be enemies,' Poseidon says, 'let's not maintain false signs of respect.'

'I certainly do not wish we become adversaries. We have learned much from you, as you have with us.'

Athena steps between the two. 'Thoth is a friend. He will make this right.'

'I shall do all that I can,' Thoth agrees.

Poseidon relents. 'Very well. Just remember that you will be measured on what you accomplish, not by what you attempt.'

'I understand.'

Poseidon and Athena's horses are brought to them. They

mount and begin to trot side-by-side.

'What did you mean by 'Odin and I'? Have you had a meeting?'

'Yes. A most pleasant one indeed.'

Athena stares at Poseidon, who appears to be ignoring her. 'Why was I not made aware? Surely, you would want the goddess of Wisdom at your side.'

Poseidon pulls the reigns and brings his horse to a halt. 'Athena, we have encountered many differences through the years. I'm never sure if I can trust you.'

'Well, I don't see you have a choice. We have to pull together now. All of us.'

'What do you need?' Poseidon asks.

'Troops. Soldiers. Anyone you can spare. There is a large lake between the front and the portal. Triton would be a most excellent choice to join us.'

'I'm afraid Triton is otherwise engaged. He is working on a special project for me. However, I can offer you Anthas and Hyperes. Of course, I will see to it that your forces have steeds in which to ride into battle. That should be sufficient for your cause.'

****

Ra is not pleased with Thoth. 'Why,' he demands, 'would you share precious knowledge of the ongoing war between Horus and Set with those Greek pretenders?'

'I believed that they should have some kind of explanation as to why our forces are not on the war front,' Thoth replies.

'What is the business of Egypt is that of Egypt and Egypt alone. Outsiders need not know our affairs.'

DEITIES

'I am sorry, my king.'

Ra grips his scepter. 'I expect for this transgression, you'll need more than a simple apology. Perhaps a little time in the Underworld would do you justice.'

Thoth is frightened. 'But the Underworld is now controlled by The Darkness. Anubis himself has claimed power over all planes. If you send me there, my safety would be jeopardised. I might never return.'

Ra stares down the god of Wisdom. 'I am sure with all your wiles, you will survive. I am banishing you as of this moment. I shall recall you when I am ready.'

10
Exit, Stage Left

'Coyote, something seems odd,' Apollo says.

Apollo and Coyote walk down one of San Francisco's steep hills. 'What's that?' Coyote asks.

'Well, it seems you're the only one on earth who knows who I am. Why is that?'

Coyote stammers. 'Well, that's actually hard to explain. You might think of me as a spiritual advisor. Or perhaps a celestial tour guide.'

'Tour guide?'

'You know, showing you around. Teaching you the ropes. Making you feel comfortable,' Coyote responds.

'Still,' Apollo says, 'My feeling is that you were waiting for me.'

'Waiting for you? Nothing could be further from the truth. These college students often have parties. They need someone of age to buy their alcohol and I am paid handsomely for it.'

'I see.'

Coyote is now walking at a slightly quicker pace than

DEITIES

Apollo, who is lagging a bit behind. 'Let's have some fun together. I know this place where we can have us a time. The girls dance naked, gyrating their hips. They swing from poles; they grind in your lap. It's a great habitat for two friends out on the town. What do you say, Apollo? You want a naked girl rubbing against your thigh?'

Apollo is silent.

'Look, we can always go somewhere else. We have time to kill. Like the old song claims, 'I got the money; you got the time."

Apollo is still silent.

'Or perhaps, we could go somewhere quiet. You can ask any question you like. And I'll be forthright in my answers.'

Apollo is still silent.

Coyote asks, 'Apollo, are you even there?'

And no, Apollo isn't.

Coyote backtracks around a corner; just in time to see Apollo ducking into a music hall. 'Damn it!'

****

Apollo's Music Room is San Francisco's answer to Los Angeles' Whiskey-A-Go-Go and The Viper Room. In the past, it featured such acts as The Talking Heads, David Bowie and countless others. Tonight, the stage is inhabited by Nine Times Blue.

Apollo's Music Room is a brick building that was once painted white, although only the bulk of the lead-based paint peeled off years ago. It sits in a shady area of town, near the Tenderloin District. A blight, to be sure; however, it certainly fits in with the neighbourhood.

STUART CLARKE

The interior leaves much to be desired as well. The wood floors seemed as if they could cave in at any time. This was a music hall where people crowd the stage; hence, seating is limited. The bar stays overcrowded, several people deep in each line. It was exactly the kind of venue you'd least expect a band to play at but, apparently, that's why they loved to play there.

To Apollo, however, this is paradise. He watches the opening band finish its last song and feels the music welling up inside him. The electric guitar, in particular, is of interest to him. He watches the lead guitarist play this foreign lute, paying particular attention to his fingers on the chords and the strings. He could do that. Of this, Apollo is certain.

The band finishes its set and leaves the stage, the curtains closing behind them. The roadies would be out soon enough to gather the instruments, so they are left behind. The musicians now have important jobs to fulfill. Finding drinks and drugs and someone innocent to share them with.

The crowd disperses after the band leaves the stage. It's time to hit the head or to get another drink. An opening appears in this jam-packed room and Apollo intends to take full advantage of it. He makes his way to the stage.

There is a girl, though. She insists on striking up a conversation. 'Hey sexy,' she says. 'Do we know each other? If not, we definitely should.'

'I don't believe we've met,' Apollo says. He is still distracted by the stage and the plan forming in his mind.

'Well then, I'm Laurel.'

'Like the tree?' Apollo asks. 'I knew a girl once that a turned into a laurel tree.'

DEITIES

'That's quite a story. How did you manage to do that exactly?'

'Well, it's quite a long story. I don't believe I have time to regale it.'

Laurel giggles. 'You still haven't told me your name.'

'Apollo, god of Music and Light.'

'A god, you say? Someone has a very high opinion of himself.'

Apollo does his best to gracefully exit the conversation. 'Yes. If you'll excuse me, there is something I must do.'

'Of course, darling,' Laurel answers, although her disappointment is evident. 'Don't go and forget about me, though. I'd like to continue our chat. I've never met a god before.'

****

Coyote strides with an intense pace, not quite a jog, more like a walking sprint to Apollo's Music Hall. Unfortunately, a line has formed outside the front entrance. He weasels his way to the front.

'Hey, little man,' the doorman says, 'Line's in the back.'

Coyote glances over his shoulder. There are at least fifty people in line. He doesn't have that kind of time. 'If you look on the VIP list, I believe you'll find my name. Check for a Coyote.'

The doorman shakes his head. 'All the VIPs done checked in. Back of the line with you.'

Coyote rips out a crisp one-hundred-dollar bill and displays it to the doorman. 'Check again, if you would.'

The doorman's eyes light up. He'd been bribed before, of

STUART CLARKE

course but he had never had a C-note placed into his hand. 'I'm sorry, sir. Coyote, was it? I see you right here. I apologise for any misunderstanding.'

'No harm; no foul.'

Coyote passes the bill to the doorman, who sticks it in his shirt pocket. On the way in, Coyote 'innocently' bumps the doorman and retrieves his money via a quick move.

Once inside, Coyote begins his search for Apollo. 'Bastard,' he gripes. 'Should have left him in the damned bed sheet. He'd be a lot easier to find.'

Coyote's short stature makes it impossible to see through the crowd. Finally, an opening emerges and he spies Apollo near the stage. He makes a beeline towards him, bumping into people as he goes without stopping to apologise. When he reaches the platform, Apollo is nowhere to be found.

****

Apollo sneaks to the right. No one is watching him as he steps onto the stage. He stands over a Fender Stratocaster, similar to the one he witnessed Jimi playing all those years ago. Apollo glances over his shoulder to ensure he is alone. He picks up the guitar carefully, almost as if it might bite him. Looking it over, he observes its neck, its strings and its tuners. He tosses the strap over his shoulder and holds it. Oh, how he holds it.

With the guitar firmly in his hand, he gingerly touches the strings. No sound is made but he can feel the vibrations running through his fingers and throughout his body. This instrument was new, many lifetimes in the making. Apollo knows he can make it sing.

He gives the guitar a full strum. Its electricity pumps

DEITIES

through his veins. He is ready to try it out for real. Thinking back to the electronics store, he mimics Jimi's fingers. Soon, 'Voodoo Child' overwhelms the house music. Apollo plays it quicker than Jimi but even still, his fingers struggle to keep up with his mind.

The musical blast coming from the stage enlivens the crowd. They rush to the front of the stage, not wanting to miss a second of this performance. Apollo is locked in the moment. His eyes are so focused on the strings that he doesn't even realise the curtains have been opened. He stands alone, center stage, mastering this beast of an instrument.

His trance is broken when the spotlight shines down on him. For a brief second, he is embarrassed that he's onstage in front of a whooping crowd. Quickly, he does what he does best. He entertains. The guitar is screaming and if Apollo knew the words, he'd be singing them as well.

Backstage, the roadies are scrambling. 'Who is this guy?' they ask each other. 'How did he get on stage?' But the headliners do not care. They dash onstage to join him. The bass player adds the backbeat, the drummer augments with percussion and the singer provides the lyrics. Their lead guitarist watches in awe.

The singer tries to keep up with Apollo but he's playing 'Voodoo' so rapidly it's impossible. Plus, Apollo learned but a fragment of the song while watching Jimi, so now he's improvising, making music out of thin air. The singer stands back and lets Apollo play. And play, he does.

Coyote elbows his way front and center. He cannot help but be amused. 'The god of Light beneath the spotlight, truly where he belongs,' he mutters to himself. But time was ticking. Coyote would have to get him off that stage.

Apollo completes his version of 'Voodoo Child' to a standing ovation. No one in the crowd had ever seen anything like it before, including those compatriots on the stage.

'Where did you learn to play that way?' the lead singer asks. 'I consider our guitarist to be among the best but that was inspired. What was that bit you did at the end? I'm certain I've never heard it.'

Apollo shrugs. 'I just played what felt right.'

Coyote crawls onto the stage and grabs Apollo. 'You've had your fun but now it's time to go.'

Reluctantly, Apollo agrees to step down. A chorus of 'boos' erupts aimed at Coyote. Coyote ignores them and ushers Apollo from the limelight.

They slowly make their way through the audience having to push to get to the exit. Everyone wants to meet Apollo, to shake his hand, to slap his back, or dole out high-fives. One person; however, is more aggressive than the rest. He is roughly fifty with a receding hairline and looks out of place at such a venue.

Jackson Tate blocks Coyote's progress. Jackson is not going to let Apollo leave the building without speaking to him. Realising this, Coyote relents.

'That was quite the show you put up there, young man. My name is Tate. Jackson Tate. I'm a talent scout. Own my own agency. I think you'd fit right in.'

'Fit in with what?' Apollo asks.

'Why with my stable of musicians. I keep them all working

DEITIES

but naturally, I keep an open eye for fresh talent. And let me tell you, son, you got it.'

Apollo is confused. 'What do you mean working?'

'It's simple, really. I get you gigs. I think I can get you a lot of them. Local, regional, national. Let me tell you, for you, son, the sky's the limit.'

'What's a gig?'

Now, Jackson realises he's dealing with an amateur and can up his percentage. All the better for him. 'It's like this. You play music to adoring fans and I give you money. Minus my twenty percent, of course.'

Apollo's eyes beam wide. 'You mean I could do this more often?' He turns to Coyote, 'That's good, right?'

Coyote shrugs. 'Yes, that would be good. But we really have to be going.'

Jackson looks at Coyote. 'You're his manager, I take it. How did you arrange to get him on this bill?'

Coyote is really mad with Apollo. 'Arrange? I arranged nothing. He's just an idiot who hopped on stage.'

'That idiot, as you call him, sure can play an axe.' Jackson reaches into his back pocket and retrieves his wallet. He looks to Apollo and hands him a business card. 'You look me up if you want representation. It'll be worth your while, I can promise you that.'

Apollo takes the card and examines it. It reads Chaos Management.

Coyote is flustered. 'Apollo,' he says, 'we really have to get going.'

Jackson latches onto Apollo's name. 'Apollo? I don't like it;

I love it! Wasn't he some sort of god or something?'

'The god of Music and Light,' Apollo answers, again peeved that he hasn't been recognised.

'Well, all I can say is, you've chosen your stage name wisely. You truly are a god of music. A virtuoso.'

'Thank you for your time,' Coyote interjects, 'but time is of the essence. We've got someplace we must be.'

'Understood,' Jackson says. 'Apollo, you keep that card. Here take two. Put them somewhere you won't lose it. Call me tomorrow and I'll take you to lunch. You can leave your buzzkill friend at home.'

Apollo sticks the card in his jeans pocket as Coyote struggles to get him out the door.

11
The Lady in Blue

Oscar Collins was a cop's cop. He worked his way up the ranks, starting with graveyard beat, to Vice and everything in between. Finally, his dream job came. Oscar worked Homicide. And he was damn good at it.

Oscar had certainly been around the block. At fifty-six, the African-American was still in better shape than the bulk of the detectives. He was tall and lean, not overwhelmingly muscular but he could flat stand his ground if need be. He was nearing retirement age but there was not one ounce of Danny Glover in him; he was not too old for this shit.

So, he was more than a bit surprised when he was assigned a new partner. And not a seasoned veteran like himself. A rookie, no less. This new detective didn't work her way up the food chain. She never walked the beat, at least not in San Francisco. She never spent nights on the street as he and his compatriots, had. She was a mystery. It was like she came out of nowhere. But the lieutenants were high on her. She was to be a shining star on the force. The flavour of the month.

STUART CLARKE

Oscar didn't care for her much. She didn't do the idle chat thing. He knew less than zero about her. Family? It never came up, so he didn't ask. Was she married? No idea. He tried to engage her on several occasions but she'd mostly respond with one-word or vague answers. If he didn't know better, he'd think she had something to hide.

****

Artemis did have something to hide. She found herself on earth several months ago, not knowing where she was or how she got there. So, she did the best she could. The Greek goddess of the Hunt could certainly do one thing well and that was hunting. Soon she realised that after being homeless for a number of weeks, she needed to do something drastic. She shed her tattered attire and braided her matted hair. She pulled herself together, stealing a set of respectable clothing from a Goodwill shop. She marched right into a police station and asked for a job. The cop behind the desk laughed at her but she was persistent, so he gave her an application.

She was stumped on the first question. What was her name? Artemis seemed too old, too archaic and too godlike for this version of earth. Diana, though, that might fit the bill. She hastily scrawled her Roman counterpart's name. But then, they wanted a last name as well. Lake Nemi was a sanctuary of Artemis's. Nemorensis, that was the full name. But it seemed a bit too long, too hard on the mortal tongue. She opted to abbreviate it. And, thus, Diana Nemo came into existence.

The other questions were challenging as well. Where did she live? What were her qualifications? Did she have any other jobs in the past? She realised she was being watched. Words were exchanged behind her back. Jokes about the homeless girl who wanted to be a cop. But opportunity always knocks, best open the door.

A crazed man entered the station, waving a gun. The officer behind the desk immediately charged him but was a tad too slow. He was shot in the face. In a quick turn of events, the man seized a younger cop and held the gun against his head. The other cops in the station held their weapons on the crazed man but could not fire. They could not risk the life of their colleague.

Artemis, now Diana Nemo, did not hesitate. She dropped the application on the floor and concocted a plan. She was clearly the last person he was expecting to make a move. So that's exactly what she did.

In a flash, Diana was behind the man. Before he could react, she kicked the back of his knees, dropping him to the ground. She rolled on top of him and quickly knocked the gun from his hand. Diana applied a rear choke lock and the man was completely incapacitated.

The police officers came running. One kicked the gun into the corner. Another checked on his dying friend. It took three officers to force Diana to remove the chokehold.

It was serendipity. The officer who had briefly been taken hostage was the stepson of the Chief of Police. The chief watched the video over and over; he loved what he saw from Diana. She was admitted to the police academy immediately, where she proved to be superior both physically and mentally. She excelled at running and tackling. She had never fired a weapon before but picked it up quickly and soon she was amongst the most accurate of shooters – it was actually easier than a bow for her. Just point and squeeze. She didn't even appear to mind when they pepper sprayed her face. It hurt, to be sure but wincing seemed a sign of weakness.

So, Diana averted all that Oscar went through. No moving up the ranks, no paying her dues. She was immediately assigned Homicide. And because she was still quite rough around the edges, Oscar was given the task of training her.

Needless to say, she was less than popular among the force. 'Who was this bitch?' the questions flew. Diana was very pretty which was not an advantage in this case. Her sandy blonde hair, perfect skin and pert, upright breasts made her the centre of attention. The station was, essentially, a 'Boys' Club'. The more gregarious men hit on her relentlessly. Naturally, she turned them down – she had never touched a mortal in her life but this was certainly not the way it was perceived. Whispers emerged. 'Lesbian' and 'Dyke' were common. Also, in choosing her last name, she had little idea what it meant from a popular culture standpoint. 'Nemo' began 'Something fishy this way comes' as she entered rooms. Still, she was a shining star with a glorious future in the making. Would she be sabotaged, or would they ride the coattails?

****

Oscar didn't give a shit either way. He was a serious man, above the partisan police locker room. He'd accomplished all he needed in this lifetime. He had made countless arrests, including two major ones – a serial rapist and a contract-for-hire killer. He had the accommodations and the pension to back it up. He'd retire and fix old cars or something like that.

DEITIES

Maybe, he'd even catch up on his Netflix.

Diana was his project; probably, his last one. She was possibly the last thing on the police bucket list. Training the new bird so she could fly on her own. And, if he did his job well, she would soar above the clouds.

In his heart, though, he was pessimistic. She was so rough and undisciplined, he feared a visit from Internal Affairs would be on her growth chart. She was quick with a punch before flashing her badge. She twisted an arm once so hard it broke. He always backed her up during questioning sessions but he was rapidly growing tired of it. She was a heartbeat away from a brutality suit and that wasn't going to drag him down.

He noted that most rookies, always wanted to drive. He wasn't having any of that but he found it odd that she never asked. She probably didn't know her way around so well but he knew for a fact that her lowest scores came on the driving section of the exam. She must have been given a pass like it seemed she did for everything else.

Still, it was hard to argue with results. Arrests increased as did his stature. Diana was a wildcard but well thought of by her superiors. They were also his superiors. No sense in fighting it, he told himself, train her the best you can.

He would subtly torment her at times. 'There's been a shooting. Diana, have you ever been in the 'hood?'

Diana shook her head. She had been in the woods. How different could it be?

12

The Great Retreat

Horus' army isn't quite ready to engage in battle. Many are still injured – some with limps, some were missing limbs and others were technically still dead. But if he were to maintain his precarious alliance with Set, there was no time to wait. He ordered a full-scale evacuation of forces. He is essentially inviting Set's troops to follow him.

Several generals question his motives. One, in particular, is Nemty. He is a minor Egyptian war god, who was very close to Horus. 'Shouldn't we stand ground? Set's army is in nearly as bad a shape as ours. He cannot launch a thorough assault at this time.'

'We need time to heal,' Horus explains. 'Set may, or may not, follow us. But we need to gather our strength. We will fight when the time is right.'

'The time is now,' Nemty replies. 'If we give ground now, Set will see it as a sign of weakness.'

'Do not question my judgment. This battle is just that – a

DEITIES

battle. It is not the war. Only a skirmish.'

Nemty is not convinced. 'We cannot back down. It is not like us.'

Horus is angered, both with Nemty and himself. 'I will engage this conversation no further. You will follow my orders.'

'Yes, my lord,' Nemty grumbles.

Horus walks in solitude. He hates himself for agreeing to Set's plan. But true glory may well await him. If he's not being played the fool.

****

Set's army is equally as confused, although they are in considerably better spirits. Their enemy was retreating, quite literally running away from further conflict. Their territory was successfully defended; it is time to advance upon Horus'.

Set's generals have much easier marching orders than those who belong to Horus. Forward is the word of the day. But every time they got close to their adversaries, the hostile troops would vanish over another hill. They wondered if this was a trap. When would the fighting begin anew?

Set, though, is remarkably calm. It seems he senses no danger, even when their nemesis turned strongly to the right, toward the Black Land, where the soil matched those of Horus' military. Soon, it is they behind enemy lines, charging onward near the Nile River. Surely, a deception must await.

****

Horus' army reached the banks of the Nile and turned north. They did not attempt to hold ground, even as his army regained its strength. Those who were dead were reanimating. Limbs showed the early signs of resurgence. Limps disappeared.

Nemty could not restrain himself. 'Horus, what is your plan? My gods are eager for conflict and I do not feel I can lead them if I do not know.'

Horus snaps. 'Nemty, they are not your gods, they are mine. Each and every one. Remember your place.'

'We are heading north. In a day's time, we will reach Heliopolis. Surely, that is not your goal.'

'Tell me the name of your finest captain.'

Nemty thinks. 'That would be Anti.'

'I have lost tolerance with you. It is Anti who shall lead your battalion. Unless you gain a newfound faith in me.'

Nemty backtracks. 'No, my lord. I just need something to report back to my gods.'

'You have your orders. Tell them to follow them.'

'Yes. I shall do just that.' However, Nemty cannot help but notice Set's demons circling overhead, like vultures. Was Horus preparing for a full-fledged surrender? He hoped not. It was not something he could be a party to.

But as the troops continue north, it seems that Horus had something drastic in mind. Maybe to seek Ra's aid in this endless civil war. With Set's army nearing the gates of Heliopolis, Ra would have no choice but to intervene.

****

Menhit, the lioness and goddess of Massacre wants Set's ear. She approaches him and is surprised to see Isis by his side. 'They are on the run,' she offers. 'Now is the time to strike and strike hard.'

Set smiles. 'I appreciate your sheer brutality; however, this is all going according to my plan. Would you rather control the

DEITIES

desert or all of Egypt? My eyes are on the larger prize.'

Menhit nods her head. She understands the stakes have been raised. 'So, are we now in league with Horus?'

Isis shushes her and whispers. 'All do not need to know. We march now on Heliopolis now, with Horus' protection. He will deliver us to the Gates of Ra. From there, we will do what we do best. We shall slaughter his guard and assume the throne.'

Menhit feels honoured to be invited into the inner circle. It is with her intelligence and ability in battle that she will improve her station. This war goddess would certainly fare well in this new leadership. Toppling Ra would not be a task for the faint hearted but no one ever accused her of that. She would serve Set well. If all works according to plan, she would become Set's favourite consort.

13

Your Destiny is Around the Corner

Apollo is somewhere between livid and confused by Coyote's actions. He was certainly having fun onstage and didn't mind hearing how great he was from one Mr. Jackson Tate. He pulls one of the cards from his jeans and reads it again. It had a pretty hieroglyphic, Jackson's name and a series of letters and numbers. Apollo isn't sure what to make out of the bottom of the card. 'What do these mean?' he asks.

'Address and telephone number. Don't worry. You don't need them.'

Apollo shoved the card into his leather jacket. He is growing more annoyed with Coyote as each moment passes. He was walking alongside Coyote but suddenly, he comes to a stop.

Exasperated, Coyote asks, 'What is it now?'

'You said you have a strict no interference policy, yet you

DEITIES

continually interfere on my behalf. Why is that?'

Coyote doesn't answer right away and when he does, he denies it. 'I have done nothing for you.'

'No, you have. You ensured I was fed. You pulled me from the music hall. And you hit that boy with a large rock. Now tell me how that is not changing my fate?'

'Technically, it was a cinder block but I won't argue semantics. You want to go back to the music hall? Fine. But first, let me show you something.'

Apollo tags along as Coyote leads him back to the music hall. However, they pass the entrance and turn down the alley adjacent to it. 'You have made quite the point, Apollo. I have been acting on your behalf. I am about to do so again. You may not like this one as much.'

Apollo turns to confront Coyote but something catches his eye. Emerging from the San Francisco fog is a menacing being. Apollo recognises him immediately.

Coyote looks to the ground. 'Sorry. I was actually beginning to like you.'

Pluto nears Apollo but is diverted briefly by a homeless man.

'Excuse me, sir,' the homeless man begs. 'Would you happen to have any spare change? I'd like to get something to drink.' Pluto ignores him but the man is persistent. 'Just a little change will do. I don't ask for much.'

Pluto puts his hand on the homeless man's face and shoves him to the ground. Pluto is focused on Apollo, walking towards him, Terminator-style.

Apollo glares momentarily at Coyote but soon finds

himself backing down the alley until he reaches the chain link fence which blocks it off. 'Pluto,' Apollo calls, 'how are you liking this new version of earth?'

Pluto grunts. 'I'll like it a lot better without you on it.'

'This earth's great. They have tacos and music and all sorts of new things to explore. We're a long way from Greece and Rome. So, let's put our pasts behind us. Come on. What do you say?'

Now the two are within a foot of each other. Pluto backhands Apollo hard across the face. 'How is that for an answer, golden boy?'

Pluto's slap stings Apollo's face. 'Look, there's no reason for us to fight. It's not like we're on the Ethereal Plane. No Light and no Darkness. Just us. Let's have fun.'

Pluto backhands Apollo again, this time with his other hand. Apollo loses his balance and nearly falls. Apollo is done begging. He punches Pluto in the gut. It has little effect on the hulking Pluto.

'That's what I want to see,' Pluto says. 'A little fight in you. I don't want this to be one-sided. Tell you what. I'll give you a free punch. Go ahead. Hit me hard. Just know, I'm going to destroy you afterwards.'

Apollo is nervous. Fight or flight is running through his mind. Against his better judgment, he decides to fight. He closes his fist and, with all of his might, throws an overhand directly into his hulking opponent's jaw.

Pluto staggers and rubs his aching chin. 'Nice punch you've got there, Apollo. Now the true beating can commence.' Pluto swings wildly at Apollo, who easily ducks it. Pluto reloads and

DEITIES

Apollo moves his head in the nick of time.

Apollo manages to get a couple of jabs in while Pluto's defenses are dropped but they only serve to anger the behemoth. He reaches and grabs Apollo by the jacket and pulls him close. 'Now that you are in my grasp, Sun god, there is no escape.' Pluto punches Apollo in the gut repeatedly, forcing the air out of Apollo's lungs. Pluto pushes Apollo onto his back and into a puddle. The Underworld god stands over him.

Pluto smiles. 'The rest of this, I am going to specifically enjoy. Ending you once and for all.' He grabs Apollo by the back of the jacket and shakes him. Everything from the frat boy's pocket falls to the ground.

Apollo realises he must do something drastic, so he headbutts Pluto squarely in the nose. There is a distinct cracking sound.

Pluto drops Apollo to the ground and rubs his nose. It hurts like hell but he is glad the Sun god has decided to fight back. Victory will be so much sweeter.

Apollo sweeps his legs and trips the hulking Pluto. Now they are both on the ground. Apollo leaps on top of his foe and begins to hit him hard in the face. Then, the strangest thing happens. Pluto is bleeding. Apollo has never seen a god bleed before; it was something only mortals did. He is momentarily stunned and this is all the opening Pluto needs. With his tremendous strength, he literally bench presses Apollo from his chest. Apollo lands on his knees and quickly staggers to his feet.

Pluto wipes his nose and looks at his hand. He is furious to see that he is bleeding. 'What did you do to me?' he demands.

Apollo remains in a defensive position. 'I'm really not sure.'

Pluto charges at Apollo but Apollo deftly sidesteps him and watches as Pluto runs headlong into the brick wall.

Apollo is on him in an instant, punching Pluto in the ribs. But his advantage is quickly reversed. Soon. it is Pluto smashing Apollo's head into the bricks. Pluto is no longer enjoying this fight and wants it to end. He leaves Apollo leaning against the wall and searches for a weapon. He finds an empty bottle of MD 20/20 and breaks it. Now, he has a dagger. He holds it to Apollo's neck. 'Enjoy the taste of death,' he says. 'See you in the Underworld.' Pluto pulls back the jagged bottle and is ready to thrust…

BANG!

Pluto feels a pain in his side like he has never felt before. He drops the bottle and sees more blood, this time seeping from his midsection. He looks angrily at Apollo.

Two more gunshots ring into the night. BANG! BANG! Pluto falls and finds he cannot get up. He lays quietly in misery, only gasping a few last words to Apollo. 'You will never win this war.' And with that, he rolls over and takes his final breath.

From the mist, emerges Freya. She is carrying a Glock 40 and it is still smoking. She rushes to Apollo's aid. Both are shocked to see blood, much less such a copious amount.

Apollo is surprised and relieved to see Freya, mostly relieved. Still, he is dazed. 'What are you doing here?'

'Saving your life,' she replies.

'Don't be absurd,' Apollo says, 'I'm immortal. You know I cannot die.'

DEITIES

Freya motions to Pluto. 'Maybe you should ask him.'

'No. He's powerful; he'll reanimate soon. And he is going to be very, very angry.'

'No, Apollo. The rules are different here. Do you really think I would resort to this human weapon if I could magically produce a broadsword? That's far more my style. And believe me, I tried.'

'I do not understand.'

Freya does not have the patience for Apollo. 'Quickly, this weapon makes a loud boom. I do not think we have a lot of time for discussion. Grab your coat and let's move. Are you able to walk?'

Apollo straightens himself up and takes a few staggering steps. 'Not particularly.'

Freya sighs. 'Fine, hold onto me. Let's go somewhere safe until you heal.'

'Where?'

'Anywhere but here.'

****

From a perch atop a nearby building, Coyote watched the action take place. He observes Apollo and Freya limp off into the night. He smiles. 'Way to go, Apollo,' he says softly. But he soon realises he is not alone. The man with the hood is standing behind him.

'Shaman,' the hooded figure says, 'there is much to discuss.'

Coyote doesn't turn around to acknowledge him. 'I don't know what there is to discuss. I delivered the package. Just like I was instructed to do.'

'The outcome was not a desired one.'

'Sounds like a personal problem to me. I did my part. I expect my payment.'

The hooded man is unwavering. 'Your payment shall be bestowed upon you when the contract is complete. Until then, you will continue to be in my employ. Do you understand my mandate?'

Coyote turns and thinks he's staring the man down but the hood obscures his vision. He assumes their eyes are locked. 'I want more. You hired me for a certain service which I performed. If you want to continue this arrangement, you must be willing to offer more.'

'That can be decided when the time comes. Your reward will be great. But necessity dictates that Apollo must die. You will find him again. Do you understand what you must do?'

Coyote turns back around and stares into the night. He understood his role. And he did not like it.

14

The Meeting of the Minds

Odin's emergency meeting is well attended. Gods and goddesses from many pantheons attend. The Romans, the Celtics, the Persians and the Mesopotamians send envoys. The Greeks were en route. Noticeably absent are the Egyptians.

Odin sits at the head of the grand table next to the severed head of Mimir, his chief advisor. The other great gods and goddesses whisper amongst themselves, socialising and playing 'catchup'.

Minerva, the Roman goddess of Wisdom, is agitated. She is the first to speak to the entire group. 'Can we get started here? I do not think it wise to wait until the Greeks decide to make their grand entrance.'

'No,' Odin says. 'We shall wait for them. Zeus and Athena will have much to offer in this discussion. This is as much their fight as it is any of ours.'

Minerva has been shot down. Her expression turns sour. She does not care for Athena. Like many Roman gods, she suffers from an inferiority complex when compared to her Greek counterpart.

A few minutes, later Athena enters the room. Poseidon accompanies her instead of Zeus. This turns heads. Athena immediately takes a seat while Poseidon stands, framed by the great doorway with his trident in hand.

Minerva points towards Poseidon. 'What's he doing here? I would have thought the 'Almighty' Zeus might attend such an important meeting. I suppose you are his errand boy?'

Poseidon ignores Minerva and focuses on Jupiter, the chief Roman god. 'You can silence her, right?'

Jupiter is somewhat of a shrinking violet of a god – not at all what you'd expect from a supreme ruler. He nods weakly and whispers into Minerva's ear. She pouts but relents.

'Yes,' Odin says, 'where is Zeus? His opinions are most valued here.'

Athena nods. 'They are. Or, at the very least, would be. His whereabouts are still unknown to us. But we must continue onward. This war cannot wait for any god, no matter how powerful he might be.'

Mimir rarely speaks unless spoken to but he whispers to Odin, 'Athena is correct. Our summit must continue without his presence. Time waits for no god.'

Odin agrees. 'Very well. I call this meeting to order. The first line of business concerns our friends, the Egyptians. I am most disappointed that they have chosen not to make this a top priority.'

'I can speak to that,' Poseidon says. 'Ra was very cold when Athena and I paid him a visit. He does not see that this war

DEITIES

affects him in the least.'

'Even after you explained how it would have dire consequences on his very plane of existence?'

Athena answers. 'He seemed offended that it was Poseidon and me who sought an audience. He had little tolerance for those we that he referred to as 'minor gods'. Perhaps, you should contact him yourself. He might have more patience with you.'

Odin turns to Mimir. 'Should we send an envoy to placate his ego?'

Mimir responds, 'We could; however, it is entirely possible that he is a lost cause. Perhaps, he should be isolated and treated like yet another adversary.'

Ahura Mazda, the chief Persian god, is angered by the answer. 'It is unfair that my warriors constantly face annihilation while fighting for something that benefits Ra. Would you like it if I withdrew my forces as well?'

Odin peers down the table. 'Of course not. We must remain resolute in our battles. Need I remind you of the consequences of failure?'

'No,' Ahura Mazda seethes. 'However, there must be a way to control the portal and delve out punishment at the same time. If Ra will not send his armies, he should have no ability to access it.'

Nabu, a Babylonian god of Wisdom, chimes in. 'Surely, there are pressures that could be placed upon him. His forces are very strong and it would be most advantageous to have them at our disposal.'

'Actually, his forces may not be that strong,' Poseidon

reveals. 'Egypt is in the throes of a great civil war. According to Thoth, Horus and Set are locked in an eternal struggle.'

'Which means,' Athena offers, 'that we will not have Horus fighting by our side but The Darkness, does not have Set leading its forces.'

Odin considers this. 'But still, my generals tell the tale of a vast army of Egyptian demons attacking their forces. Where are they coming from?'

Brigid, a Celtic goddess of Wisdom, believes she has the answer. 'Anubis must be sending them. My sources tell me he supplanted Set and garnered support of those in the Underworld.'

Mimir whispers to Odin. Odin nods and says, 'It is said that your assessment is correct, fair Brigid. The Underworld's armies are also being fortified by our very own Frost Giants. If the Norse cannot act as one, I fear there is little that can be done.'

Minerva lashes out. 'If the Egyptians wish to act alone, then perhaps the Romans should as well. We can see how that works out.'

Athena rolls her eyes. 'You have no idea what the battle is like, Minerva. You do not engage in it. You would not last a day on the Celestial Plane, much less a week.'

'Enough!' Odin shouts, 'No one is suggesting anything of the sort. It's just that we need to get our own houses in order before we can defeat The Darkness.'

Poseidon pounces. 'Odin, with all due respect, I could not disagree with you more. Now is the time for us to pull together as a unit and not let squabbles within our own pantheons

DEITIES

deter our movements. Ra has elected to keep out of the battle. We must all sacrifice more greatly. The defense of the portal depends upon it.'

This causes a stirring among those at the table. No one has ever seen anyone question Odin's judgment in Valhalla, especially not a secondary god. But Poseidon draws both the ire and respect of those around him. He was acting the part of the alpha, even if he technically was not.

Odin, not used to being silenced at his own table, restrains himself from reacting. He consults Mimir who tells him that Poseidon could be right. 'The defense of the portal is of the utmost importance,' Mimir explains. 'It does not matter who, or even how, this is accomplished so long as it is. All of us need to act as one.'

Odin takes the advice of his counsellor to heart. 'Poseidon, I believe you are correct in your measure. Thank you for your insight.'

'My pleasure,' Poseidon says.'

A brief moment of serenity passes before Nabu speaks. 'So, what is our best option? Should we build separate fronts? Mesopotamians fight together? Greeks with Greeks? Celts with Celts? Etcetera? Or should we intermingle our forces?'

Athena speaks up. 'The way The Darkness engages us; it is in a lump. They fight over who is among the leadership and who fights on the front. We are a smaller group than they and, I daresay, a smarter one. However, we may do better, for the short term, leading our own troops.'

Odin says, 'I agree with that to a point. All of us need to work as one. The way I see it, we should fight on different fronts but with advisors from different pantheons. That way we can learn the ways of each other without interfering in the battles. We can learn from one another and use the best tactics shown by all. In particular, Athena, I would like to see you work with the Romans. You have much in common. Your wisdom will help them fight and summarily, what you glean will only help the Greeks.'

Both Athena and Minerva sigh in disapproval.

Odin continues, 'For now, the Mesopotamians shall work with the Persians and the Celts with the Norse. Together, we shall deepen our alliances. Together, we shall defeat The Darkness.'

Poseidon smiles. This was the response he was hoping for.

15

The Demon's Lair

The hooded figure moves timidly into the chamber and hesitates for several minutes before entering the darkness of the cavern. He takes a deep breath and continues along the path. A path that he has not travelled down before.

The chamber is unlit. Darkness is all he can see ahead of him. A crack in the door allows a glimmer of ambient light.

The hooded figure reaches into his pocket and pulls out a lighter. On the third try, he succeeds in producing a spark. With great trepidation, he follows the flame until he sees the sight he's dreading.

In the distance, he can make out a huge throne. It belongs to Asag, an ancient Mesopotamian demon who is as old as time itself. Asag is asleep and the hooded figure must wake him to complete his mission. This will not prove to be an easy task, as the demon is in a deep slumber. Asag snores mightily and shows no signs of rousing.

'Hello,' the hooded figure whispers. 'I'm here.' He quickly

realises the error of his ways and repeats himself several more times, adding more volume with each iteration.

At last, Asag opens his eyes. They beam yellow and the light emitting from his pupils fills the room with an eerie glow. The beast is now in full view and the hooded figure shudders at the sight. Asag is huge. It's hard to tell how large he actually is because he is seated upon a throne but he must be over twenty feet tall. He is scaled throughout his body, save for the enormous claws on his hands and feet. His head is angular, like that of a terrifying dragon. Razor sharp teeth, that cannot be contained by his mouth, hang over his lips. Horns, like those of the Minotaur, emerge atop his head. Asag is everything the hooded figure was warned about but nothing could have prepared him for being in his presence.

Still, this monster is harmless – at least for the moment. He is chained to his throne, conquered many millennia ago by the Sumerian hero, Ninurta. This is clearly Asag's realm, although not by choice. He is, in fact, a prisoner in his own chamber.

Asag is said to have mated with mountains; hence, his offspring rock demons who are surrounding the hooded figure, hissing and breathing fire. Asag roars and the demons disperse.

The hooded figure gathers himself. 'I have brought you something, your majesty.' He reaches into his satchel and pulls out a small canister. 'But we must talk before you may have it.'

Asag roars but soon becomes quiet, intent on listening to the comparatively diminutive figure beneath him.

'I have brought you a soul, so that you may regain your power. However, it is not the soul for which we were hoping.'

The demon grumbles something in an unrecognisable,

DEITIES

ancient tongue.

'It is Apollo that concerns us. When he has been erased from existence, we shall continue bringing the spirits of gods as they die on earth. However, you shall not receive any more until Apollo ceases to be.'

A low growl escapes Asag's lips. The rock demons stir and seek shelter. They know what this sound means – Asag is angry. His anger has been known to incinerate all around him. However, he controls his temper. He needs this hooded figure alive to carry out the tasks that have been promised. Asag again speaks in the foreign language.

'Yes, your station shall be returned to you but only when the time is right.'

The demon snarls. He is not happy and lets that be known.

'I understand that you have been waiting for many lifetimes. I assure you shall be freed to do as you please. You can even destroy the earth if you like. But remember, this all depends on you devouring Apollo.'

The demon's eyes gleam.

'As an act of goodwill, I present you with this gift.' The hooded figure opens the canister. The mist of Pluto floats out; he is transparent and confused. This is all that remains of him; his body has been discarded. All that remains is his essence.

Asag inhales deeply and Pluto's soul is sucked closer to the demon's nostrils. The Roman god tries to fight the impending doom but it is hopeless. Soon, he is but feet from the monster. Asag inhales again and Pluto disappears into the demon's nose.

Asag pulls at his chains but cannot release himself. He needs more souls to feed his power.

'That is all,' the hooded figure says. 'I shall take my leave. Your strength should be such now that when a god dies on earth, you shall not need to have the soul delivered to you. Apollo will be the next god you'll digest. You will know when his death has occurred.'

Asag grunts a demonic begone as the hooded figure walks out.

****

Once safely outside, the hooded figure mutters, 'It would be devastating if that monster were released. It will not happen on my watch.'

16

The Reluctant Guest

Thoth is apprehensive about the Underworld. Actually, he is downright afraid. Many years ago, he was involved in the resurrection of Osiris, an original Egyptian god of the Afterlife and one of Set's original enemies. He is worried that his allegiance to Ra will result in horrible things.

He arrives at the poker table, stunned and frightened. He, of course, has heard the stories of the Ninth Circle. How gods and mortals are trapped in stone, cold ice. Thoth's abilities do not include withstanding extreme cold or heat. He is not well suited for punishment; he is an advisor of rulers. Nothing more, nothing less.

Hades and Hel sit at the table, mindlessly dealing cards. They are intrigued when Thoth arrives. Has someone broken through the ice, they wonder. Has Anubis found them a new playmate? Someone to torture to their hearts' desire?

Thoth makes a weak gesture and introduces himself.

'Thoth?' Hel growls. 'Never heard of you.'

Hades grabs the cards and shuffles them. 'So, Thoth, have you ever played Soul Swap?'

Thoth shakes his head no.

'It's quite an easy game really,' Hades explains. 'I deal you one card. If it's lower than mine, you lose your soul. If, however, it's higher than mine, we play again. Understand the rules?'

Thoth gulps.

Hel lights a cigar off of a burning chair. She is really sexy when she smokes, even when considering the fact that half her face is a skull with no skin. 'What if you draw the same card?'

'Great question, sweetie,' Hades says. 'In that case, we can sit quietly until Hel finishes her cigar. Then, we resume play.'

Hades deals the cards. Hades, who has a seven, flips it over. 'You've got a good shot on this one, slave of The Light.'

Thoth flips his card. It's a ten. Hades smirks. 'Next hand, then.'

Hel puffs at her cigar. She enjoys watching Hades afflicting this torture.

Hades shuffles and offers the deck to Thoth. 'Would you like to cut the cards?' Thoth shakes his head. 'Trust everyone,' Hades says. 'But always cut the deck.' Hades deals, this time face up. Thoth has an eight, while Hades has a King.'

'Pity,' Hel says. 'And to think, we were just getting to know you.'

Thoth shivers as Hades rises to devour him. 'Wait,' he says. 'You're not the typical soul, are you? No, you're special. You're from The Light. A high ranking official, if I am not mistaken. You are a long way from home.'

'I am,' Thoth replies, not knowing if this betters his

DEITIES

situation.

Hades grins. 'Then, this is special. I feed off the souls of the light.'

Hel drops her cigar. 'Hades, my dear, might I have a bite?'

'But, of course. There is no reason we should not both increase our powers. Where would you like to bite first, dearest? The face? The throat? Or somewhere else?'

'You know that I'm a big fan of somewhere else.'

Hades chuckles. 'That you are. And I love you for it.' He pushes Thoth to the floor, as Hel prepares to bite…

'Enough!' Anubis announces. Hades sneers at Anubis. Hel hisses.

'Why would you interrupt us?' Hades is fuming. 'What business is this of yours?'

Anubis circles them. 'He is an Egyptian. There must be a reason he is here.'

'Certainly.' Hel says, 'As a spy.'

Anubis shakes his head. 'No. Thoth would not be here on his own accord. He is a coward. I must find out why he is in my realm.'

Hades grouses. 'So, you'd rather stick together with your Egyptian cohorts than your Underworld brethren. Is that the way it is?'

Hel chimes in. 'Sheesh. You never let us have any fun. It's not like we were going to kill him. At least, not permanently.'

Thoth gulps. With Anubis, it is out of the frying pan and into the fire.

Anubis circles the table. 'Thoth, you have entered my domain. Surely, there cannot be trouble in paradise.'

STUART CLARKE

Thoth fears Anubis, far more than the other two. He has donned his jackal mask and is intimidating. 'No,' Thoth lies, 'all is well with Ra.'

'I doubt that. There is no reason you would be here otherwise. Is the advice you give not meeting expectations? Or is it something fouler we should discuss?'

Thoth's nerves are shaking and it is obvious. His knees knock together and his hands tremble. He hopes the truth will set him free. 'Ra and I have a disagreement about the best course of action concerning the war.'

Anubis scowls. 'You mean the war with me. Tell me more.'

Thoth wishes he'd kept quiet but now there was no way around it – he must clarify. 'We were visited by Athena and Poseidon…'

Anubis interrupts. 'Poseidon, you say?' Anubis is momentarily speechless. 'Go, on,' he finally says.

'Yes,' Thoth continues, 'Poseidon. He and Athena were trying to convince Ra to engage in the battle of the ethereal plane. Ra was insulted that he held an audience with two minor gods. He expected Zeus for such an urgent mission. I must say, I did as well.'

'What, may I ask, was your position in this talk of war?'

Thoth wishes he could read Anubis' expression; however, the mask makes this impossible. 'I explained that we were stretched too thin. Horus battles Set and cannot forsake our civil war to send troops at this time. Ra was furious that I mentioned our internal affairs to the Greeks.'

'I assume you see the error of your ways. Of course, it only serves to benefit me.' Anubis gets down to Thoth's level. His

DEITIES

jackal helmet is nearly touching Thoth's forehead. 'You have a decision to make now. You either advise me or you can be trapped in ice for eternity.'

Thoth doesn't need to think about this for long. 'I would be honoured to be in your service, master.'

'Good. I think you will find me to be a reasonable god.'

Hel rolls her eyes. 'I wouldn't expect too much in the way of reasonableness.'

Anubis turns to Hel. 'If you weren't so much fun to look at, I would have banished you centuries ago. But that tongue of yours is beginning to make you seem less attractive.'

Hel rises. She slowly turns around, displaying her attributes. 'It would take many more centuries for me to be banished.'

Hades has been silent for some time but he takes a lull in the conversation as an opportunity to speak. 'Anubis, Hel and I have assumed that Pluto was fighting on the front. But it's not like him to stay away so long. Do you have any inkling as to when he might return?'

Anubis doesn't answer this. He simply motions to Thoth to join him.

****

Hades and Hel quickly tire of the conversation between Anubis and Thoth. They excuse themselves to the bar, which is packed full of those from The Darkness. However, the crowd parts like the Red Sea as they make their way through. There are no barstools available; all have patrons seated in them. But when a Frost Giant recognises Hades, he immediately gives up his stool.

Inanna pretends not to notice Hel, who is standing

impatiently behind her. Hel taps her shoulder. 'Excuse me,' Hel says, 'but you need to move. Now.'

Inanna hisses and feigns superiority. But once she sees the fire in Hel's eyes, she relents.

Hel laughs in her face. 'You silly, little demon. Go before I destroy you in front of all these gods and goddesses. Actually, that would be rather enjoyable. Feel free to stick around.'

Inanna leaves quietly but this action has not gone unnoticed. It is viewed as an invitation by the male gods to console her, to hit upon her. She'd be leaving with one of them, naturally. But the question is with who.

Sucellus is the Treachery Bar's permanent bartender. He was kidnapped hundreds of years ago and put to work. But he's a jovial creature – the middle-aged Celtic god of Alcohol. There are plenty of worse gigs in the Ninth Circle of Hell.

When he eyes Hades and Hel sitting without drinks in front of them, he hurries over. 'Mead for the lady,' he says. 'And Hades, what is your pleasure? Nectar or wine?'

Hades is unsure. 'Mix me up a concoction that you think will please me.'

Sucellus nods. 'That I can do.' He grabs several bottles of various flavours and creates a drink with a cerulean hue. He proudly passes it to Hades.

'What is it?'

'I call it a Blue Valium. Be forewarned though, it's stronger than what you're used to.'

Hades takes a sip from the goblet. His eyes water. He takes another sip. He likes it. 'What is in this?'

Sucellus shakes his head. 'Sorry, can't tell. Trade secret.

DEITIES

Besides, you probably don't want to know.'

Hades takes a large gulp. 'So, what do you hear about the war?'

Sucellus smiles. 'Only good things. Your side is winning.'

Hel laughs. 'Come now. You've been here so long, you're one of us.'

Sucellus muses. 'I suppose I am. But how I miss the sunshine. Maybe one day, I'll return to the sky.'

Hades needles him. 'I wouldn't count on it. You're too good a bartender.'

'If that's my curse, I'm happy to oblige. I do so have fun with you hellions.'

Hel asks, 'So, you say the war is going well. Is Pluto dominating them up on that Ethereal Plane?'

Sucellus looks confused. 'No one has said anything about Pluto. If he were there, I would have heard about it.'

Hades looks concerned. 'What do you mean you haven't heard anything about Pluto? You hear everything.'

'I do. You pour a few drinks into your typical war god, they tell you everything that happened that day. Sometimes, I take a drink myself every time the word 'decapitated' is uttered. I stay pretty soused.'

'Pluto is not on the Ethereal Plane?' Hel demands.

'Hey, I'm just telling you what I've heard. Or, in this case, haven't heard.'

A Frost Giant seated next to them has been eavesdropping on the conversation. 'Pluto hasn't been to the front in years. Certainly, not in the last few days.'

Hades looks at Sucellus. 'I'm going to need another of these blue drinks. A little liquid courage is in order before I approach Anubis with this tidbit of information.'

Hel agrees. 'Hit me again.'

Sucellus grins. 'You're going to confront Anubis? Tell you what, I'll make them doubles.'

****

Anubis is sitting at a table grilling Thoth about the war when Hades and Hel burst in. Anubis is annoyed to see them. 'I thought I made it clear that I should not be disturbed,' he barks.

Hades is furious. 'Where is Pluto? You led us to believe he was fighting the war. Is he?'

Anubis and Thoth answer at the same time.

'Yes,' Anubis says.

'No,' Thoth says.

Hel is angered as well as a little drunk. 'Which is it?' she demands.

Thoth deflects. 'I'm sorry. I spoke out of turn.'

Hades is adamant. 'No, Thoth. You did well. Tell me what you know.'

Thoth looks nervously to Anubis. Anubis shakes his head. Thoth is free to speak. 'He was sent to earth.'

'Earth? Why? That is not even our realm any longer. That makes no sense whatsoever.'

Thoth shuts up. Anubis answers, 'To kill Apollo.'

Hades laughs. 'Why would it matter if Apollo lived or died? And why earth? I'm getting the distinct impression you're not telling us something.'

'There are forces at work here beyond your feeble

DEITIES

comprehension.'

Hel snaps, 'That feeble comprehension line might have worked with the simpleton, Pluto but not with us.'

Hades sits down at Anubis' table and turns to Thoth. 'You. You tell me all that you know.'

Anubis stares down Hades. 'He shall not utter a single syllable, or I shall strike him down where he sits.'

Hades glowers. 'Then, I shall wait until he regenerates and ask again. And again. And again. Until I get the answer I want.'

Hel is staring at Anubis. 'Give us the answer, boss man. Or we shall rip it out of his throat.'

Thoth is quite anxious. Hell is far worse than he imagined. 'Shall I tell them?' he asks of Anubis.

'No,' Anubis replies. 'Allow me. Apollo is on earth. I dispatched Pluto through the Spheri Eternus to kill him.'

Hades glares at Anubis. 'So far, so good. But where I ask you, is Pluto now?'

'Apollo has killed him.'

'Killed him? Whatever do you mean?'

Anubis doesn't have this answer. He turns to Thoth. 'Could you please explain this?'

'Yes,' Hel says, 'by all mean, clear this up.'

Thoth takes a deep breath. 'In the Heavens and I assume the Underworld, death is not permanent. However, in the earthly realm, where we are no longer worshipped, our existence can be completely erased. Pluto has met with this fate.'

Hades interjects. 'At the hands of Apollo?'

'That is my understanding of the situation.'

STUART CLARKE

Hades is fuming. 'Anubis, you fool. You knew that Pluto was not the brightest ember in the fire. Why would you send such a guileless half-wit to fulfill this task? Why would you not go yourself?'

Anubis is fuming as well. 'I do not appreciate being spoken to in this tone. I sent Pluto so that he might gain experience. Maybe I should have sent you.'

'I would still be alive and Apollo would be dead. But you, you jackal-headed coward, you should have handled this yourself.'

Hel realises something. 'You sent Pluto through the Spheri Eternus. The Darkness does not even control the portal. Who are you working with? Who is your counterpart in The Light?'

Anubis stares down Thoth. 'That I cannot reveal,' Anubis says.

Hades is becoming more enraged by the second. 'Well, can you reveal how you can send me and Hel to earth to avenge Pluto's death?'

'That, I believe, could be arranged.'

'Well, then arrange it,' Hel says.

17

The Fall of the House of Ra

Horus' army flees through Heliopolis and closes in on the very doorstep of a slumbering Ra. Ra's guards are on high alert, noting the troop movements of both Horus and Set. The guards have created a defensive formation around Ra's pyramid. There is no way Set was getting through to their Sun god. Especially, once they are reinforced with Horus' troops.

Horus' sun worn army arrives near the pyramid and the defensive creates an opening for them to pass. They immediately close ranks and wait. It is a hot day in Heliopolis; thus, Horus and his troops are given water and fresh linens to wear. Set's troops will be sunburnt and dehydrated – at a stark disadvantage against this newly fortified guard. This battle could well be the last.

Nekhbet, Ra's chief protector, goes to Horus. 'What does the landscape look like out there?' she asks. 'How many?'

STUART CLARKE

'His army is large,' Horus warns. 'They are very bloodthirsty. I have seen terrible things happen in this chapter of war.'

Nekhbet looks around and notices weakness among Horus' ranks. Some are still bleeding from open wounds, some have scars that have not healed and some have stumps instead of limbs. 'What did he do to your forces?'

'It was like nothing I'd ever seen,' Horus admits. 'When you've been battling as long as we have, a mutual respect is the expectation. But recently, the sheer ferocity has escalated. Set's troops do not merely slay; they dismember first. As you can see, the healing process takes a great deal of time.'

One of Nekhbet's scouts returns with dire news. 'They are coming rapidly through the desert,' she warns.

Nekhbet nods. 'This was to be expected.'

'But,' the scout continues, 'they saw me and made no effort to capture me. I find that rather odd.'

Nekhbet considers this. 'It is.' She turns to Horus. 'You must send your falcons to get an aerial view. I need to know approximate numbers and if their army is as injured as yours.'

Horus summons his falcons and gives the order. They fly off over the horizon.

****

Two falcons arrive as Set's forces march. One lands on Set's right shoulder and looks at him quizzically. 'You still working for Horus?' Set asks the raptor.

The bird, naturally, does not answer. Its mate has landed on the shoulder of Isis. It is she who can communicate with them. 'Tell me, dear falcon, is my son well?'

The bird screeches. 'Ra's forces anxiously await your arrival.

DEITIES

They are armed with spears and have dug in defensively. Horus is safely behind their lines and being treated as the royalty he will soon be.'

Isis smiles. 'The plan is working!' she calls to Set.

Set orders his troops to halt. It is time to explain the mission. His generals gather the troops together, so they can hear their leader speak. The demons lay on their hindquarters. The warriors take a knee.

'Today,' Set says, 'we no longer wage war against Horus. Today, we fight with him.'

These statements cause grumbling and confusion amongst the rank and file. They are curtly hushed by their superiors.

'We are going to march into Heliopolis and defeat Ra himself. No one shall attack any of Horus' army unless they attack you first. Do you understand?' Set's audience is silent. 'Horus will fight with us as we attack Ra's guardians. However, be forewarned, we are moving in an unprecedented direction. If you stand beside me, the reward will be great. But if you have fears let them be known to me now. No harm will befall you.'

Set looks through the rows upon rows of unsettled, yet silent, troops. The demons flap their wings; they are ready to fight. Most of the warriors are steadfast; however, a few show signs of weakness.

Set walks through the crowded formation and stops in front of a combatant. This soldier is shaking. He is nervous about going against Ra. What if Horus has laid a trap? What if Ra conquers them all? What if…

Set looks down upon the warrior. 'What is your name?'
'Senbi, your majesty.'

'Senbi, you say. If I am not mistaken, your name translates to the personification of health.'

'Yes, your majesty.'

'You do not look healthy to me,' Set says, before driving his spear into the warrior's skull. Some of the troops gasp but others, the heartier, cheer. Set looks to the warrior sitting next to the impaled Senbi. 'You. Gather my weapon.'

The warrior does as requested. It is an effort to remove the spear from Senbi's skull. This soldier fights with it, turning and twisting it to no avail. Finally, with all his might, he wrenches it. Senbi's head is still attached to the weapon. But Senbi's head is no longer connected to Senbi.

'I'm sorry, your majesty. Maybe, if you gave me a little more time I could pry it out for you.'

Set laughs. 'Nonsense, I think I prefer it this way.' He calls to Menhit. 'I doubt anyone else wants to meet Senbi's fate but please ensure they are ready. It is time to march onwards.'

****

The falcons return and land on Horus' outstretched arms. They squawk loudly. Horus turns to Nekhbet. 'Set's army approaches.'

Nekhbet looks out over the horizon. She can see the enemy advancing. 'Should we attack?' she asks of Horus.

'My army is still weak,' he answers. 'Perhaps, we should take a more defensive posture.'

Nekhbet disagrees. 'You do that if you must but my guards will not wait. We shall take the fight to them.'

Nekhbet's troops dash out into the battlefield, while Horus sits back. His forces murmur amongst themselves. They do

DEITIES

not understand why they are not actively engaged. These are warrior-gods of The Light. They should be defending Heliopolis with great intensity regardless of how wounded they are. With Nekhbet's troops, they reasoned, the numbers are finally in their favour.

The battle commences in front of Horus. It is hard for him to watch Set's vastly superior army attack Nekhbet's forces but he cannot look away.

Nemty can no longer endure it. 'Horus,' he screams, 'they are getting murdered out there! We must dash to their aid at once.'

'No. I will not give that order. We stand down. It is we who defend the gates of Heliopolis now.'

'With all due respect, I cannot abide by that. I shall lead my regiment into battle at once.'

'Nemty,' Horus explains. 'We are not here to conquer Set. We are going to depose Ra. Now, do you want a high seat in my new regime? Or would you rather fight for a lost cause?'

Nemty is stunned. 'What are you suggesting? Have you reached an accord with Set to oust Ra? That's not who we are! We are The Light. We fight evil! We do not conspire with them!'

'That was then. Now, I fight for a unified Egypt.'

'With you as leader, I take it. I cannot accept that. I am sending my forces into battle this minute.'

Nemty turns his back to Horus and Horus impales him with his spear. 'Why are you doing this?'

Horus frowns. 'It hurts me that you will not join me. Ra has kept us at war for far too long. It is time we made peace.

Set and I shall rule equally and an everlasting peace shall come to pass.'

Nemty begins to lose consciousness. 'He's only going to stab you in the back as you have done to me.'

'We'll see about that. Goodbye, Nemty.' Horus withdraws his spear.

****

Nekhbet's forces are no match for Set's war-hardened desert warriors. A few of Horus' confused troops dash out into the fray but most stay silent, wondering what they should do. Some witnessed Horus slaying Nemty and the rumours are flying.

On the battlefield, only a small cadre of Ra's palace guard remains. They flee back to the gates of Heliopolis. There, Horus' army decimates the remainder of Ra's guard.

Set enters Heliopolis with Isis by his side. She hugs Horus. 'I know this was hard for you but you will make a far better ruler than Ra.'

Set points to the entrance of Ra's pyramid. 'He's in there. He probably slept through the entire battle. I'm ready when you are.'

Horus stares at the ornate, diamond and ruby encrusted door. He is apprehensive about entering it. He turns to look at his mother.

Isis nods. 'Look to the future,' she says. 'Not to the past. Now go in and make me proud.'

Together with Set and Isis, Horus pries open the door. Now, there is no turning back.

Set gestures. 'After you, my nephew.'

Horus enters the crypt and grabs an already lit torch from

DEITIES

the wall. He knows these corridors well. As Ra's primary general, he had been welcomed into this inner circle thousands of times. Naturally, this time would be different.

They reach the center atrium. Ra's throne is vacant. 'See, I told you,' Set says. 'The Sun god slumbered during his demise.' Set is grinning widely. 'Shall we wake him?'

Horus pauses. He feels a wide range of emotions – guilt, nervousness, fear and exhilaration. 'Yes,' he finally says. 'It is time to finish what we have started.'

Set points the way. 'He sleeps down this hallway.'

A large golden door stands before them. It is locked from the inside and its handle will not budge. 'Should we wait?' Horus asks.

'Not when we could break it down. I would rather enjoy seeing the eye of Ra when he realises who's entered his sacred chamber.'

Isis joins them. The goddess of Magic has a most interesting idea. 'This gold has been consecrated. You will not be able to simply wrest it open. However, what if it were not gold at all?'

'I'm not sure what you mean but I always enjoy your notions,' Set says.

Isis stands back and concentrates. Soon, the gold door has been transformed into a large block of flaming ice. She smiles. 'Soon the ice shall melt and we may enter. Ra will have no choice but to yield his power.'

Within minutes, the ice dissipates. Set steps through the ice-cold fire. It is a different type of burn. Bitter cold but with the smell of ash.

Isis warns. 'Move through it quickly, Set. It will burn you.'

Horus quickly hops through it and Isis follows. True enough, Ra is asleep; his youthful looking body is wrapped beneath a linen sheet. 'Nudge him,' Isis suggests.

Set pushes the shoulder of the Sun god. He rolls over, still a slumber. Set finds this funny. 'He must be dreaming he's still the king.'

Horus is sullen but Isis is adamant. 'Let's get this over with.' She instructs Horus to awaken him, which he does.

Ra is barely conscious – still in a dreamlike state. He sees Horus. 'Horus, my friend, what brings you here?' Ra then looks and notices Isis and grows a bit concerned. When he sees Set, he sits up in bed. 'This must be some kind of nightmare.'

Set laughs. 'No. You slept through the nightmare. Now, you're experiencing the hangover known as reality.'

Ra is angry. He sits up and flashes a sun bolt through Set, plastering him against the wall. He readies another and aims it at Horus, who ducks and it narrowly misses him.

Isis smiles, 'You're forgetting something, Ra.' She blinks and a thousand deadly scorpions, poisonous spiders and venomous asps appear in his bed. She leans in and whispers into his ear. 'I know your secret name. I can utter it and your powers will dissipate. We wouldn't want that, would we?'

The spiders are walking up his arms. The scorpions scale his legs and crawl beneath his tunic. The snakes prepare to strike. Ra is naturally shaken. 'What is it you want? I can give you anything you need.'

Set has gathered himself. 'Anything, you say? Well, we're going to need you to abdicate. It is time for you to step aside.'

DEITIES

'You cannot be serious. I am the Creator of all life. I am the sole being responsible for all existence.'

'Careful,' Isis says, 'those scorpions are getting awfully close to your genitalia.'

Ra is sweating furiously. 'I will do what you ask. Please withdraw the reptiles and the arachnids.'

Isis blinks her eyes and it is done. The spiders, snakes and scorpions vanish. 'While it would be far more entertaining to watch poison reap through your pores and wounds, this can be accomplished peacefully. You will accompany Set to the Underworld.'

'Yes, my ruler,' Set says, sarcasm dripping from his lips, 'an eternity of suffering awaits. Horus, prepare a sarcophagus.'

Horus searches the room and locates several. The first he opens contains the mummified remains of a minor pharaoh. It is ornately decorated, beautifully carved in gold. 'Something like this?'

Set nods in the negative. 'No. I was thinking something suiting a slave. Something wooden. Something without ornamentation.'

'I think I see just the one.' He points to common timber box, similar to the type a slave might in which be buried. 'Will this suffice?'

'That's more like what I envisioned.'

Isis approves as well. 'Ra, you should get inside this without any fuss. As I recall, you recoil at the very sight of asps. I can always provide some reptilian company if you like.'

Ra realises that resistance is futile. His fate is sealed. He must sacrifice his dignity and hope for the best. Although, to be honest, the future looked bleak.

Ra is now inside the coffin and it is hoisted upon the shoulders of Horus and Set. Isis leads them back out into the sunlight. Seeing the two gods together gives pause to the previously warring factions.

Set's soldiers and Horus' troops have been engaging in verbal assaults and minor skirmishes. This is, of course, expected from enemy factions who engaged in mortal combat for thousands of years. Peace is a foreign concept for them. War is all they have ever known.

However, when Horus and Set step out of Ra's pyramid, they stop squabbling. Has a new dawn emerged? Do thousands of years of reconciliation lie ahead?

Horus and Set pass the casket to Set's most trusted allies. Together, they address the masses.

'A longstanding war has reached its end,' Horus announces. 'Today, we are no longer Darkness or Light! Today, we are Egyptians!'

Set takes center stage. 'My friends, both old and new, we resurrect what once made Egypt the most powerful pantheon the universe has ever known. No longer shall we fight amongst ourselves. We shall become one. There is no good. There is no evil. There is only Egypt.'

Horus resumes. 'Turn to your enemy and treat them as your comrade. Trust in each other as we trust in you. Together, we shall change history.'

Set continues. 'There is still much work to be done but together it can be accomplished. The war between us is in the past. We look to the future. Horus is now your leader.'

DEITIES

Horus adds. 'As is Set. We share power. We share vision. We share the goal of a superior Egyptian pantheon.'

The crowd roars in approval. An armistice could not be any sweeter.

****

Isis advises Horus. 'We must act quickly. Gather the scribes and have messages sent to the major gods in each realm. We must inform them that Ra has stepped down and that you are now the chief among all Egyptian gods.'

Horus is puzzled. 'But what of Set? He is also empowered.'

Isis smiles. 'We have performed the first of many tasks. The alliance between you and Set cannot be known. It must remain a secret. And that secret will reveal itself in due time.'

Set's army has reformed. They have chained Ra's coffin to the back of a chariot. They are ready to move.

Horus approaches Set. 'Where are you going?'

'I have an Underworld to take by storm. It has been a long time since I saw that opportunist Anubis. I suspect I should visit him before word reaches him.'

Horus is impressed. 'You're going to conquer the Underworld? A very bold move. I like it.'

Set is smug. 'The toppling of Ra was only the first phase. Restoring my place in the Underworld is the second. I rather suspect you'll like the third.' Set turns to leave but stops. 'Horus, I'm also going to need your falcon helmet.'

Reluctantly, Horus passes it over.

18

Barter

While Apollo sleeps, Freya goes out for supplies. She emerges from the equivalent of a metropolitan hovel and begins walking the street outside. She spies what must be an earthly market and heads in its direction.

Once inside the minimart, she sees a plethora of items, none of which she is familiar with. She picks up box after box, reading the labels. There are a few things she needs – healing ointments, pain suppressant, bandages and food. She finds that the bright lights and multitude of objects are disorientating. She's aghast.

Fortunately, when you are a buxom blonde wearing little more than a satin robe, it is easy to find help. A man approaches her. 'I'm Miles,' he says. 'You seem a bit, um, overwhelmed.'

'I am,' she says. She regales the list of necessities.

'Let me see how I can help but it will cost you.'

Freya agrees. Being a goddess of Beauty has trained her in

DEITIES

the art of barter. If it's sex he wants, it's sex he will get.

Miles grabs a handheld shopping basket. 'Do you have a preference between Tylenol and Advil? I always go with Advil.' He tosses it in the basket. 'You said you needed bandages. Ace or Band-Aids?'

Freya shrugs. She doesn't know. So, he tosses in some of each.

'Neosporin is good for open wounds. Helps them heal. Won't leave a scar.'

Freya laughs. 'He's so vain; he's definitely not going to want a blemish.'

Miles is a little peeved at the word 'he's'. However, he continues to help her. 'This is the candy aisle.' He picks up a package of Skittles. 'Now, these are my favourite,' he explains. 'However, I can't say they make much of a meal. Let's get some of this as well. It's beef jerky. Lots of protein.'

Freya nods.

'Are you thirsty?' He guides her to the beverage section. 'Do you like beer?'

'Not especially. I do like a good mead. And Apollo drinks mostly nectar. But, if there's wine, I suppose that would suffice.'

'I don't expect the wine here to be very good,' Miles says. He looks around the shelf. 'This Australian bottle is the best you'll find at a minimart.'

'At a minimart,' Freya repeats. 'Let's get some.'

He drops a bottle into the cart. 'Need water? Soda? Red Bull? They say Red Bull gives you wings.'

'I could use wings.'

Water and Red Bull pile up. 'Anything else?'

'I don't suppose so.'

Miles leads her to the register. The cashier begins to ring the items up and bag them. 'So, what's your name?' Miles asks.

'It's Freya.' She begins to disrobe, right there in the store. Miles and the cashier are in shock, not once but twice. Freya is now topless and her breasts are amazing. However, neither Miles nor the cashier focus on them for long. When she pulls the gun from her waist and lays it on the counter, lust turns to fear.

'Uh, what is that?' Miles asks, worried.

'It's a weapon of some sort,' Freya answers. 'Have you ever seen one before? I think it's good at killing.'

Miles sprints out the door. Freya turns to the cashier as she pulls her robe back on. 'I thought he wanted to have sex. It's been centuries since I've been with a mortal.'

The cashier is nervous. He is a middle-aged Mexican man. He is not a legal resident and wants no trouble. He opens the register and puts all the bills into one of Freya's bags.

Freya peers inside the bag. 'What's this?'

'It's all there is in the drawer. I do not have access to the safe.'

'Oh,' she says, not at all understanding what he means. 'Well, I suppose I'll be going then. You have a good day.'

She takes a couple of steps away, then turns and retrieves the gun. 'Better not forget this. It comes in handy.'

****

Apollo awakes when he hears the door creak. It is Freya returning from her unintentional robbery. He sits up on the mite-riddled sofa. The pain is incredible. He winces.

DEITIES

Freya reaches into the bag and pulls out the Advil. 'This is supposed to help with the pain.' She claws her way through the box and grabs the hard, plastic bottle. The childproof lid proves to be quite the challenge but eventually, she manages it. She claws through the metallic cover and is confused by the cotton. She yanks it out and sees many little pills inside. Apollo is in a lot of pain, so she hands him the largest one.

Apollo examines it. 'It says do not eat.'

Freya snatches it back and verifies his interpretation then tosses it over her shoulder. 'Try some of the smaller ones.'

Apollo swallows them and washes them down with bottled water. 'Any other earthly delights?'

'These are, evidently, called Skittles. This is beef jerky. I suggest we try it.'

They each take a stick. It is chewy. 'Tastes like elk,' Freya remarks.

'We need to find tacos,' Apollo says, in between bites. 'They are apparently a delicacy. Trust me, they are quite good.'

Freya looks over Apollo. An open wound still exists on his forehead, just above his right eye. She wets her finger and rubs off the dried blood like a mother wiping her child's face. She opens the ointment and rubs it into the gash.

Apollo is apprehensive. 'You sure you know what you're doing? I mean, this is my face. You do have experience with this sort of thing, right?'

'Not exactly.'

'Pardon?'

Freya shrugs. 'I've witnessed Athena perform this action a thousand times but to be fair, I'm generally the one chopping head's off, not tending to the wounds.'

She finds the Band-Aids and, ultimately, figures out how to stick them on Apollo's forehead. She uses about ten of them.

'How do I look?' Apollo asks.

'You don't want to know.'

Apollo looks over the bags. 'Is that wine I see?'

'Supposedly, the best they have.'

'Well, then let's open it.'

Freya claws her way through the foil to the cork. It won't budge, so she pushes it down into the bottle. She takes a sip and makes a face.

Apollo laughs. 'Not to your liking? Pass that over here.' He smells it and it seems off. Still, he takes a healthy swig from the bottle. Immediately, he spits it to the ground. 'Bacchus would be mortified.'

Apollo picks up the bag and sees the money inside it. 'Where did you get all of this?'

'The man just gave it to me.'

'This is earth gold. I don't think people just give it away. Did you do anything special?'

'I did show him my breasts,' she says. 'Oh, I also showed him this weapon. He seemed afraid of it.'

'That could be it. But the important thing is we're going to need more of it. But I don't think we should go place to place taking mortal's currency.'

Freya is concerned. 'How, then?'

Apollo reaches into his back pocket and produces Jackson Tate's business card. 'This man might be able to help.'

Freya reads the card. 'How do we find him?'

DEITIES

****

Apparently, yellow motorised chariots are more than willing to drive places, especially, when the passengers have the required currency. Freya gives the driver more than four hundred dollars on a fifteen-buck fare. 'Sorry,' she explains, 'that's all we have.'

They stand outside Jackson's office building and follow a group of people inside. Apollo finds a listing for Chaos Management on a board near the elevator. It's in suite 1850. They walk aimlessly, trying to locate the stairs but cannot find them.

Finally, a security guard takes pity on the confused pair. 'The stairwell is behind that door. But I think you'll find the elevator more to your liking.' He guides them. When the elevator opens, he pushes the eighteen button. The guard is snarky. 'When the doors open, that's when you get off.'

They find suite 1850. A receptionist greets them. 'How can I help you?'

Apollo smiles. 'We're here to see Jackson Tate.'

'I see. I'm afraid he's all booked up at the moment. I can set up a meeting though.' She looks through Jackson's appointment schedule. 'How about next Friday at four?'

Actually, Friday is named for Freya, so she knows how far away that is. 'We really need to see him now,' she insists.

'I'm afraid that's impossible.'

Freya is unwavering. She leans forward on the desk and reads the receptionist's ID badge. 'Julie Davenport, where I come from, anything is possible. We must see him now.'

The receptionist gives a little. 'I'll ring him and we can see what he says. But I'm not promising anything. Who should I

STUART CLARKE

say is here?'

'Apollo. Tell him it's Apollo.'

****

Jackson Tate is on the speakerphone, arguing with a local promoter over a venue. 'It's too goddamn small. These boys can sell out an arena and you want me to put them in a sports bar?'

'I'm telling you,' the promoter explains, 'this is what's available. This town is booked up tight right now – you know that. If you can be flexible on dates, I can work something out.'

'The band is from Seattle Fucking Washington. The city is lucky to get them once every two years. They are critically acclaimed, for Christ sake.'

The promoter isn't moving. 'And they don't sell particularly well. I like their music. I really do. But I like money even more.'

Jackson's second line blinks. 'I'm putting you on hold while you figure out how to make me happy.' He picks up line two. 'Julie, this better be fucking good.'

Julie stammers. 'There's an Apollo here to see you. Seems to be urgent.'

'Apollo? Send him back!'

Julie ushers Apollo and Freya through the door and into Jackson's office. It is impressive. Framed gold and platinum records hang on the rich mahogany walls. Signed guitars are everywhere and a full drum set resides in the corner. Jackson rushes to greet Apollo. 'I wasn't sure I'd be seeing you again. Let me tell you, you are the talk of the town.'

Freya turns to Apollo. 'What's he talking about?'

Jackson smiles. 'He's only the next Jimi Hendrix, that's what I'm talking about. I'm surprised he didn't tell you, little

DEITIES

lady. You are his girlfriend, right?'

'Uh, no. More like his bodyguard.'

Apollo introduces Freya to Jackson, during which time Freya make it abundantly clear that she is not to be called 'little lady'.

'Freya, I gotta ask. You don't happen to sing? A hot lead singer fronting this guy's guitar magic would be an agent's dream come true.'

'Sorry,' Freya says. 'Singing is not among my talents.'

'Pity that.' Jackson dashes to his messy desk and pulls out a copy of the SF Weekly. He passes it to Apollo. 'This came out today. You made the cover.'

Apollo looks at the picture and smiles. There he is, onstage beneath a headline – Mystery Guitarist Blows Room Away.

Freya grabs the paper from Apollo's hands. 'This is not good,' she mutters.

Jackson cannot believe his ears. 'Are you kidding? This is outstanding. You cannot buy exposure like this and, Lord knows, I've tried. Under my management, Apollo is going to become a legend. How do you feel about that, Apollo? Stick with me and I'll make you a Rock God. Interested?'

Apollo's ears perk up at the word 'god' but Freya intervenes. 'We have to get out of here now!'

'Nonsense,' Jackson says, 'I think we should have a drink. You like single malt Scotch, Apollo?'

Freya pulls out the gun from her robe and points it at Jackson. 'Take us to your domicile.'

'My domi...you mean my apartment? Sure, we could do that. Just put down the gun.'

'I am NOT putting down the…what did you call it?'

'I think he said 'gun',' Apollo offers.

Freya nods. 'I'm not putting the gun down. We are leaving now. All of us.'

Jackson tries one last thing. He releases the hold button on the speakerphone. 'You've got to help me! I'm desperate!'

The promoter who minutes ago was being cussed out by Jackson replies, 'No way, no how. Asshole!'

Dial tone.

****

Freya stays close behind Jackson as the three walks down the staircase to the parking garage. 'That's me, over there,' he says, pointing out a brown Range Rover. 'I assume you'll want me to do the driving.'

Freya nods.

Jackson frowns. 'Okay, get in.' Apollo climbs into the front while Freya elects to sit in the back, still aiming the gun at Jackson's head.

They pull out of the parking garage and make a left. Freya suddenly becomes concerned. 'How far away do you live?'

Jackson sighs. 'About ten minutes away with traffic.'

'That's too close.' She notices a sticker on the Range Rover's windshield. 'What's a Calistoga Resort?'

'It's a place I go sometimes. I own property there. It's in the wine country.'

'Is it far away?'

'This time of year? Probably about three hours,' Jackson replies.

'Sounds perfect. That's where we're going.'

DEITIES

Jackson drives for about an hour. They cross the Golden Gate Bridge which offers magnificent views of Sausalito and Alcatraz.

'Alcatraz used to be a prison,' Jackson says. Apparently, he has his tour guide hat on.

Apollo finds this interesting; however, Freya does not. 'Keep quiet and drive,' she says.

'Can we at least turn on some music?' Jackson asks.

While Freya is mentally debating this, Apollo answers, 'Please do.'

The Range Rover is equipped with Pandora. Jackson selects his classic rock station. Led Zeppelin's 'Whole Lotta Love' plays. Immediately, Apollo loves it. He visualises Jimmy Page's fingers skillfully moving up and down the guitar neck. Actually, he visualises his own fingers. Soon, Apollo is singing the chorus, matching Robert Plant's voice nearly note for note.

Despite his predicament, Jackson is impressed. 'You gotta future, kid. I'm willing to put this little kidnapping thing behind us if you sign with me. Besides, you're going to like where I am taking you. There's a special room just for you.'

Freya is still in the back seat holding the gun but her eyelids are getting heavy. Unlike Apollo, she has yet to sleep. She is quickly growing weary and soon drifts off.

Jackson notices this but keeps driving. He figures he'll win her over soon enough. Watching Apollo play air guitar in the front seat overcomes any reservations he might still have. This boy is a goldmine.

The Range Rover pulls into a service station. When it stops, it jars Freya awake. She immediately gathers the gun and points it at Jackson's head. He is almost condescending. 'Easy. Just fueling up.'

Jackson finishes filling the tank with gas and hops back in. 'You two hungry?' he asks. 'I know I am. Let me show you the beauty of the In-n-Out Burger.'

The Range Rover kicks up loose gravel as it pulls out onto the main road. This results in a cloud of smoke. It disperses onto an Indian Chief Classic motorcycle. Its rider watches the SUV vanish over a hill. Coyote smiles, then kick starts the bike and pulls out to follow it.

19
A Future Cold Case

'Move along, nothing to see here,' Officer Juan Carlos says. He really likes saying that to onlookers, especially when there is something to see. In this case, a six-foot-six, three-hundred-pound man is lying face down in a pool of his own blood.

One man, in particular, is getting on Juan's last nerve. 'Tell me what happened,' the man demands. 'I have a family here and I need to know if there's a serial killer.'

'Did you see anything? Did you hear anything? If not, I have no use for you.'

A drunk, homeless man walks up. 'I seen it. I seen the whole thing.'

Juan thought he could get inebriated just by inhaling the man's breath. He gives the homeless man the once over. 'I'm sure you did. I'm sure you see lots of things.'

'No. These two boys were fighting. Then, this pretty lady comes with a piece and offs that motherfucker.'

'I'll be sure to add that to the report.'

'Man,' the homeless man yells, 'I speak the truth!'

The detectives, Oscar Collins and Diana Nemo arrive. Oscar makes a big show of stepping over the 'Police Line Do Not Cross' tape while Diana ducks under it. They hurry over to where the EMTs are examining the body.

Oscar yawns. 'Did you move anything?'

The older of the EMTs answers, 'Not yet. Checked for a pulse. Nada. Waiting for you to take your sweet time in getting here before we called the meat wagon.'

Oscar laughs. 'Better call a big one 'cause that's one hell of a passenger.'

Diana busies herself inspecting the alley. She finds something. 'A bullet exited the body and hit here.'

Oscar and the EMT exchange an eye roll. Oscar walks over and picks up one bullet and then another. 'You see, Diana, it took two bullets to bring this monster down. And here they are. Police work ain't that hard.'

Diana walks back to the body and examines it. 'You're wrong. This man was shot three times but it appears two went in the same hole. So, in all likelihood, there's still a bullet inside him.'

'No way a .40 is still in there. Two were fired. Two brought him down. And the bullets are useless. They hit the wall hard and are scuffed beyond all recognition.'

'It's possible,' the EMT said, 'that one hit a rib and lodged inside. Remember, this is one big boy we're talking about.'

Diana looks momentarily justified. Oscar tells the EMT to send the carcass to autopsy. He glares at Diana, 'This isn't for

DEITIES

you.'

Finally, the EMTs roll the dead man over. There on the slab is Pluto. Diana sees him and gasps. This wasn't just a corpse; this was her uncle. Her estranged, evil uncle. Yet a god of the Underworld. What was he doing on earth? And more importantly, what was he doing dead?

Oscar is supercilious. 'Someone you know from your homeless days?' he asks.

Diana pauses. She can't answer straight away. 'No, never seen him around here.'

Oscar relishes in this. 'I guess that our Mighty Joe Doe Young is just a regular John Doe. I'm sure we can find something out, next week at the earliest. It's not like this guy is going anywhere.'

'This could be important,' Diana insists, standing up for herself. 'Don't make me call the Captain.'

Diana had a special relationship with the Captain. Her cases always got top priority. Maybe because she saved the chief's stepson. Maybe because he had a thing for her. But in the end, it didn't matter – what Diana wants, Diana gets.

'Fine, 'Oscar says, 'send the meat wagon priority one. I'm sure Digby won't mind.'

The EMT comments, 'Like you said, I'll make sure they send a big one.'

The homeless man is still shouting. 'I seen the entire thing! Why won't nobody listen to me?'

Juan attempts to quieten him down but it's useless. Diana hears him and quickly makes a beeline towards him. 'What did you see?'

STUART CLARKE

Finally, someone is taking him seriously. 'That big motherfucker comes walking in here like he owns the place. I asked him for some change and he pushed me down. Ain't no one gonna treat me that way, so I hung around a bit. You know, from, like, a distance.'

'And then what?'

'He and this smaller guy start a-jawin'. Then, they start with the fists. Smaller guy does his best and all but he ain't no match. He about to die. Then, this honey shows up, gun a-flarin'. She offs that big guy and takes the smaller one with her.'

Oscar joins Diana during this diatribe. He admits it seems feasible.

Diana takes umbrage. 'It sounds exactly like what happened. I hope you took notes.'

Oscar has no interest in being treated this way by the junior detective. 'You write down anything you like when we get back to the station.

Diana ducks back under the tape. Amid the pool of blood, she notices something small and rectangular. A business card from Jackson Tate. She puts it in her pocket deciding to keep this little clue to herself.

****

After Diana files her report, Oscar and herself drive to the morgue. Once there, Oscar nods to the receptionist and she buzzes them past the door.

George Digby is the finest coroner in the city. He takes his work very seriously. Some of the others left the job. They now serve as expert witnesses during trials. Apparently, there is a lot of money in the field.

Digby is dressed in green scrubs. A mask obscures his face and a white cap covers his dark hair. He motions Oscar and Diana over.

'I've seen some interesting cases but this one takes the cake. You find any ID on this guy?'

'No,' Oscar answers. 'No wallet; no ID. We're hoping you can solve this little riddle.'

'Gonna be hard. This one's got no fingerprints. Can't trace to the DMV or the arrest databases without them.'

'Maybe he filed them off,' Oscar suggests.

'Nope. There'd be abrasions if he had. I've taken an imprint of his teeth. Maybe dental records will give us a match.'

'So basically, you have no idea.'

"Fraid not. And get this – he has no identifiable blood type.'

Oscar scratches his head. 'Is that even possible?'

'Not really. There are some pretty rare types other than the ones you know. Doesn't match any of them either.'

Oscar leans in and examines Pluto's face. There is a sizable scar on the forehead. 'This your work?' he asks Digby.

'Yeah, that's me. Circular saw wouldn't go through that thick skull. I got another one I'll try.'

'Handsome enough fellow. Wonder what he did before he was dead.'

Digby nods. 'This guy doesn't have a single blemish on his body, either. It's like he's the perfect specimen. Here, I got something for you.' Using forceps, Digby retrieves the bullet from a dish. 'Thought this might come in handy.'

STUART CLARKE

'Thanks.' Oscar places the bullet in an evidence bag and sticks it in a plastic bag. 'We'll see what Ballistics finds out.'

Digby removes the sheet from Pluto's body. Pluto is really carved up.

Diana gags at the sight of her fellow god. His blood is everywhere.

Oscar laughs. 'You want to sit this one out?' Diana nods and exits the room, her hands covering her mouth as though she might vomit. 'She usually has a stronger stomach,' Oscar explains.

'She's a nice-looking girl. You wanna put in a word for me? The only ladies I usually see are dead ones.'

'I think you might be barking up the wrong tree. She's turned down the entire force. Personally, I think she's a vagitarian.'

'Pity that.'

****

Diana doesn't really need to heave but it was certainly a graceful exit. She reaches into her pocket and retrieves Jackson Tate's bloody business card. She's going to have a meeting with that man, so she hails a cab.

Once in the office, she flashes her badge to the receptionist. 'I must speak to Jackson Tate,' she says.

'I'm afraid he's out of the office at the moment,' Julie, the receptionist, responds.

'When will he be back?'

'I must say, I do not know. He must have left during my lunch. Sometimes, he does that and doesn't return. He'll probably be here tomorrow but I can't be sure. He was meeting with a new client today, so anything is possible.'

'Where does he usually take his clients?'

'Le Tryst is his favourite. French food, very good. But he usually has me call ahead, so I doubt he went there.'

Diana sighs. 'I need his cell number.'

Julie scrawls down his number. 'I can dial it if you like.'

'Please.'

Julie enters the digits. It goes straight to voicemail. 'No answer.'

'Tell me about this new client.'

Julie exhales. 'He was gorgeous. I would have cozied up to him, except he had this vixen with him. She was an absolute knockout. There was no way I could compete with her.'

'Do you keep records as to who meets with him? An appointment book, perhaps?'

'Of course but he came in without one. I let Jackson know that he was here and I was told to usher him back immediately. Jackson never does that.'

Diana feels she's onto something. 'You don't happen to remember this client's name, do you?'

'It's not one I'd ever forget. Apollo. Very unusual, don't you think?'

Diana's eyes widen. 'Yes, that's a very odd name.' It is good that Julie has no idea how unusual. 'Where else would Jackson have taken him?'

'He has a place in Calistoga that he visits frequently. He was very excited about Apollo. Perhaps, he took him there.'

'I'm going to need a map.'

20

Hel on Earth

Hades and Hel materialise outside a biker bar in the Mission District. This was a particularly dangerous part of town – one that the Hell's Angels ruled. They take stock of their surroundings. Litter, cigarette butts, used needles. Not all that different from hell. Hades noted that they might actually like it here.

Two Harleys pull up alongside them. The younger of the riders dismounts first, he eyes them suspiciously. But he can't take his eyes off the beautiful creature that is Hel. A Goth girl near a biker bar. This was something worth seeing.

The older biker places his helmet on his handlebars. He motions to Hades to join him. 'You two are a long way from home.'

'You have no idea,' Hades answers.

The older biker, whom Hades will come to know as Doc, is coarse. 'You're sort of a pretty boy to be bringing a girl to a place like this. You lose a bet or something?'

DEITIES

Doc is filthy. Unwashed, with tobacco breath. What could have been last night's meal still hangs prominently in his scraggly beard. Hades is unsure what to make of him. Certainly, a god of the Underworld would find solace amongst earth's refugees.

'No bet,' Hades says. 'Just got here.'

Doc notices his friend chatting up Hel. This younger biker was known as Groom because he passed out during what was supposed to be his wedding. Heroin can do that to you. 'Let's go and get you a drink,' Doc says. 'Just don't get mad if you don't get out of here alive.'

'I think I can handle myself.'

Doc breaks into laughter. 'We'll see about that.'

Hades and Hel are escorted into the bar by Doc and Groom. The place is packed, full of criminals and parolees. Hades takes note that the crowd does not part upon his arrival. Do they have no respect on earth? Do they not recognise him for the god he is?

Doc has no such problems. Everybody wants to talk to him. 'When did you get out?' a scruffy biker asks.

'Just a few days ago. Parole officer is a friend of ours. Thinks he's a motorcyclist 'cause he bought a Hog. Won't give me any trouble as long as I stay off the hard stuff.'

The biker grins. 'Only the finest whiskey for you, my friend. Gentleman Jack, all around.' He notices Hades and Hel. 'Who are those fucks? They ain't undercovers, are they?'

Doc is a little concerned he hadn't considered that possibility. He stared down Hades. Hades stared back.

Doc pulls Hades aside. 'I've invited you into my home. I

hope you intend on keeping your nose clean.'

Hades has no idea what that means. 'I always do,' he replied.

'It's a good thing for you that you brought that hot piece of tail with you. Otherwise, the boys might take you outside.'

'I've been outside. I must say I prefer it in here.'

Doc finds this funny. 'What are you drinking?'

'Nothing yet.'

'I'm going to get you a Jack and Coke. Next round's on you.'

Meanwhile, Groom is making time with Hel. 'Where you from?'

'The Underworld,' she answers. 'But originally, Norway.'

'The Underworld. I like it. You just might fit in here. Not too sure about your boyfriend.'

'Hades? He's not my boyfriend. We're just together.'

Groom likes the sound of this. 'Of course, we can't call him Hades. That name's already been chosen.'

'I'm not sure if he'd be angered or honoured.'

Groom looks over at Hades. 'Believe me, the Hades I know would kick his arse all the way to the Tenderloin.' Groom decides he wants to get Hel really drunk and see where that leads. 'You wanna shot of tequila?'

'I'm sure whatever you're having will be fine.'

Groom heads off to the bar. During this time, Hel catches a glimpse of herself in the mirror. No longer is she wearing two faces. The skull half has vanished, replaced by a replica of the beautiful side. She could not be happier.

A few minutes later, he returns with two double Jose Cuervos and a shaker of salt. He passes Hel a lime.

DEITIES

'What am I supposed to do with this?' she asks.

Groom thinks for a moment. 'They're called body shots. Wet your neck and sprinkle the salt on it. And hold the lime between your teeth.'

She does as instructed. Groom licks her neck, drinks his shot and takes the lime from Hel's mouth. She rather likes this little mortal ceremony.

'Now you do me,' Groom says.

Hel licks the salt off his sweaty skin. She lifts up her glass and downs the shot. But she starts coughing uncontrollably, leaving Groom hanging with a lime in his mouth.

Groom tosses the lime over his shoulder. 'Not a tequila girl, I take it?'

'I've drank some terrible things in my lifetime but this is by far the worst.'

'It does taste pretty terrible but it does get you good and drunk.'

Hel frowns. 'So does mead.'

'Mead?'

'Never mind. What is that mechanical stallion you rode in on? It looks like fun.'

It takes Groom a few seconds to realise what she's talking about. 'The motorcycle? That's a Hog – an HD Dyna. Best bike on the planet.'

'I see. Where does one acquire a Hog?'

Groom is actually a little embarrassed about the story behind it. 'My stepdad's in prison. He sorta 'loaned' it to me. But I take really good care of her, so no worries.'

'Can you teach me to ride one?'

STUART CLARKE

'Sure, darling. You say when.'
'Now.'

****

It turns out that Hades likes Jack and Cokes. The sweetness followed by the bite really warms him up. He is enjoying Doc and his friends, oblivious to the fact that they are planning on beating him up and robbing him.

'Here's to Hades,' Doc toasts. 'I don't know where you came from but we're glad you showed up.'

Hades is a little drunk by now. The liquor hits his system harder than he is used to. The other bikers plot. They will soon take Hades outside. He'll be drunk and helpless. Whatever cash he has on him will belong to them.

They introduce Hades to a drink known as a Kamikaze – Vodka, Triple Sec and Rose's Lime Juice. It is sweet and appears to have no taste of alcohol. Hades drinks three more. He starts to see double.

****

Hel is outside with Groom. He lights a cigarette and offers the pack to Hel. She observes him and puts it in her mouth. He lights it for her with a butane lighter. She is amazed at how easily he produces a flame.

She takes her first drag of a cigarette. It is lighter and easier to smoke than a cigar. She rather likes it. But she's still interested in the lighter. 'Can you show me the fire again?'

Groom obliges. He pops open the lighter and spark – there is the flame again. He passes it to her. She flicks it open and, voila, fire. 'Interesting,' she says. She rubs her hand over the flame and feels its heat. This is fire. The real deal.

DEITIES

'It's amazing to me that you can light a joint anywhere in this town but, god forbid, you smoke a cig. The cops care about shit like that.

They finish their cigarettes. 'You wanna take a ride?' Groom asks.

'That I do.'

Groom straddles the bike. 'Hop on back.' She does. 'Now let me show you what this cycle can do.'

He kicks it. The tires squeal as he makes a quick U-turn. Her arms are locked solidly around him and Groom loves it. Where to take her, he wonders. His place? Hers? Or right up against a wall?

They approach a stop sign and he slows down. Hel taps his shoulder. 'My turn.'

Groom is dismissive at first. Nobody rides his bike. But then nobody looked like Hel either. Maybe, just this once. 'You know how to handle one of these?'

'I'll figure it out. I'm a fast learner.'

Against his better judgment, he lets her drive. She's slow, to be sure but surprisingly adept. She doesn't take the corners too harshly. She accelerates through the turns. If she hadn't told him otherwise, he'd think she'd done this before.

Hel stops the bike about a block away from the bar. 'I hope you don't take this personally but I need this vehicle.'

'Sorry, honey, she's not for sale.'

'Wasn't exactly planning on trading for it.'

Hel and Groom get off the motorcycle. 'Listen,' Groom says. 'I don't know what you have in mind but it's only fair to warn you, I'm packing.'

STUART CLARKE

'Packing what?'

He reaches behind his waist and pulls out a Smith & Wesson. 'I always keep one on hand. You never know when you'll meet a pyscho bitch.'

'So, that's a weapon? I'm going to need that too.'

Groom is now pointing the gun directly at Hel. 'I don't know what your damage is sister, but I think it's best you walk away right now.'

Hel's fingernails are like claws. She lunges and pierces Groom's throat. He makes a gurgling sound and drops the gun.

Groom is choking on his own blood. Hel kicks him to the ground and retrieves the weapon. She kickstarts the bike and goes to collect Hades.

****

Hel peeks in the bar but Hades is nowhere to be found. One particularly helpful biker laughs at her. 'Doc and the boys took your friend out back. Gonna teach him a lesson about whose turf you stumbled into.'

Hel's smile is like saccharin. She exits and walks around the corner. There, she sees Hades lying on the ground. He's being kicked by Doc and three other men.

She pulls out the Smith & Wesson. 'I think you should stop now.'

They realise that they are staring down a barrel. 'You think you can shoot all of us?' Doc asks. We've all got guns just like that.'

She pulls the trigger and shoots Doc in the knee. He falls down, squawking in pain. The remaining three pull out their weapons. 'You shouldn't have done that, little girl. Time to pay

DEITIES

the piper.'

Hel doesn't blink. She quickly shoots two of the other men in the chest. They fall to the ground, mortally wounded. The last man standing is in a bit of shock. Still, he stands his ground. He prepares to fire on Hel but he is pulled by the jacket from behind. Hades has dragged him to the ground.

The man has dropped his gun but has another weapon in his arsenal. He flicks open a switchblade and attempts to stab Hades with it. He misses. Hades grabs the man's wrist with such force that it dislocates. The switchblade falls harmlessly.

The man is crying in agony. Hades picks up the knife and stabs him several times – in the eyes, the throat and the chest.

Hel gathers all the guns. Weapons like these, she reasons, may be hard to come by.

'I have a Hog a little ways down,' Hel says. 'We should go.'

'You mean that mechanical horse?'

'Yes. But let's call it a Hog. Like the locals do.'

21

Following the Past

The Range Rover takes a shortcut by cutting through the city of Napa – a wily shortcut. It is tourist season now and Highway 29 is not the way to go. There reside the bulk of the Valley's wineries and the thoroughfare divides the largest and most popular vineyards. The vacationers drive their rentals as if they were a bumper car ride at an alcoholic Disneyland for adults. Automobiles weave in and out of lanes.

Napa runs a pretty fragile economy, much like that of an island nation. The tourist season fills the hotels and restaurants. The wineries sell bottle after bottle and case after case. And of course, the 'tasting tours'. These amount to little more than five-dollar sips from commemorative wine glasses bearing the winery's logo. Proof they can keep. Been there; done that; got the t-shirt.

Of course, no self-respecting city could withstand that many drunk drivers without doing something about it. Law enforcement is enlisted to keep the roads safe for other

DEITIES

motorists and pedestrians. To protect drivers from themselves. And to earn the county a pretty penny in the process. The unofficial motto of Napa county is 'Come on Vacation; Leave on Probation'.

****

Coyote trails the Range Rover keeping a distance of about two hundred yards. He speeds up when necessary but mostly just hangs back. He gets closer to the SUV when it turns left onto the Silverado Trail. He may have been seen – seen but not noticed. He can see Apollo riding in the 'death seat' with the blonde in the back. Coyote looks but has no idea who the driver is. He's not sure how this newcomer plays out in this strange scenario but it seems likely that he has a part. Coyote hopes it's not a very large one.

The road winds past lesser known wineries – no Mondavi's or Beringer's on this side. Few drivers meant higher visibility for Coyote. Nothing to do but watch the road; watch the road…

Coyote finds his mind wandering. Here he is, tracking Apollo into the Valley, because someone and he's not even sure who, is paying him to do it. Coyote would be paid well, of course. There would be money but more importantly, his station would rise. Coyote would become more powerful and could return to the reservation. Those who ostracised him all those years ago, would kneel before him.

****

Hundreds of years ago, Coyote was considered a great god amongst the Native Americans' in California. Some traditional folklore had him linked to the creation of light, of man and even the earth. But that was before the invasion of the white man into the Native American territories. The white man brought with them their own religion and killed off those who did not convert. The natives were given two choices – turn your back on your faith or die. Often, they were killed regardless.

Coyote is reputed to have created Napa and Sonoma counties. He knew this area well but still marvelled at the changes. The crops were obviously quite different. Wine was not held in high regard in those days. In that time, Coyote carried pemmican – dried meat pounded together with kidney fat and berries. It must taste better than it sounds. But today, wine rules the Valley. It was not to be this way. Of this, Coyote is sure.

Coyote was not always a bad guy in the Native American pantheon. Like the Greek Titan Prometheus, he stole fire so that humans could use it to keep warm during the winter months. Like Persephone, the goddess of the Spring, he taught Eagle about the renewal of the earth every six months. Like the Christian god, he is fabled to have created mankind itself. And this may be where the trouble begins.

Christian settlers conquered those Western tribes. They came with rifles, weapons that seemed to shoot blazes of fire from their very tip. The Native American gods fled. Crow and Eagle to the skies; Cougar to the safety of the mountains. The gods of Thunder and Lightning passed their reigns over. Soon, it was but Coyote standing for the people.

But those people betrayed him. They were weak; they feared death at the hands of the white man. Coyote could not, or rather would not, defend such a group of cowards. They had

DEITIES

lost belief in him; thus, he lost belief in them. He would merge into the city. He would become a criminal. He became the Trickster god and my, what tricks he would play.

However, humanity tricked the Trickster. It was grown far more self-reliant than any god could reckon. These new humans prayed but once a week. They did not hold their idols in regard. Perhaps, the other gods had been right to disperse.

Coyote does not do that. He chooses to live amongst the humans. He takes advantage of them, one at a time or in groups. Coyote became a thief; he became a spy; and, in this bizarre case, became a tracker.

****

The Range Rover slows as it reaches Calistoga. There on the right is the Calistoga Resort – an exclusive country club. Jackson Tate is a founding member. He drives past the security gate and the guard waves him in.

'Put the gun away, Freya,' Jackson says. 'If I wanted you dead, that man would have handled it for me. Let's all be friends now.'

Apollo looks to the backseat. He shrugs. 'He may have a point.'

Freya holds the gun close. She's not giving it up but at least she's not aiming it at anyone.

Finally, the Range Rover comes to a stop in front of what's known in the club as a 'cottage'. This particular cottage boasts eight bedrooms and six full baths. The trio enters the enormous foyer behind the front door. Jackson is very proud of his success and loves watching the expressions of those seeing it for the first time. However, this was no Olympus or Valhalla. To

STUART CLARKE

Apollo and Freya, it was what was to be expected on earth for gods such as them. Somewhere between the flophouse where Apollo regained his consciousness and an acceptable place. Jackson is trying, they thought. Good on him.

'Come,' Jackson says. He wants to give a tour. Apollo and Freya acquiesce to this although neither appears interested in his granite countertops or leather seating arrangements. They are, however, amazed that he has a cool breeze in the form of air conditioning and refrigerators and a stove that produces heat at the turn of a switch.

Jackson notices Freya playing with the stove eyes. 'You hungry?' he asks. 'How do you feel about sea bass? My favourite fish.'

'Never had it. I eat a lot of salmon,' she says.

'Love salmon,' Jackson says. 'The Norwegian smoked it the best.' Did they just bond? Freya looks Scandinavian. But these days, you never could tell.

'Smoked salmon is my favourite. We have to get some. It is so much better than Skittles.'

Jackpot!…wait what? 'There is little comparison.' Jackson momentarily thought of a Skittle wrapped in cream cheese. The thought did not stay with him long.

Apollo is playing with the burners. 'Watch it, Apollo. That fish is twenty-seven dollars a pound. Let's not cook it unevenly.'

Apollo backs away from the stove and Jackson takes over. One good thing about this man, is that he can cook. He serves three plates of sea bass accompanied by a shrimp risotto and something called kale. Kale, it turns out, is green and is meant

DEITIES

to be pushed aside on a plate.

Freya consumes the sea bass. It is unlike anything from the oceans she has ever encountered. Apollo as well devours the dish. There is nothing remotely like it on Olympus.

'This is not from the Aegean,' Apollo says definitively.

'Nor from the North Sea,' Freya confirms.

Jackson has a large mouthful of risotto he is contending with. He swallows hard. 'This fish is Chilean.'

Apollo and Freya look at each other, confused.

'You know, Chile? South America?'

Apollo nods. He recalls something that Coyote said about new lands. South America must be among them. And if sea bass was any indication, its cuisine was outstanding. He tried to explain this to Freya. She was adamant that there was no such place as South America; else, the Vikings would have discovered it.

'Our Vikings founded Greenland. And Iceland. They named them backward because they are sneaky.'

'Who's to say who discovered what?' Jackson says. 'They like to say Columbus discovered America but people already lived here. Something's rotten in the state of Denmark if you know what I mean.'

Freya has no idea what he means but he is disparaging a Scandinavian territory, so that is enough to aim the gun at his chest again.

Jackson is startled. 'What did I say? Not a big Shakespeare fan, I take it?'

'Denmark is a holy land. There is nothing rotten about it!' Freya exclaims.

'It's just an expression. Like 'all roads lead to Rome',' Jackson explains.

This upsets Apollo. 'They most certainly do not!'

Jackson makes a mental note to never discuss anything even vaguely associated with geography with them again. 'None of the roads here do, in any event.'

Apollo nods. He is satisfied. Freya, however, still fumes. 'When Rome fell, word reached the Germanic people slowly. It took many more years for us to learn of its demise.'

Jackson nods, although he's really not sure why. They eat the rest of the meal in silence.

After dinner, Jackson shows Apollo a special room. It has around thirty guitars lining the walls. Autographed photos with musical legends, including Paul McCartney and Mick Jagger, are prominently displayed. But what confuses Apollo the most is the walls. They are white and soft to the touch.

'They're soundproof,' Jackson explains. 'Please play to your heart's content.'

****

Coyote ditches the Indian bike deep in the bushes where it is essentially invisible. Somewhere inside that gated access point, the Range Rover is parked. There would be no walking in the Calistoga Resort's front door. It's a good thing he carries bolt cutters for such an occasion. The chain link fence doesn't stand a chance.

22

This is a Good Thing, Right?

Hermes appears at Mount Olympus with the most interesting news. Trouble is, he refuses to share it with anyone but Zeus. And Zeus is still missing.

A number of gods and goddesses are on Olympus today. Ares, the Greek god of War threatens him. Athena attempts to trick him but Hermes is too savvy for her verbal traps. She then tries to reason with him but that gets her nowhere as well. Poseidon wants to physically beat it out of him but Hera intervenes.

'Surely, in lieu of Zeus, his wife would be sufficient,' Hera says.

'I am sorry,' Hermes replies. 'My orders are to deliver the message to Zeus and only to Zeus.' It soon becomes apparent that Hermes is enjoying this little repartee. For once, he is the most important god in the room.

Athena disputes Hermes sense of entitlement. 'If Zeus were here, he'd tell us whatever this great secret is.'

'Ah,' Hermes says. 'Of that, I cannot be certain.'

Aphrodite, the Greek goddess of Beauty, watches from afar. She decides to get involved. She has her own means of persuasion – the kind for which Hermes will be no match. She slinks behind him and puts her hands up his toga. She rubs her hands on his thighs. Hermes gasps as her fingers massage their way past his groin to his testicles and rapidly rising shaft. Aphrodite kisses his neck while playing with his manhood, driving him to the brink…

She suddenly stops.

Hermes is left high and dry. 'Wait,' he pleads. 'Don't stop.'

Aphrodite cocks her head. 'I believe you have something you need to tell us.'

Against his better judgment, Hermes relents. He is thinking with his smaller head now. 'Very well. But remember, this is meant for Zeus' ears. You didn't hear it from me.'

'Fine,' Athena says. 'Convey the message.'

Hermes hates himself right now. He hates that the promise of a mere hand job is clouding his thinking. But really, where's the harm? 'It seems that Horus has defeated Set.'

'That's fantastic news!' Athena exclaims. 'Does this mean he will be joining us on the war front?'

'I am not certain but feel it is a safe assumption. There is more, though. In honour of Horus' victory, Ra has stepped aside. It is Horus who shall lead the Egyptians from this day forward.'

This statement causes murmurs amongst the Olympians.

DEITIES

This is truly noteworthy. It is also grounds for concern. Very rarely are gods replaced willingly. However, Horus did end a war that lasted several thousands of years.

Poseidon is not entirely convinced. 'It is a matter of record that I am not pleased with Ra. He was extremely rude to Athena and me. But to be appointed a new ruler during such a time of crisis is worrisome. While I am confident he is trustworthy, I suspect he has much to learn.'

Athena does not share the same fears. 'Remember, Horus will have Thoth to guide his decisions. And I feel certain that Ra will be extremely willing to help with those matters of utmost importance.'

Hermes stands, somewhat impatiently, as the discussions take place. He is still hard and wants relief. 'Uh, Aphrodite? Weren't we in the midst of something?'

Aphrodite doesn't exactly blush. Hermes was used. She doesn't even seek to intervene. Neither does Hephaestus, her husband. He is accustomed to her infidelities. They sadden him but the crippled god of Blacksmiths knows nothing else.

It is Ares, Aphrodite's longtime lover, who intervenes. 'I think she was just making a point,' he says. 'You, like many, are powerless against her charms. I knew what was happening all along. I am surprised you did not.'

Hermes sulks. He has been played the fool.

'Cheer up, Hermes,' Poseidon says. 'You have work to do. Send a message to Horus congratulating him on his new station. Explain that those brethren from Olympus are excited to aid in any way he desires.'

Athena smiles. 'The scribes shall compose a scroll in the

hieroglyphic language for his reading pleasure. Hermes shall deliver it with our commendation.'

Hermes, the messenger, knows his place.

****

Odin stares out the window of the great hall of Valhalla. He does not sit; he has scarcely sat these several days. He paces the granite-tiled floors incessantly, stopping only to gather his thoughts, before resuming his pacing. Many thoughts run through his brain – thoughts of hope and thoughts of dread. Ra's displacement means something important, of this he is sure but he cannot fathom its magnitude.

The severed head of Mimir, Odin's advisor, has little to offer Odin. 'I'm afraid we will need to wait. Horus is an honourable general but whether or not he is a leader remains to be seen.'

Odin agrees. 'I have always held Horus in the highest esteem. However, I fear what the future may bring.'

Odin summons Njord. As a member of the Vanir, he may have glimpses into the future. Njord makes haste and appears before Odin.

Uncharacteristically, Njord speaks before Odin requests. 'I know why I am here,' he says. 'Horus has conquered Ra.'

'Conquered?'

'Perhaps that was a poor choice of words. I should have meant to say succeeded.'

Odin rubs his long beard. 'Succession plans rarely do not involve bloodshed. Tell me what you see.'

Njord concentrates. 'It is hard to see. The Egyptian desert winds carry sandstorms. But Horus' troops are not involved in the attack. They wait. They wait for Ra to step aside.'

DEITIES

Odin is most concerned. 'Was Ra challenged?'

'Yes. But he was guarded. It would appear that he freely relinquished his throne.'

'Can you help arrange a meeting?'

Njord shakes his head. 'I no longer detect him. Just as I no longer detect Zeus. It would seem that Ra has taken leave.'

'And Zeus?'

'He is also beyond my vision.'

This troubles Odin. 'Ra has stepped aside. Zeus is missing. Are there other gods whose place is in question?'

Njord smiles. 'There is no one plotting to topple you if that's what you mean. The Light needs you more than ever. It is you now and only you, that can prevent Ragnarok.'

'And Horus?'

'Horus just may be the hero The Light has needed.'

This answer satisfies Odin.

'There is one other thing. When will my daughter, Freya, be returning? I see that she went to earth. Was there a reason?'

Odin nods. 'She is to retrieve Apollo. I am certain she will return soon.'

'What about this son of Zeus? Why would we risk our own kind for his safety?'

'Apollo is going to aid in the fight against The Darkness. Poseidon and Athena named him as an important leader in the war.'

'Apollo has not raised a bow in millennia. What makes you think he will now?'

Odin smiles. 'Because Freya can convince anyone of anything.'

STUART CLARKE

****

Hermes arrives in Heliopolis, carrying the scroll penned by the Greek scribes. This is not the same city he recalled. Gone were the armed guards surrounding Ra's palace. Instead, a festive atmosphere exists. Street vendors sell their merchandise freely. Dancing gods and goddesses form a parade. The new regime of Horus is as exciting as it is fearless.

Horus sits on a balcony observing the revelry. He smiles and tosses golden trinkets onto his adoring public. War is over; peace exists.

Hermes cannot remember a place he has witnessed such merriment. The defeat of Set has created an ongoing festival. Egypt is, at last, in harmony.

When Hermes is spotted, he is immediately led to Horus. Horus opens his arms to him, with an embrace that nearly crushes the Greek messenger. Horus is drunk on beer. He offers a glass to Hermes, which he readily accepts. The scroll is passed into Horus' eager hands. At best, Horus skims it.

Once Horus has completed his 'read', he hugs Hermes again. 'The Greeks,' he toasts, 'and the Egyptians shall be allies until time no longer passes.'

Hermes grins. This reception is even better than expected. But soon it would be even better.

Horus makes eye contact with a trio of fertility demigods. They are dancing along the loose sand streets, attracting the attention of a great many revellers. Horus motions them up the veranda.

As they arrive, they kiss Horus. It is instantly clear that Horus' wife, Hathor, disapproves. Horus points them in the

DEITIES

direction of Hermes. 'Spread the love amongst our Greek friend.' The demigods dance for Hermes. Each is sexier than the previous. They caress his skin, taste the sweat from his neck and place their enthusiastic hands inside his toga. None are as beautiful as Aphrodite but this is an instance where the sum is not greater than the whole of the parts.

'We don't usually engage in public trysts here in Egypt. We leave that activity for the Romans,' Horus says. 'Why do you not visit one of the private chamber rooms?'

Hermes rises and follows them indoors. Sometimes, it may be good to be the king. But, in a pinch, being the messenger does just fine.

23

Return to Darkness

Anubis is lonely. Pluto is gone. Gone forever. Hades and Hel have left to avenge Pluto's death. Thoth is little more than a yes-man but he has adapted quite readily to advising Anubis on matters of the war. Thoth didn't have a great deal of choice in the matter. Eternal servitude trumps eternal punishment.

There are still plenty of minor gods and goddesses roaming the rooms of the Treachery Bar but all things considered, the Ninth Circle is dead.

This thought amuses Anubis. He has no equals and no challengers. So, there is really nothing to keep him busy. He spends his time speaking to his troops – the ones actually engaged in the battles. The Frost Giants, the Demons and the minor gods of war hang on his every sentence. He offers words of wisdom and strategy. They admire him. Anubis is the one fashioning the charge against The Light. And, under Anubis' guidance, they are winning.

However, because he is not actively on the war front, much

DEITIES

of the discussion is lost upon him. Although, he tries to keep up. A popular Frost Giant met her doom today. Her body has been brought to the Underworld for reanimation. This was a particularly nasty death. A Welsh war god's spear pierced her heart. This is not an abnormal occurrence. These legions of The Darkness, like their enemies from The Light, die thousands of times on the battlefield. What makes this casualty so grisly, though, is the fact that the Frost Giant's heart was still impaled on the demigod's spear. It would take a week or longer until she would be capable of returning to war.

Anubis spends more and more time with Inanna. Though she is far from an intellectual equal, her sexual prowess knows no bounds. There are worse ways to spend eternity. The Lord of the Underworld disappears with her to a secluded room. There, they pass time.

Less than an hour passes and there is a knock on the door. Who would possibly have the gall to disturb the great Anubis? He rises, naked and fuming. This had better be important.

He flings the door open and there stands Menhit, the Egyptian goddess of Massacre. He is shocked to see her; his erection dies. Menhit notices this and laughs. She gestures to the bed and the voluptuous Inanna. 'Careful with that one. As the old saying goes, you are known by the company you keep.'

Inanna hisses, bringing a smirk to Menhit's sun-chapped lips.

Anubis is speechless for a few moments. Menhit is an unlikely guest to the Underworld. She stays in the desert with Set. There is no reason for her to be here. He puts on his brave face. 'Why Menhit, how good to see you. The war with Horus must be going well for you to pay me a visit. Let me gather my tunic and we shall celebrate your arrival.'

'Yes,' Menhit says. 'Let's.'

****

Set's entourage could best be described as a militia. They command respect as soon as they enter The Treachery. Most do not know Set. There had been rumours, of course, of the previous ruler of the Underworld. But that was thousands of years ago and they had pledged their allegiance to Anubis. They view Set as a curiosity, an ancient memory – the stuff ghost tales are made of.

Still, they show respect. They clear a pathway for Set and his generals so that they may approach the bar.

Set leans against the rail and is not immediately served. He quickly grows impatient. Sucellus, the bartender, is occupied with a minor deity. She is pretty and laughing at his jokes. Set will not be getting service any time soon. Unless he demands it.

Set slams his fist on the bar and shouts 'Get over here now! My troops are thirsty!'

Sucellus looks briefly at Set and ignores him. No one speaks to him like this, not even Anubis. Sucellus goes right back to chatting with the demigod.

One of Set's generals grins. 'He has no idea what he's in for, does he?'

Set glares daggers at Sucellus. Finally, Sucellus concedes and walks over. 'Can I get you something?'

Set growls. 'You have no idea who I am, do you?'

Sucellus shakes his head. 'Should I?'

DEITIES

Set smiles. 'My friend, I can assure you it is best that you don't. Now bring a round of your finest Egyptian beers for me and my compatriots.'

Menhit and Anubis approach Set. Anubis is shocked to see Set.

Menhit is giddy. 'I'm sure you two have much to discuss. Don't mind me. I'll be just around the corner.'

Anubis is nervous. A barstool becomes empty next to Set but still, he elects to stand. 'It is good to see you,' Anubis lies. 'Tell me stories of the war with Horus.'

Set reaches down by his side and passes Horus' falcon mask to Anubis. 'This should answer any questions you may have.'

Anubis studies the mask. It is clear that Horus has been defeated. Anubis motions for Thoth to join them.

The meek Thoth is equally surprised to see Set. He looks at the falcon mask. Horus would never allow it to be taken. 'Congratulations on your victory.'

Set raises his glass. 'It was hard fought. Horus was a magnificent opponent. The clash lasted thousands of years.'

'And still, you are the vanquisher,' Anubis exclaims.

'That I am. I cannot help but wonder, however, if this conflict could have been completed sooner.'

Anubis shrugs. 'I am not sure what you mean.'

Set stares him down. 'You are an opportunistic god, Anubis. You knew that the longer I was away, the firmer grasp you would gain on the Underworld. You could have sent forces to fight Horus at any time and yet, you chose not to.'

'There is the war to consider. The Spheri Eternus is at stake. If The Darkness could gain control over it, then we would control all realms. That is where I concentrated my forces.'

Set shakes his head. 'When you say The Darkness, you speak only of yourself. You fancy yourself their leader. I cannot tell you how little I care about The Darkness or The Light. What impresses me is leadership and strength. My enemy Horus showed more fortitude than you could ever muster.'

'Set, while it is good to see you and revel in your success, I urge you to tread lightly. You are now in my realm.'

'You actually believe that, don't you? I expect you've always rued the day that I would return to reclaim my place. Today is that day.'

Anubis chuckles. 'Look around you, Set. That small cadre you've brought with you is vastly outnumbered. They must also be war-weary after thousands of years of battle. The gods in my realm are committed to me wholeheartedly. They will not hesitate to engage your small force.'

Set smiles at this. 'Anubis, I have an entire army outside waiting for my word to storm the Underworld. The sole reason they have not is I'd prefer not to destroy the interior of this habitation. It is to be mine, after all.' Set looks around The Treachery Bar. 'I do like what you've done with the place. It would be a shame to destroy it.'

Anubis becomes incensed. 'This will stay under my control. Your army shall recognise me as the true leader. They shall join with me. You will be trapped in the ice for all eternity.'

Set summons Menhit and tells her to open the floodgates. She barks the order, 'Invade.' The doors fly open and dozens of Set's soldiers enter. 'Try not to kill them all.'

The Frost Giants pick up their battleaxes. They swing

DEITIES

wildly at the attacking Egyptians. However, the Egyptian demigods are unsure what to do. Some engage the fracas but many do not. They are confused. Set has returned. What does this mean to them? Should their allegiance change?

The Frost Giants are no match for Set's forces. They are quickly overwhelmed. The Egyptian demons who had been sitting on the sidelines now actively engage on behalf of Set's army. Soon, it is just Anubis standing alone.

Set is smiling. 'So, you were discussing an eternity trapped in ice. Is that what you want for yourself? Or are you ready to admit defeat?'

Anubis looks to Thoth. Thoth whispers in his ear. Anubis, it seems, has no choice. Still, he attempts a negotiation. 'The Darkness has gained much ground under my leadership. Soon, we shall control the portal. My suggestion is that I continue to lead the battle.'

Set considers this. 'Gaining control of the portal would be most advantageous. Can you guarantee this?'

Anubis answers without thinking. 'I can. I have trained this arm of The Darkness well. They will accomplish the task.'

'Good. You shall be on the battlefield with them as will I. Together, we shall conquer. But it is I that am the ruler of the Underworld. Do you understand?'

'I do. I shall follow your commands to the letter.'

Set smiles. 'I am pleased that you see things as crystalline as I. We wouldn't want you to end up like those who do not.'

Anubis is momentarily confused. 'What do you mean?' But then he sees Ra's sarcophagus lowered into the icy pit of flame. From that moment, Anubis knows who's in control.

24

Quiet

Jackson Tate has overcome his fear of Freya. He realises she only wants the best for Apollo. And this is something he can most certainly deliver.

Jackson shows him around his Calistoga townhouse. Like his office, it is adorned with music paraphernalia, gold records and signed guitars. He rationalises that Apollo should be more impressed – we're talking Eddie Van Halen, Jimmy Page and Jeff Beck. Apollo glosses over them as if he'd never heard of them. He looks at pictures of bands – Bon Jovi, Aerosmith and Metallica, to name a few. Again, Apollo is unimpressed.

'Don't like what you see?' Jackson finally asks.

'They look like minstrels,' Apollo answers.

'Minstrels?' Jackson laughs. 'These are some of the greatest musicians of the last five decades.'

'Five decades isn't a very long time.'

'While I like where you are going with this, you must respect the past. I heard you play Hendrix. Until you have your

DEITIES

own mixes, honour those who came before you.'

'Why? I can play much better than what I heard in your automobile. Give me a chance to create my own songs.'

Jackson is stunned. Those guitarists were the best in history. 'Well, you're in luck, Apollo. I have a soundproof room. Knock yourself out. But don't learn their songs. I don't represent cover bands.'

Apollo has no idea what a cover band is. Instead, he follows Jackson into a room where guitars are lined up against a wall. Microphones are ready. Bass guitars occupy a smaller portion of the room and two full drum sets lie in the corner.

'You think you can do something with this? Be my guest.'

Apollo soaks in the room. There are instruments he's never seen, he makes a beeline towards the bass and thumps it. Little noise comes out.

Jackson is sarcastic. 'Let me plug you in.'

Apollo enjoys the bass. He had heard Deep Purple during the ride. He strums 'Smoke on the Water' to perfection.

'No covers,' Jackson reminds. 'Make your own music.'

Apollo nods. Jackson shuts the door.

With Apollo safely behind the doors, Jackson must face Freya and her gun. 'Certainly, we're past this,' he explains. 'I mean no harm to you or to Apollo. Apollo may well be the next big rock star if you'll just let him.'

'Is currency possible? I have a feeling we may need it.'

'I don't ordinarily front money. But we'll see what Apollo comes up with. I can put him on the local circuit soon and then who knows?'

'I'm not sure that's going to be such a good idea.'

Jackson rolls his eyes. 'You're a tough sell, aren't you?'

A solid knock bangs on Jackson's door. 'Expecting anyone?' he asks Freya.

Freya shakes her head.

Cautiously, Jackson peers through the peephole. He doesn't immediately recognise the scruffy Native American on the other side of the door. 'Who are you?' he says, attempting to sound aggressive.

Coyote takes a crowbar and busts through the door. Freya is up in a flash. She points her gun and fires.

Click.

Freya is out of ammo. She pulls the trigger several more times but the result is the same. Nothing. Nothing at all.

Coyote cannot help but laugh at Freya's predicament. 'You're out of bullets, sweet cheeks. And I am fully loaded.'

Jackson feels a wave of anger wash over him but it's mostly directed at himself. He's been held hostage by a hot chick with an empty gun. Still, he was able to spend time with Apollo, the most promising musician he'd seen in his thirty-year career.

Coyote instructs Freya and Jackson to sit on the sofa. 'Where is Apollo?' he demands.

Jackson answers quickly. 'He's not here. We left him behind. I thought I'd get to know his girlfriend a little better.'

'You know something, Jackson Tate. I don't know whether to be furious or honoured that you'd choose to lie to me. I mean, I don't even play an instrument unless you count an elk skin drum. Now I'm not naïve enough to believe that you only lie to clients but still.' Coyote turns his attention to Freya. 'Now you. You are a particularly good shot. Dropped that behemoth

DEITIES

dead right there in the street. I can't say I was surprised that you tried to kill me on sight but I am disappointed that you do not even know how to use the weapon. You were out of bullets, or if I may translate, arrows.'

'Well, I'd have to say, you're extremely lucky,' Freya responds.

Coyote snickers. 'Always am. But you, not so much.' He raises the gun and aims it between Freya's eyes. Naturally, she refuses to sit still. Coyote fires and misses. But he is on her like a flash. The gun pointed to her head. 'If you have any last words, now would be an excellent time to say them.'

Freya struggles and looks to Jackson but he is parked on the sofa, trembling in fear. Freya closes her eyes and accepts her fate.

Whomp!

Diana coldcocks Coyote. He drops the gun and falls unconscious. Freya scoops up the gun but Diana insists she hand it over to her. 'Freya, what brings you to earth?'

'I'm on a rescue mission. You, I heard, were banished.'

Jackson cannot believe his ears. 'Earth? Just where are you ladies from?'

Diana answers 'Greece.'

Freya responds with 'Fólkvangr.' Jackson stares blankly. 'You know it as Norway.'

'Hand me your phone. You've had both an intruder and an attempted murder here tonight. I need to call this in to Napa's finest.'

Freya doesn't understand the ramifications of this but Jackson certainly does. Reluctantly, he hands Diana the phone.

STUART CLARKE

Diana dials 911. She identifies herself as an SFPD officer and describes the situation to the dispatcher. A black-and-white will be along momentarily, she is assured.

Seconds after she hangs up the phone, Apollo emerges from the soundproof room. 'Now that was fun,' he announces to Jackson.

Apollo accesses the room. Coyote is lying unconscious. Freya and Jackson sit on the couch. And his twin sister is holding a weapon like Freya had.

'Apollo!' Diana exclaims. 'What are you doing here?'

'Artemis, I might ask you the same question. It is so good to see you!' Apollo looks at Coyote laid out on the floor. 'I assume this was your handiwork.'

'It was. Oh and as long as I am earthbound, I go by Diana. It's less godlike.'

Apollo laughs. 'That's really quite amusing. I'm sure your Roman counterpart would not approve.'

Diana has learned a few choice words from working in the Department. 'Fuck her. What's she ever done for me?'

'I've been learning to play music. That's Jackson. He's going to make me a star.'

Diana surveys the room. 'We need to leave now. Napa's police will be here any second. I don't want to explain what happened here.'

Freya and Jackson leap off the couch. They are more than ready to go. Freya, because she doesn't know what's going on but if Diana doesn't like it, she doesn't want any part of it. Jackson would like to leave because he has about a pound of marijuana and a half kilo of coke stashed in his bedroom.

DEITIES

They are prepared to flee but Apollo points to Coyote. 'What about him?'

'Damned loose ends,' Diana mutters. 'Okay, Freya and Apollo, pick him up. There's a dumpster outside with his name on it.'

****

Coyote awakens in a Waste Management green industrial sized garbage retrieval unit. It's not the first time he's been dropped in a dumpster but this is certainly the most inconvenient time. There is a ruckus outside and he peers over the walls. Three police cars are surrounding Jackson's mansion. Coyote weighs his options. He was certainly crafty enough to make an escape. Or he could hide and hope for the best. He ponders this and remembers his motorcycle. Any policeman worth his badge would find it.

The cops are focused on the house. They are likely destroying it in a desperate attempt to find some sort of evidence. Coyote touches the back of his throbbing head. There is a little blood but it will be hard to match it to him. It could have been anyone. Plus, he doesn't have an identifiable blood type or any fingerprints. Good luck catching him.

Silently, Coyote scales the walls of the garbage cube. He sits atop the side briefly to orient himself with the landscape. The police have attracted quite the crowd. The residents were up in arms. They'd heard the gunshots. 'Have you made an arrest?' they ask. 'Do you know if anyone was murdered?'

Satisfied that the cops are busy, Coyote slinks through the shadows until he reaches the security gate. Here, things would be more complicated. The guards are itching to be involved in any potential arrest. Some are dropouts of the academy. Some are looking to move out of security detail and onto the force. There are three of them. Coyote needs to get by them with as little drama as possible.

The guards are positioned in the worst possible way. One watches the entrance. Another, the exit. The third is of most concern. He walks the perimeter carrying a flashlight, a walkie-talkie and a firearm by his side.

Despite the inherent danger associated with this third guard, he is the one Coyote needs to surpass. Coyote searches himself for potential weapons but there is nothing to be found. He knows that, on this occasion, he will not be able to simply talk his way by. And as much as he eschews physical contact, there is really no other way. He waits patiently behind a bush, watching the man's every move. The guard stops in a corner and sets the flashlight and walkie-talkie down to take a piss on the wall. It's now or never. Coyote manoeuvres without a sound with one eye on the security at the entrance and the other on his intended target.

Coyote successfully sneaks past the security gate. Cautiously, he approaches the guard from behind and retrieves the flashlight. The guard turns around abruptly, urinating on Coyote in the process but this is a small price for freedom. Coyote repeatedly hits the guard in the head with the battery side of the flashlight, knocking him out. He seizes the gun. Never know when one might come in handy.

The guards at the security gate see the flashlight being shined from multiple directions. 'Everything all right over there, Mike?'

DEITIES

Coyote knows he has but seconds to react. His motorcycle is at least one hundred yards away, so he sprints. As he runs, he can hear the walkie-talkie growing more and more concerned. Soon, the other guards would come to the aid of their fallen comrade. But he'll be long gone before they put things together.

Coyote rolls his bike from behind the bushes and revs it up. It is a particularly noisy motorcycle – that is one of the things he loved about it. But tonight, it is a hindrance. There would be cops on his tail before he knew it, so he opted to retreat. To a place he swore he'd never go to again – the reservation.

****

Diana answers the unasked question. 'We're going back to San Francisco.'

Diana is driving fast. Apollo is in the front seat but Freya and Jackson are in back behind the wire metal screen.

Freya could be happier about this seating arrangement. 'Diana, why exactly am I in a cage?'

Diana sighs. 'Two reasons. You have to sit somewhere.'

'Understood. But why here?

'Because you're also my prime person-of-interest in Pluto's murder.'

Freya barks, 'Need I remind you that I am not a person but a goddess? But I am certainly of interest.'

Jackson shudders. He knew Freya had a screw loose but didn't think she was a murderer.

Freya is incensed. 'Murder? I saved Apollo from that monster. Apollo, do you think you could explain that to your sister?'

'It's true,' Apollo says. 'Pluto was sent to earth specifically to kill me. Freya arrived just before he could accomplish his mission.'

Jackson speaks up. 'So, that's why you were so beat up when you came to my office.'

Freya snaps with sarcasm dripping. 'I believe the Oracle of Delphi has just made an appearance.'

Diana interrupts. 'In any event, Freya, you shot and killed a god. My job on earth is to bring you to justice.'

'Justice was served with Pluto's death. Now, the question remains, what do you suppose will happen to me?'

Diana is quiet. 'Honestly, I'm not sure,' she finally admits. We'll need to get you a lawyer. If we can prove that you acted in defense on Apollo's behalf, you should be fine.'

'Should be,' Freya repeats. 'You do realise there are forces at work here beyond your comprehension.'

'I am beginning to suspect that. However, I have sworn an oath to protect and serve the community. That includes Apollo but not you. At the moment, you are considered a danger to society.'

Jackson intercedes. 'What about me? I know a little something about the law. This will be construed as kidnapping.'

'I think you are a material witness. Plus, you jumped at the chance to get out of that house of yours. If I didn't know better, I'd assume you have something to hide.'

Jackson shuts up for now. But Freya is still on fire. She leans back and kicks the wires separating the backseat from the front. She kicks with all her might but the screen does not budge.

DEITIES

Diana advises, 'Save your strength, Freya. Many people, stronger than you, have tried that. It never works.'

'It does make quite the noise,' Apollo observes.

'I promise to let you out in an hour or so,' Diana says. 'But let it be known that you will be locked up in a prison until this is worked out.'

Freya continues kicking until she tires herself out. Diana smiles. Freya would be a patient rider until they arrive in San Francisco.

25

Called to the Carpet

Odin realises the error of his ways. Pairing the pantheons up with one another has been an utter disaster. The Romans undermine the Greeks and Athena has a hard time leading them. The Celts are not physically able to support Tyr, a powerful war god and a son of Odin. The Celts fight mightly of course but are simply overmatched by their foes. And there is no love lost between the Persians and the Mesopotamians. Neither side will budge. They simply will not work together.

Once again, Odin calls on the severed head of Mimir. 'What am I doing wrong?' Odin asks of the disembodied Mimir.

'On the smallest of scales, the Greeks must take control of the Romans, even if it means splitting them apart. Let the Romans handle a smaller front. They should be capable of handling that. The same must be done with the Persians and Mesopotamians. They cannot fight as a unit but there are smaller battles their forces can engage.'

DEITIES

'Can the Mesopotamians fight alongside the Greeks?' Odin asks, in earnest.

'Need I remind you of the Trojan War? Old wounds heal slowly.'

Odin nods.

Mimir continues. 'The Celts can be a powerful ally but they are without proper guidance. Tyr should be able to rally them. However, there is a missing component to our leadership.'

'Freya', Odin concedes.

'Exactly.'

'I cannot reach Zeus but perhaps Poseidon and Athena have access to him.'

'Or,' Mimir suggests, 'control has been granted to Zeus' wife in his absence.'

'That is a possibility. Although a remote one, at best.'

'Summon Athena first. See if she can help us.'

****

Athena is in battle as usual. She fights a pack of wolf-gods. They surround her and take turns attacking. Each time she gets one alone, she slices its throat. The wolves whimper and fall back into the pack. Athena has a hard time killing them all. There are approximately twenty of them but only three bodies. They are attacking with purpose, hoping to tire her out. And the strategy is working. She's only slain four of the large grey and black canines. But she has a rather delicious idea. To maim and not kill.

The next wolf that attacks, she aims for the hindquarters, dicing off the tail and the left leg. The action has the wolves second-guessing themselves but a particularly brave wolf leaps into the fray. Athena's sword immediately slices off a front leg. The other wolves change their tactics. They surround her and attack at once. This was exactly what Athena was waiting for. She spins and her blade connects with most of the pack. Several are beheaded, the remaining scatter. Athena sits down amid the carnage. She is exhausted. The battles are getting more and more difficult. Being outnumbered grows tiresome. She needs rest. But what she really needs is a drink.

****

Venus is sitting at Heaven's Hotel bar. Ares is chatting her up. She notices Athena but pretends to be oblivious. 'Didn't take her long to get over Apollo,' Athena mutters. She considers approaching her but decides that it is, in no way, worth her time. Besides, she might have to lower herself to speak to Ares.

So, she heads over to Apollo's table, where Apollo is noticeably absent. Bacchus is sharing wine with Pan and Kyrene. All three are drunk but not happily so.

Bacchus rises when Athena ducks under the velvet rope. 'Please tell me you have some good news,' he says, in lieu of a greeting.

'I killed a bunch of wolf-gods today but I assume that's not what you meant.'

Bacchus sighs. 'Still no word on Apollo?'

'Sorry. I have no idea when, or even if, he'll be back.'

Kyrene speaks up. 'I've heard rumours. Apollo is on earth but both Freya and Pluto are missing.'

Athena dives on this. 'Rumours? From where?'

'From the trees and the woodland creatures. When The Darkness travels through the forest, they speak rather loudly.

DEITIES

They don't always account for the fact that we have ears everywhere.'

'What are they saying about Pluto? I haven't seen him on the battlefield.'

'That he is gone. Similar to Apollo.'

Athena thinks. 'Apollo must have vanished through a portal…'

'To earth,' Kyrene offers.

'Perhaps. But there is no portal that Pluto could pass through. Unless Poseidon is some sort of genius and duped him. But Poseidon wouldn't lower himself to that. He's brute force, not a trickster.'

'But Mercury is,' Bacchus says. 'Could the Roman to Roman connection be at play here?'

'Could Mercury lead Pluto to the Spheri Eternus?' Athena wondered out loud. 'I must say, I have my doubts but anything is possible.'

'This does bring up an interesting point,' Bacchus says. 'Where exactly is the portal?'

'Historically, it's been wherever Zeus wanted it. He kept it on Olympus, where he and Odin could best watch over it. But it's moveable. Zeus' philosophy was to transfer it to Valhalla at times, as Odin is the god he trusts the most.'

'Given how angry Zeus has been with Apollo, it's possible that he could have moved it here to punish his son.'

Athena considers this. 'Very possible. In fact, as much as I hate to admit it, you may be onto something.'

'Where is the portal now?' Bacchus asks.

'It is on the Ethereal Plane. Which makes me really miss

Freya. We cannot defend it without her.'

'Can Odin not move it?'

'No, they both need to agree to it. And because Zeus is absent, the portal will remain where it is.'

Bacchus is more serious than ever. 'Who can use it?'

'Only the chief gods but generally Odin and Zeus must agree that inter-realm travel is necessary.'

'What if Zeus were absent? Who could use it then?'

Athena has a moment of clarity. 'Poseidon. He would have the knowledge.'

'So, this is becoming clear. Zeus punished Apollo, Odin sent Freya, presumably to rescue Apollo and Poseidon banished Pluto. With Mercury's help, of course.'

Athena is shocked. Has Bacchus solved the riddle that had confounded her for so long? 'Bacchus, you're a mental virtuoso. I mean, who knew? I could kiss you.'

Bacchus grins. 'Well, by all means.'

Athena gives him a peck on the cheek. Not exactly the kiss Bacchus was hoping for. But he'd take what he could get.

Bacchus thinks. 'Kyrene, you and I are going to take a little trip to Olympus.'

'Why?' Kyrene asked.

'We're going to convince Poseidon to send us to earth. We're going to find Apollo and bring him home.'

Kyrene smiles. 'Yes!' she squeals.

Bacchus turns to Pan. 'You coming?'

'No,' he answers. 'I'm going to fight alongside Athena. You'd be surprised at the number of satyrs and fauns I can recruit. You want to see The Darkness panic? I invented panic.'

DEITIES

Athena smiles thankfully.

****

Athena receives word from Odin. To be honest, she doesn't really want to visit him. But when Odin calls, the wise thing to do is go immediately. She knew he had questions for her, questions that she could not answer. The first question would be, where is Zeus? The second would be, who was leading the Greek delegation? Whether or not he should deal exclusively with Poseidon would come up as well.

To make matters worse, Njord and Mimir were by Odin's side. She feels like a philosophy student forced to defend a paper. It takes a lot to rattle Athena; however, she is about to be rattled.

Odin speaks first. 'Athena, as I'm sure you know, the Spheri Eternus is dangerously close to falling into enemy hands.'

'Of course,' she replies.

'And I would very much like to move it. Unfortunately, neither you nor Poseidon have been able to locate Zeus. This presents a most serious problem.'

Athena is nervous. She hates asking questions she doesn't know the answer to. 'Forgive my ignorance but could another god be of aid? Jupiter? Ahura Mazda? Canopus?'

Odin bends his ear down to listen to Mimir. 'Absolutely not. Because Olympus and Valhalla currently hold control, only a god of Olympus can release it to me. I must say I am most troubled by the disappearance of Zeus.'

'I understand. But you should know that I am equally troubled by Freya's disappearance. I suspect that you sent her away.'

'Silence! You have no business questioning my intentions. This act was done to rescue your unworthy brother. He was supposed to join our fight but I suppose that is not the case.'

'He is purported to be on earth,' Athena said.

'Of course, he is on earth.' Odin is seething. 'As is Freya. But without Zeus, I cannot bring either one back.'

'Perhaps, Poseidon could be of aid. He understands the portal in ways I do not.'

'Well then, you have wasted enough of my time,' Odin barks. 'Get back to the battlefield and do something useful.'

Athena is not used to bowing before any god but she has little choice. 'Yes, my lord.'

****

While Athena sulks to her chariot, Odin discusses what has happened with his advisors.

Njord shows concern. 'There was little reason for you to be so angry with her,' he says. 'She is doing the best she can with limited resources.'

Mimir agrees. 'It was a mistake to send Freya to retrieve Apollo. Her presence is needed now more than ever on the Ethereal Plane.'

Odin listens intently to the most trusted of his circle. 'You are both correct. Please see to it that an apology is delivered to Olympus for Athena. And perhaps, the time has come to meet with Poseidon again. If we can move the portal here, we will buy time until our forces reach full capacity.

26

Wings

Oscar is, of course, wondering where the hell Diana is. But something new just ran across the blotter. Four bikers were killed outside a Hell's Angels turf bar. This had no markings of an inter-gang squabble. The Gypsy Jokers motorcycle gang members would naturally be questioned but Oscar was a pro. These were outsiders.

Donnie 'Doc' Adams was in the hospital in serious pain. A gunshot to the knee will do that to you. Ordinarily, bikers won't speak to police. They are not exactly above the law, more like around it. But Doc was more than ready to sing about this incident. He was happy to go on record.

'There was this couple,' he explained. 'I guess I think they were a couple. She didn't show much interest in him.'

Oscar is taking notes, something he wishes Diana was with him to do. 'Did you catch any names?'

'Yeah but clearly fake ones. The chick called herself Hel. He went by Hades. Hel took off with Groom.'

STUART CLARKE

'Groom?'

Doc clarifies. 'Yeah, David Chambliss. We call him Groom because of a wedding fiasco.'

Oscar doesn't even bother to write that part down. 'David Chambliss is dead. Throat slashed by what looks like claws.'

'Groom's dead? Fuck it! What a fucking waste. I loved that kid.'

'The gun that shot you is actually registered to him.'

Doc is shocked, 'Groom registered a gun?'

'I'm as surprised as you.'

'Groom was a good kid. We made sure he kept his nose clean.'

'I can see that. Chambliss had virtually no rap sheet. Minor marijuana possession charge about three years ago. Got tossed out of court.'

Doc laughs. 'Judge fancied himself a biker. What a fuckin' joke.'

Oscar is angered. 'You're the one with the dead friends here. You want SFPD help? Tell me all that you know. I mean everything. Spill!'

'Fine. Groom took off with Hel, or whatever her name is and he didn't come back. We got the Hades character pretty good and drunk and the boys and I thought we'd have a little fun with him.'

Oscar stares down Doc. 'You were beating him? Like four on one?'

Doc sighs. 'Yeah. Just thought we'd work him over a bit. No big thing.'

'Four of you punching and kicking a defenseless man is "no

big thing."'

'You gotta look at it in context. He was a stranger in our hangout. He needed to be taught a lesson.'

'Looks like you're the ones who learned it.'

'Fuck you, Oscar. I lost four good men that night. Don't you think the Gypsy Jokers know that already? I'm scared for my people.'

'Looks like you'll have to recruit some meth-heads.'

'Don't even joke about that. The Gypsy Jokers won't be playing games. You want a full-scale war on your watch?'

Oscar laughs. 'Doc, what does the real doc say about your knee?'

'Permanent limp unless I get it replaced. And that's expensive.'

'I'm sure you'll raise the cash somehow. Trouble is, very few surgeons take cash.'

Doc grins. 'Oh, you'd be surprised.'

As much as Oscar has enjoyed verbally torturing the wounded biker, he knows he has to get back to business. 'You want to work with our sketch artist? Maybe help us, help you?'

'You're on.'

The sketch artist has been waiting rather impatiently in the hallway. Finally, he is called in to do his job.

'So,' he says, 'Hades and Hel? Classical names. You sure you got them, right?'

Doc nods. 'Oh, that's them all right.'

The sketch artist starts by drawing Hades. Black hair, black eyebrows, slight nose, goatee. 'How tall was he?'

'Probably five-ten. Maybe a little shorter. It was hard to tell because he was doubled over getting his arse kicked.'

The sketch artist jots down five-nine. 'Weight?'

'Couldn't have been more than one seventy.'

'So, four of you beat him up? Class acts, all of you.'

'Yeah, well fuck off.'

The sketch artist finishes up his Hades mockup. 'This look like him?'

'Close enough.'

Oscar interrupts, 'I think I know what you're planning on doing. You're going to get your little gang of villains together and find him yourselves, aren't you?'

'Never said that,' Doc says.

'Well, let me tell you something. If either one of these two shows up dead before I have a chance to arrest them, I'll bring the entire San Francisco PD down on you so hard, you won't be able to sell a single joint.'

'Duly noted.'

The sketch artist is ready to move on. 'Do you think you can describe the girl? The one who capped you, I mean.'

'Oh, yeah. You don't forget a fine piece of tail like that.'

'Especially, after she put a bullet in your knee.'

Doc grumbles. 'She was about five-three, spiked black hair, green eyes, pale skin and wore some sort of satanic symbol around her neck. Nice tits but a little on the small side. Great arse. Couldn't have weighed more than one-ten.'

Oscar finds this funny. 'This hot, little muffin shot up your gang and left you hobbled? I love it. I'm not sure whether to arrest her or offer her a job.'

****

DEITIES

It's no big trick stealing a motorcycle in San Francisco. Stealing a good one though, well there's a challenge.

Hades quickly grows tired of riding behind Hel. To make matters worse, Hades is quite particular. The bike Hel acquired is very sleek and very fast. Hades needs something to compete with or at least keep up.

Hel mocks him. She points out mopeds and asks if they should get that one. He grouses; he pouts; he comes dangerously close to smacking her. Then, he sees the bike he wants. Like Hel's, it's a Harley but this one has some features hers is missing.

The motorcycle pulls into a parking garage. Hel follows him inside. She pulls up alongside the driver as he dismounts. 'Nice bike,' Hel says.

The driver checks her out before checking her bike out. 'Thanks. Yours too'

Hades hops off the Hog and closely inspects the bike. It is fire engine red. A little larger than the Dyna that Hel rides. This soothes his ego. 'Mind if I take it for a quick ride?'

The rider is stunned to hear such a question. 'Uh, yeah, I mind.'

'Just a little ride and nobody gets hurt.'

'Look, just let me go about my business and we'll call it even. I'm not looking for any trouble.'

'Too bad,' Hel says. 'Trouble just found you.'

Hades is still looking over the bike. 'What kind is this?'

'It's a CVO. Look, it cost me an arm and a leg. Please don't steal it.'

'An arm and a leg, you say? Seems like a fair trade to me.'

The rider becomes hostile. 'Even if you steal it, the bike is equipped with a tracking device. A simple phone call and you'll be busted.'

'What if you don't make the call?' Hel asks. She is pointing a gun at him.

The man shakes nervously but Hades calls Hel off. 'Put away that noisemaker,' he says. Hades pulls out the switchblade. 'I rather like this. It's so much more…personal.'

Hades stabs the man in the neck. He immediately falls to his knees. The blood makes Hades excited.

Hel grabs Hades. 'You realise we have a problem, right?'

Hades raises an eyebrow. 'And what would that be?'

'We need to hide this body. Or else they will find us.'

'Good point. Ideas?'

Hel looks around at all the cars parked in the garage. 'In one of those.'

They search the lot and come upon a Ford Mustang convertible with its top down. 'I'll just bet there is a button in that contraption that opens the back,' Hades says.

Hades steps over the door. He locates a lever and pulls it. The back hatch pops.

Hel looks inside. Essentially, the trunk is full. There are laundry bags and golf clubs. 'No room for a dead guy,' Hel gripes.

Hades is more optimistic. 'It's easy. We just throw the rubbish from the back into the front. Plenty of room for a body.'

Hel smiles. She loves it when Hades takes control.

****

DEITIES

A rather cowardly security guard has been watching the development on the screen. There was no way in hell she was going down there. But she did dial 911. This is not a job for a rent-a-cop. She described the action on the screen but even as she did, Hel and Hades rode past her. Hades even shot her an evil grin; one that sent a chill down her spine.

The 911 unit arrives; however, Hades and Hel are long gone. They review the tape. 'Did you physically see anything? Even a glimpse?'

'Just what I saw on the tape. But the man did look at me as they drove by.'

'What did he look like?'

'Black hair, goatee, probably average build.'

'Were they wearing helmets?' the 911 responder asks.

'No. And it appeared that she knew how to ride a lot better than he did.'

The 911 responder smiles. 'A newbie on a Hog with no helmet. Shouldn't be too hard to find.'

The security guard gestures. 'They left the helmet in that corner.'

'Bag it and tag it,' the 911 responder orders his underling. 'I doubt there's anything resembling a print on it but it's worth a shot.' He stares at the tape and suddenly asks for a rewind. 'There! They're wearing Hell's Angels jackets. This is definitely not the way the Angels work. They'd never steal a bike in broad daylight. Especially from a civilian.'

'What does that mean?' the security guard asks.

'It means they're not Angels at all. But I just had a case where four Angels were killed and one injured. 'We're going to have to take this tape.'

****

Hades is having fun on this mechanical horse. He and Hel ride side-by-side, paying little attention to transportation laws. Traffic builds up in front of them, so Hades follows Hel's lead and use the sidewalks instead. They'd find Apollo soon enough but there is no sense in not having some fun along the way.

27

The Roman on the Mountain

As a rule, the Roman gods are forbidden from Mount Olympus unless specifically invited. However, Bacchus feels his reasons override the longstanding sense of etiquette. Plus, having Kyrene, a Greek forest nymph by his side presents at least a semblance of an offer to visit.

Olympus is the tallest mountain in all of Greece. Its summit is far above the clouds. The throne room is immaculate. White on white on white is the décor. Tall pillars separate the marble floor from the ceiling. The only gods in the room are Poseidon and Hera. Poseidon sits on Zeus' throne, so he may be beside Hera. The two are engaging in civil, yet somewhat heated conversation. They do not notice Bacchus and Kyrene until Bacchus speaks.

'I beg your majesties' pardons…' Bacchus begins.

Poseidon rises from Zeus' throne. 'What business do you

have here, Roman?'

'I was hoping to ask a favour from you,' Bacchus says nervously. 'I have brought several jugs of my finest vintage as a gift.'

Poseidon laughs at the proposal. 'Surely, you do not think your Roman wine will win you a favour from me.'

Kyrene is practically hiding behind Bacchus. She does not fear Poseidon; she fears Hera. But Hera has spotted her. 'Why are you here, little nymph? Have you been consorting with my husband and would like to beg forgiveness?'

'No, you're majesty. I would never do that.'

'Well, what then?' Hera presses. 'What possible reason would you have to bring a Roman into my domain?'

Kyrene is too intimidated to answer. But Bacchus is not. 'It concerns Apollo,' he says. 'We have been searching for him but cannot find him. I was hoping that, maybe, you could be of aid.'

Hera's eyes flash. 'Why would we help you?'

Bacchus wasn't expecting such an uphill battle. 'We are worried, as I'm sure you are as well, that he is in danger. We would like to visit the realm he is in and try to bring him back.'

'And how is that possible?' Hera asks.

'It is rumoured that, in Zeus' absence, you and Poseidon control the portal. Please grant us the opportunity to support his return.'

Poseidon smirks. 'What makes you think that you could be of any assistance? Neither of you are what I should call, powerful gods. Bacchus, you drink yourself into oblivion. As for you, nymph, my guess is you do your best work on your back.'

DEITIES

'Apollo is our friend,' Bacchus says. 'We feel that he would do anything for us, so we owe him to try to help him now. We may not be powerful gods like you and Hera but we have to make an attempt.'

'I sincerely doubt that Apollo would lift a finger to benefit anyone other than Apollo,' Hera says.

Poseidon looks to Hera. 'Give us a minute,' he says.

Bacchus and Kyrene back away from earshot, so that Hera and Poseidon can whisper amongst themselves. From where Bacchus and Kyrene stand, it appears to be getting quite animated. Poseidon seems to be arguing on their behalf while Hera rolls her eyes. Finally, she shakes her head.

'Come hither, minor gods,' Poseidon says.

Bacchus and Kyrene slowly approach the Olympians.

'I have decided to grant you this favour,' Poseidon says. 'Your condition is that I will pull you back anytime I desire.'

Kyrene is ecstatic 'You'll send us to Apollo?'

'Not exactly. I'll send you to where I believe Apollo is. You must find him yourselves.'

'Thank you, Poseidon and Hera. You are truly gods among gods.' Bacchus says.

'Leave the wine. I am certain that Dionysus will find it amusing.' Hera says.

'Yes, by all means,' Poseidon chimes. 'Place it on his throne. I will rather enjoy his facial expression.'

****

There is no battle on the Ethereal Plane today. Things are quiet; too quiet for Athena's taste. Where were the Frost Giants? The Demons? The warlike demigods?

Pan is by her side. 'I'm assuming it isn't usually like this.'

Athena is too perplexed to answer. She walks swiftly to Tyr.

'I don't like this,' Tyr says.

'Me either. If there's one thing The Darkness can be counted on, it's showing up for battle. They're so close to the Spheri Eternus, they can probably taste it. There is no rational reason they wouldn't be here.'

Tyr considers this. 'There is, actually. Set's army was defeated; however, they will soon be regaining strength. Anubis will lead them. There will be more of them. Angrier after their loss. They will be out for blood.'

'Yes but Horus will return as well. His forces will have a renewed sense of power. Believe me, there is nothing more exhilarating than winning an extended war,' Athena responds.

'Your Trojan war did drag on for several years, did it not?'

'Ten long ones. I can only imagine the war between Horus and Set,' Athena replies.

Tyr turns deadly serious. 'What do you really think of Horus? Is he going to take the reins and save the day? Are we to follow his orders?'

Athena has wondered about this herself. 'We're losing this war but not for lack of leadership. It's being utterly overwhelmed by numbers. It's like fighting a hydra. Cut off one head; two more grow back.'

Tyr agrees. 'It is hard fighting a war where your enemies are immortal. Kill them and they are back a week later. I'm just glad the same applies to us.'

Pan walks over and disturbs the two generals. 'My satyrs are bored. They seek conflict.'

DEITIES

Tyr doesn't know Pan and is angry with his interruption. 'Sometimes, things don't go as planned. But you should be thankful. I doubt your herd would fair very well.'

Pan is taken aback. 'My herd? We know more battle tactics than you can fathom.'

Athena comes to Pan's defense. 'Listen, both of you. Pan may not have experience on the Ethereal Plane but I've seen him fight in the woodlands. There, he is without compare.'

Tyr is unimpressed. 'Look around, Athena. Do you see any trees here?'

Pan is close to losing his temper which would be a very bad thing. However, Athena spots something on the horizon. 'Look,' she says. 'That's Poseidon's stallion and it's pulling a chariot.'

As Poseidon grows closer, Athena cannot believe her eyes. Bacchus and Kyrene are riding in the back. She turns to Pan, who is also in shock. 'What are they doing here? Is this your doing?'

Pan has to gather himself. 'No. Not at all.'

Poseidon stops short of Pan, Tyr and Athena. A mere hundred or so yards away. Directly aside the Spheri Eternus.

Bacchus and Kyrene exit the chariot. Pan and Athena make double time racing to see them.

'Poseidon! Why would you bring them here? They cannot fight!' Athena exclaims.

Poseidon looks around, disinterested. 'Doesn't look like much fighting is going on.'

'Purely coincidental. And what are you even…doing with them?'

Poseidon smiles. 'They'd like to use the portal.'

Kyrene is excited. 'We're going to see Apollo!'

Bacchus shakes his head. He is excited as well.

'So, where are you sending them?' Athena demands.

'Kyrene wants to go to earth, so that's where they're going. Believe me, I've thought this through.' Poseidon replies. 'However, had they not crashed Olympus, they wouldn't be here now. I say good for them.'

'Where on earth are you sending them?'

Poseidon laughs. 'I can't tell you that. It would spoil the surprise. But I assure you, it's someplace nice.'

Athena is aghast but Pan is supportive. 'Find our friend and bring him back unharmed. We'll be guarding the portal to ensure your safe return.'

Bacchus hugs Pan. 'The four of us shall be reunited at Apollo's VIP table before you know it.'

Pan tears up and does not even try to hide it. 'I look forward to it.'

Poseidon makes a swirling motion with his hand. Bacchus and Kyrene are nervous but there is no turning back. They begin to fade in and out of view. To Athena and Pan, it looks startlingly similar to Apollo's disappearance.

Bacchus and Kyrene are now staring at each other. Kyrene giggles. She's going to see, no save, Apollo. Bacchus experiences some trepidation. He hopes this was a good idea.

After the two have completely vanished, Athena speaks to Poseidon very directly. 'Poseidon, I am going to ask you this just once. Do you control the portal?'

Poseidon looks directly into her eyes. 'I do not control it but

DEITIES

I do know how to use it. Only Zeus can move it. Ra can move it. More than anything, I would love to move it to Olympus or Valhalla or any place but here. Somewhere else. Somewhere safe.'

'Teach me then. Teach me to use the portal.'

'I am sorry but I cannot do that. Zeus trusted me with the knowledge and I will not let him down. Especially, in this time of war.'

****

Bacchus and Kyrene materialise on earth deep in Napa Valley. They are both amazed by the rows upon rows of grapes of differing colours and sizes. Bacchus picks a Chardonnay grape from a nearby vine. He studies it closely before biting into it. It doesn't taste like any white grape he's encountered before. He wonders if he's in Gaul. They are known for their fine wine.

Kyrene could not be happier. They've arrived on earth, one step closer to finding Apollo. She dances among the vines, twirling and pirouetting. She enjoys the feel of the soil on her bare feet. Kyrene spies a ladybug crawling on a leaf. She allows it onto her fingers and it slowly makes its way up her exposed arm. The red and black insect must have been taking a liking to her, as it disappears beneath her forest-green blouse.

Bacchus finds this amusing. He has never seen such a creature but finds it fascinating. Of course, he is also fascinated by what lies beneath the green leaves covering her chest. Perhaps, seeing them both together would be a possibility. But probably not.

He looks past the giggling Kyrene and spies a tall hill. 'There.'

Kyrene looks quizzically at the peak. 'What about it?'

'We should climb it. We might have a better chance of seeing Apollo from an elevated height.'

Kyrene begins bounding her way towards the knoll. Bacchus, in his toga, cannot keep up. This puts him in a singular advantage. Forest nymphs have never encountered panties.

Kyrene reaches the summit about ten minutes before Bacchus does. Bacchus is perspiring and panting. Somewhere along the hike, he lost a sandal. When he reaches the top, he is exhausted and sits for a spell.

Kyrene is not interested in Bacchus having any reprieve. 'Get up!' she insists. Her four-foot frame does not offer her much of a vista.

Bacchus struggles to his feet. Now he sees how enormous this valley is. His expression turns from hopeful to overwhelmed. There look to be hundreds of vineyards and buildings the size of great temples. Apollo could be in any one of them.

Kyrene jumps at his side. She tries, despite her small size, to see what Bacchus sees to no avail. 'Pick me up.'

Bacchus hunches over and Kyrene leaps upon his back. There, she climbs on his shoulders and gazes across the wonder that is Napa Valley. 'Wow,' she says. 'Where could he be?'

Bacchus isn't sure what to say. He doesn't want to allude to the fact that they may be on a fool's errand but discovering Apollo's whereabouts in such an imposing amount of acreage bordered on the impossible.

'Hold still,' Kyrene says. She manoeuvres her feet onto his

DEITIES

shoulders and soon she stands atop him. She points. 'There,' she says. 'We're going that way.'

Bacchus sighs. 'Why there?' He points in another direction. 'Is it better than this way?' He points in another. 'Or perhaps this way would be better?'

'No. There is movement in that direction. Movement may mean mortals. And if a mortal met a god, it would certainly leave a lasting impression. And Apollo would leave just that.'

28

You Can't Go Home Again

The paved road ended several miles ago. The Indian Chief Classic bike kicks up dust as it bumps its way down the trail. This bike, like most motorised vehicles, is not meant to use these back paths. His front tire tears and air seeps out. But Coyote doesn't care about his motorcycle right now. He has important business to attend to.

He comes to a stop and climbs off his bike, lowering the kickstand. The rest of this journey would be on foot. Coyote searches the back fence for an opening. The fence is relatively new. It must have been replaced since he was last here so many moons ago.

Finally, he spots an opening where he can slide through. He slinks his body through the rift and gets his jacket caught on a barb. He fights it and succeeds in gaining his freedom, at the expense of the leather on the sleeve.

DEITIES

When he is able to turn around, he realises he is not alone. Two Pomo teenagers are holding him at gunpoint. Coyote exhales. 'What is it you want?'

'We're sort of wondering what you're doing on our property,' the younger one answers. He has a smile on his face befitting a youth with a firearm.

Coyote shows no fear but instead looks at his jacket sleeve. It is going to be expensive to replace. However, a far more likely scenario involves Coyote stealing one.

The older teenager barks, 'My friend asked you a question. Why are you on our property?'

'I was not raised with much respect for personal property,' Coyote says. 'But let me assess this situation for you. There are two of you and one of me. You both have guns and I have none. Yet, it is you who is nervous for reasons I cannot fathom.'

The teenagers look at one another. 'You said it. We both have guns. And we are not afraid to use them,' the younger one says.

'Yes, you are.' Coyote paces back and forth. 'There was a time when my people would not hesitate to shoot. A time when they were brave. They were at one with nature. They were at peace with right and wrong. They lived among the animals and plants with a sense of unity and dignity.'

The teenagers laugh. 'Whatever it is you're smoking,' the older teenager says, 'I want a toke.'

Coyote reaches into his jacket pocket and pulls out a pack of Natural American Spirit cigarettes. He lights one and puts the lighter back into the pack. He tosses it back to the older boy. 'I'd offer matches but I'd fear you couldn't light one.'

Each teenager takes a cigarette from Coyote's pack. They toss the box back to him. Still, they hold their guns. Any worry Coyote might have had about being shot vanishes into the breeze. Now, if they kept the cigarettes, the game would still be on. 'What are you boys named?'

'John,' the older answers.

'Michael.'

Coyote sighs. 'Those names disgust me. Christian names. White man names. Isn't anyone named for animals any longer?'

'What about you? You got some kind of animal name? Earthworm, maybe?' John asks.

'I am Coyote.'

This draws a chorus of laughter from the teenagers. 'So, you're like, our Creator god?'

'Creator Spirit,' Coyote corrects. 'Do they teach you nothing here?'

'If you're the Creator, why would you lower yourself to sneak through the back gate? I would expect you'd want to make your presence known.'

This was a question that Coyote neither expected nor wanted to hear. 'I'm less welcome here these days than you might expect.'

The teenagers laugh. 'I suppose you'd like to meet with the elders?'

'I thought you'd never ask.'

****

Chief Stillwater is ninety-four years old. His sunburnt red skin is still tight across his face but sags along his arms and legs and his most uncomfortable places. Stillwater sits alone, watching.

DEITIES

He is always watching. Just in case.

He is the eldest of the Pomo on this reservation. His interactions with the others are minimal. They feed, wash and clothe him but he is in no one's inner circle. He is a duty; a toleration. At this age, he is decrepit. He no longer moves well on his own. He can stand and hobble a few yards at a time but essentially awaits the freedom that death will bring him.

Except today. He senses urgency. His eyes widen from their usual squint. He is aware; he is alive. Something is amiss. Something that he can set right.

Chief Stillwater is but a figurehead in this tribe. While the reservation is, itself, a sovereign nation within the United States, its leadership is much different than it once was. Stillwater, nonetheless, is its chief. But democracy has reared its ugly head. The reservation is no longer governed by a single member. It is controlled by a Senate-like structure. Stillwater, effectively, acts as a rubber stamp for the tribe.

But still, he holds veto power. This he will enact today.

John and Michael bring Coyote to the Chief. Stillwater's eyes are focused on the outsider's frame. 'It has been many years since I've seen you, Coyote.'

'This is true,' Coyote answers. 'You were very young, not much older than these two who hold their weapons on me.'

Stillwater observes John and Michael. 'You should leave us. If Coyote has risked coming here to speak with me, it must be something worth hearing.'

John and Michael take their leave. They can be heard saying as they walk away, 'Bringing one crazy to another.'

'I trust our young greeted you appropriately?' Stillwater asks

STUART CLARKE

Coyote.

'They wanted to kill me.'

'That I call appropriate.'

Coyote was hoping for an easy meet-and-greet with the old man. It appears that is not going to be happening. 'Are there things from our past you wish to bury?' Coyote asks.

Stillwater does not smile. 'Our people exist in squalor. We live in poverty. We pray to you and you do not come.'

'Perhaps you pray to me but you also pray to the Christian god. You want nature to provide but you insult it by taking money from the government. You call yourselves sovereign, yet you live like dependents,' Coyote snaps.

Stillwater is angered. 'My father's father told me of a time where all of the animals protected us. Then, they scattered. The white man with their machines and technologies chased the protector spirits away. Why did you leave us? Were you not worthy to the task?'

Coyote rants. 'You went willingly. Not all, of course. Many died. How do you think it was for me to see my indigenous creation, my humans, overrun? But faith was traded for tangible quantities. A day's work for food, for shelter. How many mines did our people dig? And for what? Gold? It carries no value. Not then.'

'Ah but now you have changed your ways.'

'Have you looked around your nation recently? Both John and Michael carry what is called iPhones, pieces of technology built off the backs of poor foreign workers. This entire nation is running on your fumes. What will your successor bring?'

Chief Stillwater locks eyes with Coyote. 'Tonight, we shall

DEITIES

discover together.'

****

The ceremonial tribal fire was lit. Rumours circulate through camp that Coyote is here. Would others purporting to be ancient spirits arrive as well? Bear? Eagle? Crow?

Doubtful. The entire ceremony is laughable, really. Chief Stillwater is crazy. He has succumbed to the madness that often afflicts the aged.

And this meeting will prove it. It is little more than a setup, really. Let the old man speak his peace. Then, overwhelmingly vote him from the circle.

At dusk, the elders and the most promising of the younger generation meet. As instructed, they take their places around the campfire. Stillwater sits in his wheelchair and Coyote pushes him over the gravelly earth to the most prominent position in the semicircle.

The others whisper amongst themselves. Stillwater has selected his ritualistic headdress for this occasion. Jokes are cracked, albeit quietly, at his expense. However, he is nevertheless the Chief and at least, a modicum of respect must be shown.

Stillwater addresses the nine-member group. 'I gather you here tonight to introduce an unexpected visitor. He is the Spirit of the creation of humanity. Coyote has long been absent from our nation but today he graced us with his very presence. I trust you will show him all the respect that he is due.'

Samuel Redmond is Chief Stillwater's primary rival. Redmond opted out of ceremonial attire and sits wearing a cowboy button-up shirt and ripped jeans. 'I am confused,' he says. 'Just how much respect is he due?'

Laughter erupts amongst the tribesmen. Any reverence that Coyote held vanished decades ago. Now, he is viewed with disdain. Most of the tribesmen, in fact, believe him to be a fraud.

Stillwater ignores Redmond. Even though his antagonist is several decades younger, he commands tremendous influence. He is arguably the most important man present. His cement company employs over half the tribe. He pays them poorly but a bad job is often better than none at all.

Coyote breaks the awkward silence by standing on the tree stump at the top of the circle. He has spoken on this very stump hundreds of times throughout his vast existence. He's drawn audiences into a warlike frenzy to attack their neighbours or defend their lands. He's negotiated treaties between warring factions and tribes. He's presided over funerals and celebrated weddings and births. And this would be his toughest speech to date.

'I sense many doubters among the group this evening,' Coyote says. 'And I have to say I do not hold them in contempt. I have not been a manifestation in your lives. I have not made my presence felt. But this knife cuts both ways. I have not felt a connection with this nation in a great many years.'

His audience breaks into hoots and hollers. This speaker actually thinks he's the true Coyote. But what difference would it make if he were? They didn't believe in the old ways anyhow.

Coyote's agreeable expression turns to one of repugnance. How dare they respond to him in this fashion? 'I do not think

DEITIES

you realise what is at stake here.'

Redmond can't help but interrupt. 'And what would that be, Mr. Coyote?'

Coyote senses that this man has a great deal of power in the tribe but this only serves to anger him. 'Tell me your name.'

'Name's Samuel Redmond. I'm surprised you didn't know that, you being a Spirit and all that nonsense.'

'Redmond is not exactly a Pomo name. But I do believe I know who you are. One of your great-grandparents went by Red Moon. I suppose you had reason to change it.'

Redmond chuckles nervously. How did this Coyote know that? 'Made it a lot easier to get a small business loan.'

'Ah, so you're the businessman on the reservation. Tell me, which of these trailers is yours.'

'I don't live on the reservation. I have a two storey in a nearby subdivision. Bought it free and clear.'

Coyote nods his head. 'You're a rich man. And those who sit amongst you are your employees?'

Redmond looks around. 'Some of them,' he replies.

'And their children?'

'Some of them as well.'

Coyote takes a step off the stump and stands above Redmond. 'And you will be buying homes for your employees in the near future from your profits, I take it?'

Redmond shakes his head. 'Don't work like that. They save their money; they get their homes.'

Coyote frowns. 'Doesn't sound very fair to me. It seems like you have plenty and they have little.'

All eyes are suddenly on Redmond. 'Sorry. I'm a capitalist.

STUART CLARKE

A lot has changed since your Creator Spirit invented humans. That is your claim, isn't it? That you invented us?'

At least someone gets it. 'Red Moon, you are what I like to call an 'apple.' You may be red on the outside but inside you are white. Your values do not support those of your ancestors. You think about money more than community. Tell me, what if you could not rely on the grossly underpaid labour of your fellow Pomo?'

Redmond stands up and walks past Coyote. He looks at an audience that is both shocked and slightly hostile towards him. Coyote has raised some interesting points – things they all knew were true but somehow hearing these grievances aloud added tremendous impact. 'I'd replace every single one with Mexican immigrant labourers. I look after their interests but I look after my own first.'

Coyote smiles. 'Red Moon, you have fallen directly into my verbal trap. I knew if I let you speak long enough, your true colours would emerge.' Coyote addresses the audience. 'Would you like higher wages? Better living conditions?'

Surprisingly, all are quiet except one younger member of the tribe. 'We'd just like to keep our jobs.'

Redmond laughs. 'They certainly know where their bread is buttered.'

Stillwater motions to Coyote. 'I think we're done here.'

'Not quite,' Redmond says. 'I'd like to make a movement that Chief Stillwater steps down from his post. I rather think that I am the one who supports this nation. I should be given the honourary title to match. I'd like to put this to a vote. There's a slight raise to sweeten the pot.'

DEITIES

It takes a unanimous decision to remove a Chief. Slowly but surely, the tribe casts their stones in favour of Redmond. A teardrop emerges from Stillwater's eye. Coyote moves quickly and wheels the old man away.

Once they reach the awning of Stillwater's trailer, Coyote apologises. 'I'm sorry. I don't think that went well.'

'I disagree,' Stillwater says. 'They heard exactly what they needed to hear and made their choice. You can lead a horse to water…'

'Right. You going to be all right?'

Stillwater cracks the slightest of smiles. 'You have no idea how tired this old man is. I expect I shall die happy in the coming days. I believe I lived this long to experience this very moment.'

Coyote is saddened. 'I shall miss you.'

'Fear not. I will be in a better place. Remember what the elders always said.'

Coyote and Stillwater recite the verbal tradition together. 'There is no afterlife for those who do not believe.'

Stillwater reaches up and touches Coyote's face. 'There are things you must do, are there not?'

'Yes. I have to get back to San Francisco. Trouble is, my motorcycle is missing a tire.'

'Take my truck. I won't be needing it.'

Coyote looks across the way at a truck that could have been as old as Stillwater himself.

Stillwater smiles. 'Keys are above the visor. Provided it starts, it's yours.'

Coyote hugs the old man. Tears well up in his eyes.

'And one more thing. I have a little money.'

'I couldn't.'

Stillwater is adamant. 'I have no use for it. These kids will find it and use it to buy drugs. I'd much rather it go to you.'

'I'll pay you back in the afterlife,' Coyote insists.

'Where I'm going, money will not be a priority. But you be careful. You're up to something. I fear you're in over your head.'

'That I am. Perhaps, I should finish what I started though.'

Stillwater closes his eyes. 'You can be great once again. The path is for your choosing.'

'I have a mission and will see it to fruition,' Coyote says.

'You always did. Before you lost your way. It was good to see you, my friend. We shall smoke a pipe in the afterlife.'

'That we shall.'

Coyote takes his leave and crawls inside the pick-up. Three times it takes to turn over but then it hums. The gas gauge is full. He leaves the reservation but he has a feeling he will be back.

29

Back to the City

Diana arrives back at the Precinct. She opens the door for Apollo and allows Jackson Tate to come inside. Freya, however, is left locked in the back of the car, kicking and screaming. All eyes fall on Diana when she makes her entrance.

Oscar sees her first. 'Where the fuck have you been?' he demands.

Diana wasn't expecting this type of greeting. 'I was apprehending a suspect.'

'Where exactly?'

Diana thinks. 'I'm not exactly sure. Somewhere in Napa.'

'That's a little out of our jurisdiction. Why did the Napa police not make the arrest?' Oscar looks at Apollo and Jackson. 'And who exactly are these two people?'

'That's Apollo. He was the intended victim of the John Doe we can't identify. This is Jackson…'

'Tate,' Jackson finishes her sentence, sensing she is struggling.

Oscar is obviously pissed off. 'Who?'

'I was a hostage,' Jackson explains, bending the truth just a bit.

'I've got so many questions for you, Diana. You do know, we don't just drive off whenever we like. There are procedures we have to follow.'

Diana stands up for herself and does it quite well. 'I thought our job was catching criminals.'

Oscar is incensed. 'Were it up to me, Diana, I'd fire you this minute. But sadly, we'll have to take this up with the Captain.'

'Don't you want to see the suspect?'

Oscar is speechless. 'Where is he?'

'She. And she's in the squad car outside.'

'Tell me you at least read her Miranda.'

Diana stammers. 'Uh.'

Oscar is appalled. 'I'm not sure how many laws you've broken. You didn't advise her she could remain silent. You didn't advise her of her right to an attorney. Fuck, you've committed what amounts to kidnapping. And where'd you get the squad car? Should we add grand theft auto to your charges?'

'She confessed. She had a weapon and admitted to the crime. What else was I supposed to do? Set her free?'

'You were supposed to follow the law. Any lawyer will be able to spring her. Probably, sue the Department as well. Didn't exactly think this one through, did you?'

Diana is livid. 'Don't you at least want to interview her?'

Oscar cannot contain his anger. 'There's going to be an interview all right. Between you and the Captain. Now set that

DEITIES

suspect free and we'll hope for the best.'

****

Diana waits alone in the Captain's office for what seems like an eternity. Through the glass, she can see that a very animated Oscar has cornered the Captain. She only hears bits and pieces of the conversation, not enough to gauge what is going on between the two of them. Other officers have surrounded the conversation. They cast disapproving glances through the office window, toward Diana.

Finally, it seems the Captain has heard enough. He leaves the discussion and enters his office. Diana doesn't know whether to be relieved to see him or not.

'Seems like you've been on quite the adventure, Miss Nemo,' the Captain says. 'Not one I approve of, I might add.'

Captain Adams is a twenty-five-year veteran of the SFPD. He'd seen his share of cops going rogue but nothing quite like this. Typically, the rogue officers were the undercovers; those who dug into their assignments so deeply that there was a seismic reality shift. Never, in his wildest dreams, did he imagine one of his trusted detectives would perform such an action. 'Would you like to explain yourself?'

'I just wanted to bring a shooter to justice.'

Adams runs his hands through what was left of his rapidly greying hair. He smiles sadly, eliciting crow's feet near his brown eyes. 'You do realise how many laws you've broken, don't you?'

'I'm beginning to see that.'

'I'm curious. How did you know where the suspect would be?'

Diana is silent for several seconds. She couldn't let it slip that she conducted her own investigation of Jackson Tate and that's what led her to Napa. 'Just a hunch,' she finally answers.

'A hunch?' Captain Adams repeats in disbelief. 'A hunch that took you all the way to Calistoga? I don't know whether or not to be impressed. Still, you broke so many jurisdictional and procedural laws, my hands are tied. I'm going to have to ask for your badge and gun. I hope you understand.'

Diana is aghast. 'You're releasing me from the force?'

'For now it's called 'Suspension Pending Investigation.' But, to be honest, this isn't going to play out well for you. I'm afraid that your days with the SFPD are over. It's a shame, really. You were such a good detective. Loaded with potential.'

Diana realises there is little point in arguing. She slides her badge across the table and passes her gun over as well. She gets up to leave.

'Actually, I need all your weapons. I'm betting there's another gun strapped to your ankle.'

Diana complies.

As she leaves the office, all conversation comes to a halt. It is eerily silent. It's not until she reaches the lobby, that she hears the muffled whispers.

Apollo, Jackson and now Freya wait for her, sitting on the most uncomfortable benches the city has to offer. They leap to greet her.

Freya has words for her. 'I take it I'm not going to prison?'

'Doesn't look like it. For now, anyway,' Diana replies.

Freya seems satisfied with this response. 'So, what should we do now?'

DEITIES

'Drink. Heavily.'

'I know a place near here,' Apollo says. 'Coyote took me there.'

'And you want to go back,' Freya says incredulously. 'That Coyote friend of yours tried to kill you. Twice.'

'Exactly,' Apollo says. 'It might be refreshing to find out why.'

'Well, count me out,' Jackson says. 'I need to go home, shower and see if my office is being searched. By the way, Apollo, did you figure out any of the instruments in the music room?'

'Why, yes. All of them. Can't say I was very interested in the drums.'

'No worries there. Drummers are a dime a dozen. But you can play guitar. How about the longer guitar – the bass?'

'That was easy as well. The big thing with the white and black keys took some time but I got the hang of it.'

'Did you learn any of the songs I laid out for you to listen to?'

'I really like the one that starts with "A modern-day warrior…"'

Jackson is astounded. 'You learned to play 'Tom Sawyer'? That's pretty advanced stuff.'

'Wasn't terribly difficult. Just a different algorithm.'

'It takes people years to play that song. And even then, they play it badly. Listen, I don't want to push my luck here but you didn't happen to write any original songs, did you?'

'Thirty-seven of them.'

Jackson smiles. If he can pry Apollo away from the pyscho

230

bitches, he's got a winner on his hands.

****

Apollo leads Freya and Diana a few blocks. He makes several wrong turns but eventually, they find themselves outside Joe's Dive Bar.

'Apollo, this place is nasty,' Diana says.

Freya shrugs and opens the door. 'I've seen worse.'

Joe spots them immediately. Especially Freya. It's not every day that someone with her beauty and ample cleavage walks through his door. He is drawn in and cannot stop gazing.

Joe is not the only one. Everybody else sets down their drinks. No furtive glances. Just blatant stares.

Freya settles on a stool, her breasts resting on the bar. Apollo and Diana flank her but Joe pays minimal attention to them. 'Can I get you something from the bar, sweetie?'

'I would literally kill for a mead.'

'Kill, huh?'

'Wouldn't be the first time,' Freya says.

'I'm not exactly sure what mead is but I'm pretty sure we don't have it. But not to worry. I got you covered. You look like a tequila girl to me.' Joe reaches above the bar and pulls down the Cuervo 1800 Gold. 'Nothing but the best for you, babe.'

Diana pipes up. 'I wasn't aware that Cuervo was the best on the market.'

Joe briefly glances at Diana. 'Best this joint can afford to carry.' He pours for Freya and Diana. He grabs another glass and sets it down in front of Apollo. Suddenly, he remembers him. 'You,' Joe says. 'You were with that deadbeat Coyote. I hope you listened to me. Coyote is trouble.'

DEITIES

Apollo nods. 'You were right. But I must find him. I was under the impression that he frequented this location.'

'More than I'd care to admit,' Joe grumbles.

'When do you expect him?' Apollo asks.

'You never know. He comes and goes. Might not come in for months, then he'll be here every night. Never can tell with that one.'

Freya hops in. 'Do you know where we can find him? I've got a few things I'd like to discuss with him. Unless I beat him to death first.'

Joe cracks up. 'Listen, Sweet Cheeks, you'd have to get in line. A lot of people want to see Coyote dead. What's your beef? He owe you money? He steal from you?'

'It's not that simple,' Freya says. 'He tried to hurt someone close to me. Someone I'm here to protect.' She gestures towards Apollo.

'Damn! You two are together? I thought I had a shot at you.'

'Everybody has a shot at me. But believe me; the risk is not always worth the reward.'

Joe grins. 'Find that hard to believe.'

'Believe it,' Diana interjects.

Joe pours a glass for Apollo and one for himself. 'All right, everyone. Bottoms up.' Joe slams back the tequila. The other three follow suit. Apollo and Freya cough as the liquid burns their throat. Only Diana shows no effects.

'Hit us again,' Diana demands.

Joe pours. 'These aren't free shots. Someone's paying this round.'

Diana drops her purse on the bar. 'We're here to get good and drunk. I got you covered.'

'All right, then. Tell you what; I'll sell you the bottle for $125. You can drink 'til you've had your fill. Sound like a plan?'

Diana reprimands. 'Selling bottles is illegal in the city. You should know that.'

'Well, you're not a cop or anything are you?'

Diana sighs. 'Not anymore,' she says beneath her breath.

****

They drink until the early evening. All three are experiencing varying degrees of inebriation. Freya, in particular, is wobbly. Tequila is much stronger than the mead to which she is accustomed. It appears she could pass out at any moment.

Joe realises this and passes her some tap water. 'Hey Sweet Cheeks, drink some of this. It will make you feel better.'

A guitar player and a drummer enter the bar. There is clearly something awry. Joe leaves to find out what it is. The conversation becomes energetic. Joe is obviously unhappy about something. The band members are apologetic but Joe is furious.

Diana waves him over. 'Got a problem?'

Joe seethes. 'Fucking lead singer ain't coming. They're telling me he's sick or something. This is really going to fuck up my night.'

Freya nudges Apollo. 'Why don't you sing?' she asks.

Joe laughs. 'I doubt your friend can stand up long enough to even hold a microphone. I'm sending the assholes home.'

Apollo shakes his head. 'Let me try.'

Joe shrugs. 'Ain't like I got nothing to lose. But if you suck,

DEITIES

I'm pulling the plug right away, got it?'

The band sets up like they're going to play instrumentals. As if that would be enough.

Apollo approaches them cautiously and steps onto the stage.

'Who the hell are you?' the rhythm guitarist asks.

'I'm Apollo. I'm your singer tonight.'

'Like hell you are.'

Joe trails behind Apollo. 'Actually, he is your singer. If he does well, you'll still get paid. Otherwise, I can send you home penniless right now.'

Dave, the drummer, intercedes. 'We'll give it a shot.'

The bass player, Matt, huffs. 'And why would we do that?'

'Look, I need the cash. Rent's past due. I'm counting on this.'

'Whatever,' Matt glares at Apollo. 'We play mostly covers. Zep, Aerosmith, VH, toss in the occasional oldie. Think you can handle it?'

'I don't see why not.' Apollo answers. He's a little loopy from the tequila but certainly loves being on stage. 'You guys have a guitar? I play.'

'You're hammered,' Matt says. 'I'm not letting you near my equipment. And the guitar is Steve's.'

Joe says. 'Oh yes, you are.'

'Fine.' Matt passes Apollo a Rickenbacker. 'Try not to break it. You need a pick?'

'What's a pick?' Apollo asks.

Matt stares at the floor. Dave grabs him by the shoulder. 'I need the money,' he insists.

STUART CLARKE

Apollo is handed a set list. 'I hope you know some of these songs; otherwise, it's going to be a very short show.'

Apollo studies the scrawling. 'Whole Lotta Love' is the only one he knows. 'We may want to start with this one,' he says.

'We don't play that until later.'

'It's the one I know. Unless you can play Rush or Hendrix.'

'Whole Lotta Love, it is.'

Apollo launches into the opening of the Led Zeppelin classic. The crowd is impressed. Dave is impressed. So is Matt. Apollo's voice matches Robert Plant's note for note. The screeches and screams are, without a doubt, the best a cover band could ever hope for. Apollo's vocal range seems to have no bounds. A hearty round of applause erupts from the rapidly growing audience.

After the song is over, Matt grabs the microphone. 'We're, uh, auditioning a new lead singer tonight. We've never played together before, so forgive us if we have a few starts and stops.' Matt reaches down and grabs the set list and tears it up. 'We're going to play this set from the hip.'

The three congregate on stage. Apollo doesn't know 'Love in an Elevator' but has a firm grasp on 'Dream On'. Steven Tyler would have been proud. They segue into a mash-up of Roger Clyne's 'Girly' and The Who's 'Baba O'Riley'. They finish the short set with Apollo strumming an acoustic and crooning 'Beth' just like Peter Criss. Dave gets up from behind the drums but Apollo is far from finished. He grabs the electric and commences with 'Voodoo Child' with Matt and Dave struggling to keep up. Suddenly, Matt realises who he's playing

DEITIES

with.

When an eight-and-a-half-minute version of 'Voodoo' wraps up, Matt pulls him aside. 'I know who you are. You're that guy who jumped on stage with Nine Times Blue. What is your name?'

'Apollo.'

'Like the god of Music?'

'The very same.'

Matt is amazed. He'd heard the rumours, of course but nothing could have prepared him for what he witnessed. Forget that. Who he'd just backed up. 'Let's take a short break,' Matt suggests. 'We'll figure out what to play next.'

Apollo reaches for the acoustic. 'I'd like to play one original song if you don't mind. Then, we can talk.'

'By all means.'

Apollo reaches off the stage and snags a barstool. He sits alone on the stage. 'This song is for a very special friend. I think she knows who she is.'

Apollo grabs the acoustic and strums a love ballad about falling from Heaven and into love.

Apollo closes out the song. 'That's all I have thus far.'

Freya rushes to the stage and leaps atop it. Before she quite realises it, she is kissing Apollo. And not a small kiss. Open-mouthed, passionate and hungry. This catches Apollo off guard but only for the briefest of moments. He returns her appetite with his own.

Apollo hadn't detected the slightest sexual tension between the two of them. Freya, he thought, would find him too arrogant. Or after his debacle with Pluto, too weak. But here she is, exploring his mouth with her tongue. It isn't often that he is surprised where the female of the species is concerned. But, he likes being surprised pleasantly.

Joe's Dive Bar is far from the quintessential place for a first kiss. Most of the patrons are ignoring the Public Display of Affection taking place onstage. They return to their games of pool or darts or Golden Tee. Joe, however, feels slight tinges of jealousy. He was under the false impression that he was making headway with this, dare he call her, goddess. Joe looks to Diana, 'I thought you were with Apollo.'

Diana laughs. 'Apollo is my brother. My twin brother. Now tell me you don't see the family resemblance.'

Freya suddenly peels herself away from Apollo. 'I'm sorry,' she says.

Apollo is astonished. 'Why?' he finally manages.

Freya blushes. 'I've heard tales. You are now consorting with Venus. Her beauty exceeds that of mine.'

Apollo measures the two in his mind. Venus is the Roman goddess of Beauty. Freya, the Norse. But Freya has features in which Venus is lacking. Freya is smart and strong. She is quick-witted. But she can also be soft and tender. 'No Freya,' Apollo says. 'There is no one as desirable as you.'

****

The bass player finally arrived mid-way through the second set and his licks made a difference in the overall sound. Apollo belts out covers of U2, David Bowie, Nine Times Blue, Springsteen and Petty. But he really won the audience over by nailing 'It's the End of the World as We Know It' without garbling a single word. Not bad, after slamming six tequila

DEITIES

shots.

After the show, Matt pulls Apollo aside. 'I can honestly say I've never played with anyone as good as you. Do you want to become a permanent fixture?'

Apollo sits on the barstool and considers this. He is a bit distracted, though. Freya is sitting on his lap and it's causing some movement inside his jeans. 'I think so but we should ask Jackson and see what he thinks.'

Matt is at a loss. 'Jackson. Jackson Tate?'

'Yes. I guess he's sort of my friend. He thinks I can make a lot of money.'

Matt goes into marketing mode. 'Tell him you've got a band. We were called The Coverboys but now we should be…'

'Delphi,' Freya answers and turns her face to Apollo. 'You'd like that wouldn't you?'

Matt agrees it sounds like a great name but is already worried about a beautiful Yoko Ono with huge tits getting in the way.

30

New Shoes

Hades and Hel spent the night in an abandoned warehouse. Apparently, it once stored cardboard boxes. Hades imagined that, at some time, things were put in these boxes and shipping crates and plats. Hel, on the other hand, could not have cared less. She's enamoured by their bikes; the shiny new motorcycles they have acquired. She rubs Hades' bike, feeling it's steel. However, she cannot help but gaze at herself in the rearview mirror. Her face. It's so perfectly symmetrical. Gone is the skull encompassing her left side. She's beautiful and for the first time in many lifetimes, she feels it.

Hades props himself up on one elbow and watches Hel admire her reflection. 'Don't go fogging my mirrors, bitch.' Hades picked up some rather colourful language during his near-fatal mixer with the Angels.

Hel protests. 'A female dog? Honestly? If referring to me as a canine is so important, you could have gone with something

DEITIES

like a she-wolf.'

Hades laughs. 'Of course, I could have. But what would be the fun in that? Besides, I'm just using a term those criminals used to describe you. They seemed to think it suited you.'

'You mean those criminals I saved you from?'

Hades is deflated. 'Yes. Those would be the ones.'

'You know sex last night was quite good. It's been a while since you've been that passionate.'

'Well, under Anubis' control, it was hard to feel very passionate about anything.'

Hel presses. 'You're sure it's not because I'm beautiful now?'

'You were always beautiful. But now you're stunning.'

Hel smiles. Hades answered correctly.

Hades walks over to check out his bike. It is true that Hel has fogged the mirrors but he doesn't mind so much. 'We should really look for a base camp,' he says. 'This location is a little too dreary, even for me.'

Hel agrees. 'A place with a little more style would be nice. I hate to say it but what I really miss is the Underworld, especially the Treachery Bar.'

'I'm sure they have similar places where one can imbibe all they please. We may have some exploring to do before we find it. As for the Underworld, Apollo is our mission. Once we exact our revenge, Anubis will have no choice but to call us back.'

'First, we find mead. Then, lodgings. Apollo can wait. Our paths will cross soon enough.'

****

Hel and Hades leave their motorcycles behind and set out on

foot. It is hot outside, so their Hell's Angels jackets remain draped over the handlebars. After an hour of walking, they arrive at the northern portion of Market Street. There they observe hundreds, if not thousands, of humans walking in various directions. Each seems to have his or her own agenda, a specific destination in mind.

Hel focuses in on a girl who is roughly her exact size. She is enamoured with this girl's clothing. A tight black top paired with a short black leather miniskirt. Thigh high black boots complete the look. 'I want to look like her,' Hel says.

Hades stares at her dyed blonde hair. 'You want to discover where she traded for her garments?'

'No. I want to take them.'

They follow the girl and she turns down an alley. Apparently, the wrong alley. The 11th Street Hispanic gang is holding some kind of ritual. They rule the Tenderloin and a pretty white girl has just made the wrong turn.

'Hola, Bonita,' the leader says. He is grinning ear-to-ear. 'Why don't you come over here and show us a good time?'

'Sorry,' the girl says nervously. 'I'm in a hurry. Late for work. Perhaps another time.'

'No time like the present, muchacha. Come over here give me un beso. That's a kiss if your Español is poor.'

The girl turns to escape but Hades and Hel block her way. 'Now is not the time to run from your enemies,' Hades insists. He grasps her firmly by the shoulders. 'Not to worry, you are among friends.'

Hel approaches the gang. 'Am I not beautiful enough for you?'

DEITIES

'I like the way you think,' the gang leader says.

The other three members are laughing out loud. Hel smiles and draws her weapon. She shoots their leader in the gut. Hel fires two more shots, fatally wounding two others.

The third is in shock. 'What are you doing to my primos?' he gasps.

Hel fires her fourth bullet into his kneecap; this was becoming somewhat of a trademark for her – a calling card. The gang member cries out in pain. Hel puts her finger to her lips. 'If you make any more noise, I shall shoot your other one.'

Hades leads the girl to the scene. She is crying, having never witnessed anything like this before.

Hades pushes her towards Hel. 'I've saved your life, or at minimum, your chastity. Now, there is something I'd like in return.'

'Anything,' the girl says between sobs.

'I'd like your clothing. I quite fancy it and I want it.'

The girl isn't sure she heard correctly. 'You want my clothes?'

'I sincerely doubt Hel would have saved you if she didn't. So, go ahead. Remove them,' Hades commands.

The girl slowly strips starting with her blouse. Hel, likewise, is removing her clothing. Unlike the girl, she wears no bra. Her pert, dark nipples stick straight up in the air. Hel slips on the blouse and waits impatiently for the skirt.

The transaction is nearly complete. Except Hel wants the boots. She pays particular attention to how they are unzipped as she has never seen anything like them before.

'They're kind of hard to get on,' the girl says. 'Do you want some help?'

Hel relents and the girl kneels, zipping the boots up Hel's shapely legs. Hel tosses her clothes at the girl.

'I can't wear these clothes to my job,' the girl says.

Hades smirks. 'I doubt that had you been murdered or raped, you wouldn't be going to your job at all. So, run along dear. Consider yourself fortunate.'

While Hel admires her makeover, Hades searches the bodies. He discovers five more guns, three more knives and a huge wad of cash. 'We're building quite the arsenal. Apollo will be quite the easy target.'

****

They perform a similar costume change for Hades, so now he blends in with the locals as well. The next item on the agenda is getting Hel her fill of mead. They walk aimlessly for blocks, essentially following a meandering crowd. They pass by several promising spots but none seem quite good enough for Hel.

Hades grows weary of walking. 'We're not going to find the perfect place on this crappy planet. We're stopping in the next place we see.'

Hel sighs and nods her head agreement. 'That will be fine.'

They trudge a few more yards and Hades spies a rundown bar. He opens the door. 'This way, my lady.'

Hel frowns but enters the sparsely populated bar. 'You sure know how to pick them.'

The day bartender, Todd, looks up at the beautiful Goth Hel and the well-groomed Hades. Not the typical duo to enter Joe's Dive Bar. The day bartender excuses himself and goes to the manager's office and knocks on the door.

'Yeah,' Joe hollers.

DEITIES

Todd is grinning. 'Sorry to disturb you but you have got to get a load of the couple who just popped in.'

Joe rises and follows Todd behind the bar. Seated at a table, are Hel and Hades. Joe cannot help but laugh. This is not his usual clientele. He makes his way to their table. 'You two lost?' he asks.

'Your city remains a mystery to us,' Hades answers. 'However, we were looking for a place with libations.'

'Libations?'

'Yes, drinks of the alcoholic variety.'

Joe nods. 'Well, you have come to the right place. But you might have more luck seated at the bar. No wait staff on yet.'

Hades stares Joe down. 'We are accustomed to being waited on.'

Joe is taken aback. 'All right. Suit yourselves. What will you have?'

'Red wine,' Hades answers.

Joe shakes his head. 'More specific. We have a Cab, a Merlot and a Pinot. But I'll warn you, none are very good.'

'You pick, then.'

Joe sizes up Hel. 'And for the lady?'

'Mead,' Hel answers.

Joe is momentarily frozen. 'You are the second person to ask for mead in as many days. We don't have it but please tell me what it is.'

'It's a honey-based wine. Quite delicious. I'm surprised you have none.'

Joe shakes his head. 'Sounds dreadful. But if customers are clamouring for it, I'll see what I can do with the distributors.

For now, can I offer you a beer?'

'An ale?' Hel asks.

'That I can do.' Joe walks away and disappears behind the bar.

Hades whispers to Hel. 'Someone else wanted mead? What does that tell you?'

'That this place has no taste by not carrying it.'

'No. No one likes mead other than your Norse cohorts. One may have made an appearance here.'

'I don't understand what difference that would make.'

'It means,' Hades explains, 'that someone from your pantheon may be here as well. Who is missing?'

Hel thinks. 'The Darkness is accounted for. I'm pretty sure a Frost Giant would have caused quite the stir. Someone from The Light?'

'Or Loki. He does what he pleases.'

'It would be good to see him. It's been a long time since Anubis banished him.'

Hades answers quickly. He is not a fan of Loki. 'Story is he went crawling back to Odin.'

'Yeah, I heard that too,' Hel responds.

Joe comes over carrying an Anchor Steam and a glass of hideous Pinot Noir. Hel tastes the beer and likes it. Hades tries the wine and nearly retches. 'Not to your liking?' Joe asks. 'Can't say I didn't warn you. We're a beer and whiskey joint, not a trendy City bar. Can I get you an Anchor like your companion has?'

'By all means,' Hades says. 'And I have a question.'

'Shoot.'

DEITIES

'The other person who ordered mead. Did you catch a name?'

Joe thinks. 'She had a funny sounding name. Something with an 'F'?'

'Freya?' Hel bursts out.

'That's it. You know her?'

'Only far too well.'

After the initial shock wore off, Hades asks, 'Was she alone?'

'She was in here with this lady, who I swear was an off-duty cop. Her name is Diana. But, the guy she was hanging all over. He jumped on stage and played some of the best music this city has ever seen.'

Hel gasps. 'Apollo!'

'Yeah, that was his name. You know him?'

'I do,' Hades says. 'He's my spoiled nephew. You expect him around any time soon?'

'Band plays again tomorrow tonight around ten. I'm sure he'll be here.'

'Do me a favour. Don't mention I was here. I'd like to surprise him while he's singing.'

31

Not the Plain Old Plane

The legions of The Darkness loom on the horizon. However, Athena feels much better about this battle. Time has passed and the demigods are healed. They are ready for combat.

Pan has brought his small regiment of satyrs and fauns. They fall in line behind Athena. For the time being, she commands the archers and the catapults. The archers have sharpened the tips of their arrows; their catapults are loaded with huge rocks and boulders. Once the initial assault begins, she would lead a squadron of the ground forces, attacking from the east. Tyr's army would fight from the west.

And then there was the center. Horus and his Egyptian army are finally battling at full strength. It would be a sudden show of force. The Darkness could never be prepared for what is about to occur.

Athena stares across the battlefield and sees something that causes her pause. A jackal-headed figure barks orders to an

DEITIES

eager group of Frost Giants, evil demigods and disenfranchised Titans. Could it be that Anubis, himself, will lead this charge? If this is to be the case, she wants to be the one burying her spear through his chest.

She is not the only one to have noticed this. Tyr has his eyes set on the masked Egyptian as well. It would be a great honour to capture Anubis and deliver him to Odin. He stares across the battlefield and locks eyes with Athena. It is clear they have the same target in mind.

For his part, Horus doesn't seem to care one way or another. If it is to be Athena or Tyr or anyone else aligned with The Light, the result will be the same. Horus raises his hands and points to Athena, then to Tyr. He wants to discuss strategy.

Athena arrives first. 'What is it, Lord Horus?'

'Your archers should focus primarily on the larger targets – the Frost Giants and the Titans. They will be the easiest to hit and are also the most dangerous in close combat. If you can eliminate as many as possible, our chances improve immeasurably.'

Tyr catches but a fraction of the conversation. 'My troops are ready. We await your signal.'

'Tell me about the Frost Giants,' Horus asks.

'They're much quicker than they look. But have weaknesses in their knees. If we need to fight close, swords are a very good choice as a weapon.'

Horus soaks this in. 'A good general knows not only where his opponent is strong but where he is weak as well. What are our primary flaws?'

'With your Egyptian army here, we are no longer

outnumbered. However, we do not match well with them in close quarters,' Athena explains.

'Speak for yourself, Athena. My army is well-equipped to engage in hand-to-hand warfare. And I daresay, our weapons make yours look primitive.'

'Careful, Tyr. I have certainly saved you more than a few dozen times.'

Horus is irritated. 'Silence, both of you. My army is made of skilled spearmen. If the larger beings can be pared down, then my troops will be able to handle the second wave.'

Athena capitulates. 'As you wish.'

'The enemy does not appear to be prepared. Return to your stations. Launch the catapults immediately. Then, rain arrows down upon them like a deluge.'

Tyr and Athena glare at one another the entire way back to their posts. Each wants to win Horus' favour and if it comes at the expense of the other, then so be it.

Upon Athena's order, fifty catapults release boulders into the sky, pelting the enemy force. They are reloaded quickly and a second wave fills the air.

'Archers, commence!' Athena commands.

The archers take aim and release their arrows. The skies are flooded. Upon their descent, many find targets. The flesh of many Titans and Frost Giants is pierced. They are wounded badly. Another sky of arrows hits the air.

Tyr's archers use more advanced technology than Athena's Greeks and Romans. Crossbows send their darts further and faster. Reloading takes less time. Their pointed tips cause more damage than the traditional bows. Those under Tyr's command

DEITIES

may not be as skilled or accurate as Athena's but the weapons themselves deliver a blow she cannot match. In any event, The Darkness have been caught off guard.

****

Anubis is flat-footed. He scrambles to make adjustments. His own archers take aim and send their arrows into the heart of The Light. However, because they were hurried, their aim is not true. Only a few find their mark.

Anubis orders the Titans and the Frost Giants to charge into the enemy territory. Those who are badly wounded are expected to attack as well.

They are sitting ducks for the archers of The Light. The closer they get, the easier the aim becomes. Anubis gathers the winged Egyptian Demons and sends them flying above. They swoop upon the archers, knocking the archers over in droves. The battle has changed.

The Frost Giants and Tyr's army are now fighting in close quarters. Tyr's army withstands but suffers great losses. As more and more Frost Giants charge, he has no choice but to pull his army back.

Athena's troops charge the Titans. They are grossly undersized and do not fare well against their enormous enemy. Athena charges into battle herself, successfully slaying several Titans. She flashes a quick glance at Horus. He is preparing his army to attack.

Athena needs to rally her troops and combine hers with those of Horus. 'Retreat!' she shouts. 'Retreat!'

****

Anubis sends his Egyptian forces into battle. The Greek

and Norse archers have been overrun and he's willing to risk casualties of his own. The Egyptians rush into the fray. They attack the Frost Giants and Titans from behind.

Athena watches this massacre of The Darkness by members of The Darkness themselves. She is astonished. What in the name of Zeus is happening?

She stares across the battlefield and looks at Anubis. But then, she sees a figure walking slowly across the combat zone showing no fear. It is Set. At that moment, she realises what has transpired.

She is quickly surrounded by Egyptian spearmen. One by one, she fights them off. But there are too many. She is captured and escorted to Horus.

Tyr is captured as well. He is furious. 'Why are you doing this?' he demands of Horus. 'You are sworn to defend The Light!'

'My friend, there is no Light. There is no Darkness. Now, there is only Egypt.'

'You're mad with power!' Athena exclaims. 'You take Ra's position, now you want it all! You're not the Horus I used to know!'

Set arrives. 'No. I'd say he's a much-improved version. He is what I like to call 'The Big Picture'.'

'So now what? You're going to kill us?' Tyr demands. 'You know we'll come back angrier and more united than ever.'

Set shakes his head. 'Won't be that simple. Look out on that battleground. Do you see the dead? If I left them there, sure, they'd reanimate. Might even invade at some point.' Set pauses for dramatic effect. 'But if they are imprisoned

DEITIES

somewhere Horus and I control, then you are without an army. How does that sound?'

Tyr doesn't have an answer.

Athena seethes. 'Good always wins in the end. The Light shall rise again.'

'You're so cute when you're mad,' Set says. 'Pardon me for a second.' He looks at her chains. 'Don't go running off anywhere.'

Set, Horus and Anubis have a brief meeting. It is apparent to Tyr and Athena that the conversation concerns their fates.

Set emerges from the huddle. 'The good news for you, Athena, is that you will be transported to Olympus. I want you to sing of the victory that occurred here today. Spread the information throughout the realms. As for you Tyr, I'm afraid you're going to the Underworld. I really can't have both of you running around. That is to be your fate.'

Tyr is clearly fearful but he is strong. 'I will never kneel before you.'

'Of course not. You'll be trapped in a cage of ice. You'll wish to kneel before me but I'll never allow it. I'll rob you of your station but not of your foolish pride.'

Upon Horus' order, Athena is forced to the Spheri Eternus. 'Give my regards to Zeus,' Horus says, before transporting her to the great Mount.

'And Anubis, it is time for your reward. You were quite the general on the battlefield today.'

Anubis smiles. He wonders what this reward might be.

'Guards! seize him!'

Anubis is suddenly surrounded by Set's forces. 'I don't

understand.'

'Your prize is that I'm allowing you to flourish in another domain. I am exiling you to earth.'

32

Winery Crashers

Ron Sciandri is having the time of his life. An after-hours party is taking place at his, well, his parents', winery and he's playing host. Although he's pushing forty, this is the first time he's been trusted with the keys to the Cabernet Kingdom. It's almost like the house party he threw as a teenager while his parents were on vacation. And he is certainly making the most of it. One hundred of his closest friends and their guests are in attendance. They schmooze amongst themselves, waiting for a visit from Sciandri. He's not nicknamed 'The Mayor' for nothing.

There is no specific dress code for this festivity; however, Sciandri has elected to go black-and-blue. A white tuxedo shirt, complete with bowtie, is draped by a black jacket. But he's also wearing ripped blue jeans and cowboy boots. The Mayor knows how to stand out in a crowd.

Sciandri weaves his way through the crowd, backslapping the men and air kissing the ladies. He has his eye on a cute

STUART CLARKE

little blonde, leaning against one of the columns beneath the veranda. Her glass is empty, he notices. So, he grabs a bottle and a fresh glass from one of the caterers and prepares to introduce himself.

'I notice you're empty,' Sciandri says. He begins to fill her glass but she stops him halfway.

'That's plenty,' she says.

'So, you're a glass is half full sort of girl?'

'Not really. I'm just more of a Chardonnay drinker.'

Sciandri feigns horror. 'Blasphemy!'

'I know, right? This place is noted for its reds and I'm not much a red drinker. I'm very hard to please.'

'Well, now I have a mission – to please you.'

The girl smiles. 'I'm Linda, by the way.'

Sciandri touches her shoulder. 'I'm Ron. Ron Sciandri.'

'Oh. So, this is your winery?'

'That it is. It's no Mondavi or Beringer, mind you but our winemaker makes very good Cabernet.'

'But no whites. Pity,' Linda says.

'I think I can remedy that. Would you care to accompany me to our cellar? I have some outstanding Chardonnays I'd be happy to open.'

'I think that sounds like a plan.'

The Mayor grabs her by the hand and weaves their way through the crowd. Trouble is, he's an extremely popular fellow. Everybody wants to shake his hand, joke with him and take selfies with him. What should have been a two-minute walk elapses into nearly forty-five. And it has no end in sight. Linda takes baby sips from her glass and is beginning to look

DEITIES

disinterested. He's losing her.

****

Kyrene hears music across a field. She also detects the sounds of people talking. 'Bacchus,' she says, 'we're going this way.'

Bacchus follows her through the grapevines. Soon, they are standing just on the outskirts of the Sciandri Family Vineyard. They observe the revellers on the patio. The band plays eighties dance favourites. 'I don't think we'll find Apollo here,' Bacchus says. 'But perhaps we could stay a while.'

Kyrene frowns. Finding Apollo is her primary, check that, only goal. But she could indulge Bacchus a little fun. She might even have some herself.

Amid the preppies and hipsters and co-workers who called themselves Sciandri's friends, Bacchus and Kyrene appear. It doesn't take long for them to be noticed. A man walks in wearing a toga accompanied by a four-foot tall pixie in dress seemingly made of leaves tends to stop all conversations. A caterer scrambles to find glasses for the newcomers. Bacchus is pleased to be served. Kyrene pouts.

'What's the matter, Forest Nymph?' Bacchus asks.

'I was hoping for nectar.'

'When in Rome, we say, drink what the Romans do. Or something like that.' He clinks glasses with Kyrene and tastes the wine for the first time. It is amazing, like nothing he's had before. 'It's like berries and pepper and cherries. I've never experienced anything like it.'

Kyrene takes a sip. 'Yes, it's pretty good.'

'Pretty good? I daresay that neither I nor Dionysus has produced anything of this quality. I must find the winemaker.

STUART CLARKE

I will bring clippings when we return to the Heavenly realms.'

Kyrene is taking in the music. It's new. It's different. And she likes it. She can't help but dance. She spins. She wiggles. Fun envelops her and won't let go.

Frankly, Sciandri hadn't realised that no one is listening to him any longer. Linda grabs him by the arm. 'Did you hire entertainment?'

Sciandri is shocked by what he sees. He's also a bit disappointed in himself for not thinking of the toga get up. He could pull that look off as well as that guy could. He decides to investigate and makes a beeline towards Bacchus and Kyrene. Linda follows. She has got to know what is going on.

As soon as Sciandri arrives, Bacchus greets him. 'I am Bacchus, the god of Wine. This is my friend, Kyrene.'

'Sciandri. Ron Sciandri.'

This causes Linda to laugh. 'That's very James Bond of you.'

Bacchus tilts his head in confusion. 'Who is this James Bond of which you speak?'

'You know, James Bond. Spy movies? Sean Connery? Roger Moore? Pierce Bronson? And God forbid, Timothy Dalton?'

Kyrene looks at Sciandri. 'You're a spy? I am too. Sometimes. You sit in the forest long enough, you hear things. Am I right?'

Sciandri has no answer for this, so he just nods. The spritely little girl is clearly off her rocker but she seems harmless enough.

'I'm going to dance now,' Kyrene announces and dashes off under the disco ball.

'Is she always like that?' Sciandri asks Bacchus.

DEITIES

'Oh, no. She's usually out of control.'

Sciandri sighs. 'So, Bacchus, what do you think of my latest vintage?'

'Ah,' Bacchus responds. 'You are the genius who created this sensational wine. It is foreign to me. What do you call it?'

'Uh, Cabernet Sauvignon. I would have expected the god of Wine to recognise it.'

'Allow me to apologise. You see, I am from a distant time and place. Rome. Perhaps, you've heard of it.'

Sciandri chides his ignorance. 'Well, yeah. But there are plenty of wineries in Italy that produce Cabernet.'

'As a winemaker myself,' Bacchus explains, 'I mainly grow Aminean and Nomentan. I've dabbled with Apian and while others seem to like it, I do not care for it much myself.'

'Are those actual varietals or did you just make them up?'

'Ron,' Linda says, 'be nice to your guest.'

Sciandri realises he's losing points with Linda by the second, so he tries a different tact. 'So, tell me about these grapes. What are they like?'

'Well, very often we define our wines by region rather than grape. But Aminean is a white grape I have come to love. I grow quite a bit of it. The Dulce has a sweetness that knows no match; however, I prefer the Austerum, the drier version. Both have extremely high alcohol contents, which makes everyone happy. Nomentan is a light red colour. Its quality varies greatly season to season but I like to think that mine is the best. Apian is also white but not nearly as delectable as the Aminean.'

It's smartphone time. Sciandri looks up Aminean and actual results come back. Apparently, there are a few small

Italian wineries making this wine. The more you learn about wine, he thinks, the less you find you know. 'How does this wine sell?' he asks.

'Sell? Why I give it away. It seems the neighbourly thing to do.'

'So, you make wine and don't make money? How can you afford to live that way?'

Bacchus is confused. 'Where I come from we do not need money. I am occasionally given gold but I don't need to spend it if that's what you're asking.'

Sciandri is still on the smartphone. His searches on Nomentan and Apian come up empty. 'Are you growing grapes that appear to be extinct?'

'They are certainly not extinct,' Bacchus assures. 'Their quality is produced for the demigods. They do not touch my Aminean except for rare occasions.'

'Is this like a Falanghina?' Sciandri asks.

'I call it Falernian. We may well be discussing the same thing.'

'In any event, that is one rare varietal. Nice work.'

Bacchus isn't sure how to respond. 'I have vines upon vines of it planted. I wish I had brought some with me.'

'As do I,' answered Sciandri. 'Perhaps, next time.'

The band begins playing something awful – something Sciandri certainly does not approve of. They all turn to the stage where Kyrene is on stage dancing to something called the 'Macarena'.

****

Coyote is lost in the city of Napa. He has never been good at

DEITIES

driving through this area but then, he rarely has occasion to visit. He finds himself on Coombsville Road, accidentally turns right on 4th Avenue and then out of desperation, turns onto Kreuse Canyon Road. This turns out to be a dead end. He turns around but notices someone wearing a toga. Coyote feels it necessary to investigate. Who knows? It could be Apollo.

Amin the Mercedes and the Beamers and Telsas, Coyote squeezes the rusted pickup into a tight parallel park. He's out of place but has no idea how out of place he is about to be.

First, he's refused at the door. He's not dressed properly, he is told. And he's not on the guest list. So, Coyote does what he does best. He sneaks in. He draws a crowd of onlookers; in fact, only the oblivious Kyrene seems to miss him. But he makes a beeline towards Bacchus, the one in the toga.

Sciandri intercepts him. 'I think I've reached my fill of uninvited guests.'

'Is one more going to kill you?' Linda asks.

Sciandri looks over Coyote. 'Dunno. This one might.'

Coyote ignores Sciandri and instead focuses on Bacchus. 'Tell me something I want to know. Tell me you know where Apollo is.'

'You're searching for Apollo?' Bacchus replies. 'So am I!'

'Exactly who are you?'

'I'm Bacchus. I'm Apollo's best friend.'

Coyote takes a long breath. 'Tell me you're not a god.'

'I am,' Bacchus replies. 'The god of Wine.'

'Fantastic,' Coyote says sarcastically. He did mental math. The hooded man warned him of the consequences of gods dying on earth. Pluto had been a huge mistake, he recalled.

STUART CLARKE

He would need to protect Bacchus and hunt down Apollo simultaneously. His reward should be upped substantially. Protecting one more god should be no issue.

Sciandri is again angered at the band. Who told them they could play a steel drum? Jimmy Buffett's 'Volcano' started a Conga line with Kyrene wiggling at its front. She is having so much fun; it seems she has forgotten about Apollo entirely. Bacchus cannot help but laugh.

Coyote follows his eyes to the front of the line. 'Tell me she's not with you as well.'

'Oh, Kyrene,' Bacchus replies. 'She only has eyes for Apollo.'

Coyote smiles. This he can use. 'Why don't the two of you come with me? We'll find Apollo together.'

'Do you know where he is?' Bacchus asks.

'No. But I know someone who might.'

Once Kyrene begins dancing, it is a Herculean effort to get her to stop. It isn't easy but they essentially abduct Kyrene while she performs the 'Electric Slide.' Linda is sorry to see them go; Sciandri, not so much. The trio provided an unnecessary distraction from his goal of bedding Linda. Be gone with them.

Coyote leads Bacchus and Kyrene through the parking lot. Bacchus is amazed at the array of chariots available to mortals. He touches the metallic surfaces as he passes. They are new to him. This new material is so smooth, yet so hard. He cannot help but be disappointed when he sees Coyote's truck.

'Why do we not take one of these other carriages?' Bacchus asks.

Coyote is perturbed by the question. 'Because this one is

mine.'

Bacchus shrugs. 'Okay.'

Coyote opens the passenger door. 'It's only a two-seater. One of you needs to ride in the bed.'

Bacchus looks behind the seats. 'That doesn't look particularly comfortable.'

'It isn't.'

'How about I ride in your lap?' Kyrene asks Bacchus.

This sounds much better to Bacchus. 'That okay with you, Coyote?'

'Frankly, I couldn't care less.'

Bacchus climbs into the truck's cab. Kyrene plops herself on his thighs. Bacchus gets immediately hard beneath his toga.

Kyrene turns around and glares at him.

'It's completely out of my control,' Bacchus admits.

'I'd prefer not to find Apollo with your penis poking outside your toga.'

'There are always steps you could take to force it to subside.'

Kyrene glares again.

This suits Coyote just fine. He'd prefer not to drive with a handjob going on next to him. So, he focuses on getting the rusty red Ford to turnover. Once, twice, third times a charm. He pulls out of the parking place and the three are on their way to the city.

Kyrene is excited. 'How are we going to find him?'

'We're going to track down the one mortal I've seen with him. His name is Jackson Tate. He will be most helpful, whether he wants to or not.'

33

Halloween

Halloween in San Francisco is a sight to behold. There are parades but the real action takes place at night in the bars. The Funhouse this year would be no exception. Each time, the event grows in both scope and attendance. Thus, when a shirtless Egyptian god wearing nothing but what amounted to a short skirt and a jackal mask appears, he draws little notice, other than the stray comment of 'cool costume, dude.'

Anubis doesn't like this new place. It is not the earth he remembers. The late October weather is cool and the wind causes him chills. He tries futility to transport himself back to the Ethereal Plane but has no luck. He concludes that the portal is closed. Might as well make the best of it. He would find mortals to amuse him while he waits for Set's anger to subside. Or perhaps, he would perform a deed that would ensure his return to the Underworld. He would find and kill Apollo himself.

The sun sets early here, he notices. Or more likely, its rays

DEITIES

vanished behind these tall structures – monuments the likes of which he has never encountered. The gods in this strange, new land must be very pleased with these erections created in their honour. Upon his return to his Underworld realm, he would tell the stories of these tributes. Many would be constructed to honour Set and Horus.

Anubis is particularly impressed by the Transamerica tower. Its shape is reminiscent of a very tall pyramid. Surely, it would impress Set. Anubis would return and oversee its construction and he would again be in favour. He would create one for Horus as well. If Egypt controls all, it should have new powerful monuments to remind the other pantheons of their superiority.

A man approaches Anubis. He is a beggar requesting assistance. At this moment, Anubis realises he has no currency or gold. Set has sent him here quite ill-prepared.

He shrugs off the homeless man. He is likely a slave and not the type of mortal Anubis will tolerate. Instead, he makes a beeline towards the Transamerica pyramid. When he reaches its entrance, he is baffled by the revolving door. He watches many mortals enter and exit. They flash him strange looks, which Anubis believes to be worship. Finally, he works up the courage to try it himself. His spear is caught on the door's ceiling and it snaps in half. Weapons, though, should not be difficult to come by. What he needs is currency. Surely, he could find a blacksmith to fashion a new spear.

He enters and is stopped by a white-haired man in his late fifties. 'You're taking Halloween pretty seriously. Is there something I can help you with?'

'I have come seeking your currency,' Anubis replies.

'You're here for a job interview? Hate to tell you but you're not exactly dressed as I would have imagined. Do you have an appointment?'

'I need no such thing.'

The security guard shakes his head. 'Well, the good news is Transamerica is almost always hiring. You might want to change your clothes though. You don't strike me as the insurance type.'

'I'll take my chances.'

'Your loss. Let me ring Human Resources and see what I can do.' The security guard picks up the phone. 'Mary, I've got a potential job applicant here to see you. He's dressed for Halloween. You should at least see his get up.'

The guard waits while Mary speaks, then hangs up the phone. 'You're in luck. Mary Martin says she'll see you. Best of luck to you. Go to the elevator. She's on the eighteenth floor.'

Fortunately, another person was heading towards the elevator. Anubis is surprised when the doors open. Still, he follows him inside.

'Nice outfit,' the man says. 'Where are you going?'

'To see Mary Martin. The man told me she's on the eighteenth floor.'

'That's where I'm heading as well. I'll even escort you to her office. I'm certain she'd love to meet you.'

****

Mary is working late on a Friday, something she did very frequently. She is a small woman in her fifties with very few friends, save for her house cats. Work is basically her only

DEITIES

contact with other humans, so she liked coming in early and leaving late. However, on a day such as this, she feels abandoned. Fridays are like that. People duck out early to avoid the traffic, spend time with their families or go to parties.

George leans into her office door. 'I have a young man outside who's looking for a career here. I think he'll do great.' George then shows Anubis through the door. George laughs. 'Have fun, Mary.'

Mary glances up at the shirtless, jackal-headed Anubis. Needless to say, she is stunned. She looks for George but he has quickly departed. Good thing for him. As head of Human Resources, she could write him up.

She puts on her best professional face that she can muster under these unique circumstances. 'I'm Mary Martin. I'm the Director of Human Resources here at Transamerica. How may I help you today?'

Anubis minces no words. 'I seek currency.'

That's a strange way of describing it, Mary thought. 'Should we talk about your background? Do you have experience in the insurance industry?'

'I was formerly the god of the Underworld. I've led many into battle and greatly aided in capturing the Spheri Eternus portal. I'm sure you've heard of it.'

Mary stares blankly. 'So, you're a veteran of war?'

'Yes. Of a great many battles.'

'That will certainly count in your favour. What attracts you to our company?'

'The shape of your building. It reminds me of my home.' Anubis answers.

'The pyramid shape? I must say that's quite an answer.'

'I'm an Egyptian.'

'Okay, well we do have several openings. What is your name?'

'Anubis.'

Mary is frustrated. 'No, your real name. Not your Halloween name.'

Anubis becomes angry. 'I am the great Anubis. Son of Ra and Nephthys. Master of funerals and mummification. Ruler of The Darkness. Destroyer of…'

'I'm just going to interrupt you right there. I don't believe we have a position for your, uh, skillset. You're going to have to leave.'

'What about my currency? It appears I need it on this earth of yours.'

'I'm not going to be able to offer you employment. So, there will be no currency, as you phrase it. Now you can leave willingly, or I can have security escort you out.'

Anubis reaches across Mary's desk and chokes her. Mary turns red, then blue. She collapses and, he lets her drop to the floor. He eyes a bag behind her chair – her purse. He opens it and dumps the contents onto the desk. Coins, among other things, fall out. 'So, this is the earth's currency,' he mumbles. He finds papers with 'In God, We Trust' typed on them. These are clearly meant for him, particularly those with the all-seeing pyramid on the back.

****

Night falls and Anubis wanders the street aimlessly. The sights, sounds and even the stars are foreign to him. However,

DEITIES

he trudges on with one thought in mind – locating Apollo. Little does he know how implausible his mission is. Finding a single being in a city the size of San Francisco would be nearly impossible. Anubis finds himself tiring. He requires something to quench his thirst. He requires beer.

Around the corner, he spots a line of mortals dressed outlandishly. Apparently, they are waiting to gain entrance to a bar. Anubis laughs to himself. He is the Egyptian god of the Underworld; he waits for nothing.

He bypasses the crowd and cuts in line at the front. Despite the protests of those behind him, the doorman takes one look at his garb and waves him forward. Beneath his helmet, Anubis is smiling. That is one mortal who will not be buried to his waist in ice upon death.

More strangely adorned mortals are inside. House music blares through the speakers and it hurts his ears. But he is an immediate hit with all. Everyone loves his attire.

'I love how creative you look,' a girl dressed as Lady Gaga shouts over the music. 'It's art, really, appears very authentic.'

Anubis nods politely, although he didn't quite hear her.

'Can I get you a drink?' she asks.

That he heard. 'Yes. A beer, please.'

Unfortunately, Gaga can't hear him either. His voice is muffled by the mask. She reaches to take it off and he smacks her hand.

Miley is apologetic. 'Sorry. Would you take off your mask so I can hear you?'

Reluctantly, Anubis does as requested. Long, flowing black hair contrasts his light brown skin.

STUART CLARKE

Gaga is impressed. 'You've got the looks to match your body. Please tell me you're not gay.'

Anubis is confused by this statement. 'Whatever do you mean?'

'You know, do you prefer the company of men or women?'

'Goddesses, typically.'

Gaga giggles. 'Great answer. So, about that drink. Can I get you a beer?'

Anubis nods. He likes this new earth. He can take currency as he pleases and be waited upon. Just as he's accustomed to in the Underworld.

Gaga vanishes to the bar while Anubis gets acquainted with his surroundings. Strange art and neon signs hang on the walls. There is a dance floor. Men dance with women; men dance with men; women dance with women. Four people play some sort of game with balls on a table covered in green cloth. He hopes they are gambling; otherwise, games are mere diversions.

Gaga returns carrying two beers – Sierra Nevadas. 'I'm sorry if this isn't your brand. But I thought you might like it. So, cheers.' She clinks bottles with him.

Anubis observes Gaga drink from the bottle, so he follows suit. This beer is much heavier and higher in alcohol than the Egyptian beer he's familiar with. He tries to swallow but the taste is too strong. He spits it to the floor and splashes Gaga's shoes.

'Hey! I like these hooker heels,' she says. 'It's okay, though. I figured someone would puke on them tonight. Kinda glad it's you.' She takes the beer from Anubis' hand and returns to the

DEITIES

bar. 'Something lighter, I take it?' she calls over her shoulder.

'Please,' Anubis answers. He is embarrassed that a mortal – a female one at that – could handle the stronger drink. However, he is distracted by this feeling only momentarily. A man dressed as John Travolta from Saturday Night Fever approaches him. Travolta puts his hand on his arm.

'You've got muscles on your muscles,' Travolta says. 'You here with anybody?'

'Well, no.'

'Mind if I hang around for a bit then? We could have fun.'

Gaga returns from the bar, this time carrying a Corona Light. She hands it to Anubis and gets territorial. 'Back off, Vinnie Barbarino. He's with me.'

Travolta laughs at her. 'Barbarino? I'm appalled by your lack of pop culture knowledge. I'm clearly dressed as Tony Manero. You're not exactly a walking IMDB, are you?'

She prepares to lecture Travolta. 'Maybe not. But I do know that...' Gaga realises she doesn't know the Egyptian god's name. 'What is your name again?'

'Anubis.'

'Right. I do know that he prefers the company of goddesses.'

Travolta finds this hysterical. 'Oh, so you're a goddess now? Maybe I could be a god. He might like that as well.'

Anubis interrupts this spat. 'One cannot become a god or goddess. Can you even fathom a world where that would be possible?'

Gaga and Travolta look at each other.

'What is he talking about?' Travolta mouths.

'I don't know,' Gaga mouths back.

This seemingly silent interaction confuses Anubis immensely. 'Did I miss something?'

'No,' Gaga says. 'But I think I'm going to leave you with your new friend here. Ta.'

Travolta walks away without so much as a word. Anubis now stands alone in the center of a place he hates and drinking a beer that he hates. One thing he knows for certain – Gaga and Travolta would be buried to their necks in ice.

34

Selection

Athena materialises on Mount Olympus and enters the gate of clouds. She walks through the great atrium and down the great hall. She arrives in the council room and finds the thrones are vacant. Upset, she sits down in her throne and contemplates the future order of gods and goddesses. She really needs her father right now. Zeus' wisdom would be undeniably powerful at this moment. Still, she cannot help but partially blame him. This calamity occurred during his unexplained absence. If only he were watching more closely, the Egyptians would never have gained control of the portal. If only he were fighting more fiercely, the Egyptians would never have the chance. If only…

Her thoughts are interrupted by the sight of Poseidon and Hera entering the throne room from the Southern side of Olympus. At the end of the hall was Zeus and Hera's private quarters. Poseidon certainly had no business on that side of Olympus. As far as she knew, only Zeus and Hera were even permitted beyond the hall. Something evil is going on and though she couldn't prove a thing, her suspicions were heightened.

Poseidon greets her with faux pleasure. 'Athena! How wonderful to see you! Tell us glorious news from the frontlines. Is that pesky Darkness on the run?'

'I'm afraid I have no such wondrous news to share. The situation for the portal has taken a dire turn.'

Hera makes a veiled attempt to appear interested. She walks the three crystalline steps to her ivory throne. 'It has been many centuries since I took an interest in the war. Are we not winning?'

Athena's eyes flash red.

Poseidon answers Hera in Athena's stead. 'I'm afraid, my Queen, that The Darkness has gained the upper hand in the conflict.'

'Surely, our forces are better trained than those from the Underworld,' Hera replies. She looks directly at Athena. 'Perhaps, there is a lacking of proper leadership. In any event, I'm sure it is something that can be overcome.'

Poseidon attempts to balance the room as Athena and Hera have no love lost for one another. 'It's the Egyptians, your highness. They no longer participate in the battles. The Light is vastly outnumbered.'

Hera is about to speak but Athena has no interest in anything she may say. 'The Egyptians are fighting now,' Athena reports.

Poseidon is pleased. 'Certainly, this news deserves several glasses of nectar.' He nods to a servant, who prepares goblets

DEITIES

of the fine liquid. 'Did Horus ride in and take control? I always respected that youngster. Always knew great things would come his way.'

Athena smashes her goblet to the floor. 'Yes, Horus rode in. Yes, he took control. His Egyptian army turned on us. They slaughtered us from behind while The Darkness attacked us from the front. We were ambushed.'

Poseidon's eyes widen. 'Horus is aligned with The Darkness?'

'No. Set's army slaughtered the opposing Frost Giants. What I'm telling you is there is no Light or Darkness any longer. Set and Horus joined armies and routed us. But I'm leaving out the worst part.'

'Worst part?'

'Horus and Set now control the portal. And they know how to use it. They sent me here to deliver the news.'

'So, you're what Hermes would look like were he a girl,' Hera says.

Athena glares at her stepmother.

'What darling? You don't approve of the comparison? Stronger leadership would have prevented this. You have no one to blame but yourself.'

'Where's my father?' Athena demands.

Hera chuckles. 'Your father? Why I don't know, dear. But then who am I to question his whereabouts? I am only his wife.'

'The leaders of all pantheons must meet. So, I ask you again, where is Zeus?'

Poseidon rises from his throne. 'Athena, Zeus has been

absent for some time. I cannot help but think that if he were present, we would not find ourselves in this situation. I recommend a change in leadership, a vote of no confidence.'

Athena seethes. 'I will not allow that to happen, Uncle. You will not take my father's throne. If anyone should, it should be Apollo.'

'Need I remind you that Apollo seems to be missing as well?'

Athena seethes. 'Well, I suppose it's up to me.'

Hera laughs. 'You were always such a spoiled little brat. Your father's darling. He gave birth to you himself, you know? You sprang right out of his head like a pimple. He always favoured you and his bastard son, Apollo, over our legitimate children.'

'Our mortals practice democracy. Perhaps, it is time we do it ourselves. Order Hermes to gather the other Olympians.'

Hera looks down her nose. 'Order?'

Athena swallows her pride. 'Please, my Queen.'

****

Hermes makes quick work of summoning the others. They abandon their duties and immediately make pilgrimage to Olympus as Hermes has explained the magnitude of the decision that must be made. Naturally, he is unable to locate Artemis or Apollo.

Ares, the god of War and Aphrodite, the goddess of Beauty, arrive first. They were in the midst of passion when Hermes appeared in the bedroom. Both enter the throne room disheveled and reeking of sex.

Demeter, the goddess of the Harvest, smiles at her sister,

DEITIES

Hera, then hugs her niece, Athena. She casts a furtive glance at Poseidon but turns away when he attempts eye contact.

Dionysus, the god of Wine, makes quite an entrance. He is stumbling drunk and leans against a sacred statue that crashes to the marble floor. All avert their eyes, even as Dionysus attempts a half-arsed apology.

Last to arrive is Hephaestus, the god of Fire and the Forge. The crippled god moves slowly to his throne and sits alone at the end of the semicircle.

Ares calls to Hephaestus. 'Hey, old boy. Have you seen your wife lately? I know I have.'

This causes Aphrodite to blush happily. She puts her arm around Ares, flaunting her affair in front of her husband and the other Olympians.

'Ares!' Hera shouts. 'That's enough! Hephaestus is my son just as well as you are. I do not appreciate your behaviour at the expense of your brother.'

'Half-brother,' Ares corrects. 'You made that mess of a god all by yourself.'

Hera stares disapprovingly at her son. Ares stares down to the floor.

'My sister, you've got your hands full with those two,' Demeter says to Hera.

Dionysus is annoyed. 'Can someone please explain to me why we are here? Hermes pulled me out of a perfectly good orgy that I'd like to rejoin.'

'Zeus is missing and the Egyptians have taken control of the portal,' Athena answers.

'Whoa! That's a lot to take in. But I don't see where I come into play.'

'In Zeus' absence, we need to elect a new leader. Someone with the wisdom and experience of warfare.'

Poseidon interrupts. 'Or perhaps someone with experience in actually ruling. Who controls the seas?'

'That would be you,' Dionysus slurs.

'Then, it should be clear to you all that I am the most qualified,' Poseidon boasts.

'This is a time of war and I am a war goddess. Leadership needs to focus on battle savvy,' Athena says.

'Perhaps Athena is being hasty. We do not know what changes the Egyptians will attempt to introduce. There may be none at all.'

'Better to be prepared for war and have none than to have one and not be prepared,' Athena says.

'Lest you forget who the true god of war is, Athena,' Ares says. 'I cast my vote for Poseidon.' Ares tosses his stone into Poseidon's circle.

Aphrodite smiles at Ares and follows suit. Two votes for Poseidon are tallied.

Hephaestus hobbles down from his throne. 'I cannot, with good conscience, cast a stone with my brother. Therefore, I support Athena.'

Athena nods politely.

'Must be awfully difficult having a conscience, brother,' Ares says as he hugs Aphrodite. 'Glad I don't have one.'

'I visited the Egyptians when Horus first claimed the mantle and was treated well,' Hermes recalls. 'However, what he did on the Ethereal Plane is unforgivable. I stand with

DEITIES

Athena.'

The piles are now two stones apiece. Poseidon attempts to lobby Dionysus. 'You should support me,' he says. 'I can offer your vineyards protection from earthquakes.'

'An earthquake vineyard. I already have one because of your angry shakes,' Dionysus says. 'It produces some of my finest grapes. I'll take my chances.' Dionysus lobs his stone to Athena's pile and Poseidon grows angry as Athena's votes now eclipse his own.

'Poseidon,' Demeter says. 'We have children together and you have always shown to be a good father. I'm sure you will make a fine leader as well.' Her vote is cast.

Including the votes cast by Poseidon, there are four stones in each pile. All eyes, except for those of Athena, look to Hera. Athena knows what the outcome will be.

Hera rises from her throne and walks straight to Athena. 'Here I hold the key to the future. What's it going to be Athena? Should I cast this stone for my bastard stepdaughter or my favourite brother?'

Athena is crushed. 'Please, my Queen, please use wisdom and not anger. I am better qualified for this role. I know the other pantheons well. It will appear to Odin that Poseidon is being opportunistic. Nor will Ahura Mazda as he holds wisdom in very high regard. The others will follow their leads.'

'Ahura Mazda? You must be joking,' Poseidon says. 'I have little use for that Persian. As for Odin, well, you will be of great help in convincing him that removing Zeus was necessary. I assume you will be a supportive member of the leader elected by your fellow Olympians.'

'I will but after I have said my peace. When Zeus returns, Poseidon must give up the throne. That is only right.' The others nod in agreement. 'On that day, Poseidon, you will have hell to pay.'

Hera smiles at Athena, then turns and gently places her stone in Poseidon's pile. Those who voted for Poseidon cheer.

Dionysus stumbles over and congratulates the new Chief god. 'About that earthquake. Perhaps, you could summon one to aid my crop.' He pauses. 'As my punishment, naturally.'

'Perhaps. But Hera and I shall receive the finest of your wine.'

'That only seems fair.'

Hera leads Poseidon to Zeus' throne. It is black marble, with golden ornamentation. Its seven steps contain each hue of the rainbow. A kingly chair for a kingly god.

'I think some nectar is appropriate,' Ares says, pointing to the servants.

While the goblets are being filled, Hephaestus hobbles to Athena's side. 'Anything you need, just say the word.' The crippled god limps through the atrium and past the clouded gates.

Dionysus whispers in Athena's ear. 'Wanna get drunk and go to an orgy?'

Athena sighs. 'You know, I think I might.'

****

Miles beneath the sea, a cavern exists with bars blocking the entrance. Mermaids, mermen and sea creatures of all kinds swim to the undersea prison and look upon its inhabitant as though it is a thalassic zoo. Daring mermen swim close to the

DEITIES

barricade, peering their heads inside in an attempt to show bravery to the comely young mermaids. Some hurl stones between bars at the prisoner while others rake the bars with tritons. Still, the captive shows no emotion.

Zeus has lost track of how long he's been trapped here but knows he isn't going to be released any time soon, if at all. Poseidon lured him here, claiming he had discovered a second portal deep in the ocean. The King of gods broke away from the maiden with whom he was engaging in sexual congress and followed his brother beneath the waves. There, Poseidon pointed him to this cave and Zeus swam inside. Slam went the bars and the great god became trapped. Zeus' primary weapon is the lightning bolt. Obviously, Poseidon had gambled he would be unable to utilise them underwater. And Zeus could not.

Poseidon had spoken to Hera on the matter and received her blessing to carry forward with the plan. She had long grown tired of Zeus' constant infidelities. Hera and Poseidon soon developed a romantic element to their relationship. The two of them working together resulted in the banishment of Artemis and Apollo. The one thing they could not have planned for was the Egyptian coup and subsequent capture of Spheri Eternus. Now, it was not only the intended targets trapped on earth but Poseidon's favoured son, Triton, as well.

Sea creatures talk amongst themselves and Zeus still had superior hearing. Learning that Triton was confined to the earthly realm was a singular delight he could relish.

35

By the Sea

Coyote finds himself playing tour guide again. Kyrene asks lots of questions but she's so cute and perky, Coyote cannot help but humour her.

'What kind of carriage are we riding in? And why are there no horses?'

'It's called a truck. It doesn't need horses to move. It runs on gasoline, on fuel.'

Kyrene nods as if she understands. 'But you do still have horses, right?'

'Of course.'

'So, why would you need a carriage such as this?' Kyrene looks back over her shoulder and notices a cloud of black pollution emitting from the rear. 'This one seems to be on fire. It causes a lot of smoke.'

'Probably hasn't had an emission test in the last twenty years. Also, could be running low on oil.'

'Huh?'

DEITIES

Coyote sighs. 'Never mind.'

They drive past some fields. 'Look! Cows! Can we stop and pet them?' she asks in earnest.

'No.'

Kyrene pouts. 'Why not?'

Coyote is at a loss. 'It's, it's just not the kind of thing that people do.'

'But we're not people,' Bacchus interjects. 'We're gods.'

Coyote hits the brakes. 'You want to pet the cows?'

Kyrene nods up and down rapidly.

'Fine. Do what you gotta do. Just don't take too long. And don't be surprised if a bull charges you.'

Kyrene dashes to the fence. It is wired off but she manages to squeeze through. Bacchus leans on the fence and watches her run to the bovine-filled field. Coyote soon joins him.

'What exactly is her story?' Coyote asks.

'She's a nymph. She's in love with nature,' Bacchus replies. 'And that's not all. She's also in love with Apollo.

This brings a pang of guilt to Coyote. He thinks about how he deceived Apollo and led him to a near certain death. Now, he hunts him again with the same thought in mind. But this Kyrene creature is different. She's so innocent and sexual at the same time. She must see the same in Apollo. However, Coyote has a duty to exercise. The payment offered bought his morality, such that it was and that reward would change his life. Soon, the Pomo and other neighbouring tribes would follow the old ways. Coyote would have the power to make that possible. Bear, Eagle and Crow would return as guiding spirits and the world would again be in perfect balance. Each

Native-American nation will become self-sufficient again and he would be regarded as the hero he once was.

Kyrene strokes the cows in the meadow. She discovers a docile young bull and climbs upon his back. The bull walks slowly, careful not to jostle her from her perch. She waves and giggles at Bacchus and Coyote.

Bacchus waves back. 'She has a way about her,' he tells Coyote. 'I wish she felt the same about me as she does Apollo.'

'Do I detect a hint of jealousy?' Coyote hoped so. Perhaps, Bacchus would be of use in Apollo's ultimate demise.

'Oh, there's a lot to be jealous of with Apollo. He looks absolutely perfect. Not like me.' Bacchus pats his stomach. 'He has scores of goddesses, nymphs, pixies, sprites and mortals who absolutely adore him. He excels, well excelled, in fighting and archery. His music is second to none. And damn, if he isn't also the god of Light.'

'So, he's basically Mr. Perfect. What an arse,' Coyote summarises.

'Yes. But, he's my arse.'

'What about you? You do pretty well with the goddesses, don't you?' Coyote asks.

Bacchus reflects. 'I'm not exactly a major deity,' he admits. 'I do make the finest wine in any realm – much better than that of Dionysus. I do okay.'

Coyote is planting seeds. 'You ever wish you were the focus of attention? I'm sure Apollo must cast a long shadow.'

Bacchus shakes his head sadly.

'Envy is like a wolf longing to be fed.' Coyote offers.

Bacchus gets defensive. 'I'm not envious exactly. I'd just like

DEITIES

a little more recognition.'

'When we find Apollo, you shall get the credit. Then, everyone will admire you, will they not? Or will they just relish in Apollo's return?'

Bacchus does not answer.

'Come, then,' Coyote says. 'Let's get your friend.'

Bacchus and Coyote are finally able to lure Kyrene back through the fence. They take their places back in the truck. Coyote is magically able to start the engine on the first try. They pull back onto the road.

Coyote scrunches his nose. 'What's that smell?'

Kyrene looks at her bare feet. 'Probably me. I stepped in cow droppings.'

****

Pier 39 of the San Francisco Bay was once home to over 1700 sea lions. Though that number has dwindled considerably, it remains a tourist attraction of sort. The water temperature varies from chilly to very cold, so people do not actually swim with them in this climate, save for the random happenstance of drunken Swedes.

The male sea lions can grow to be well over eight hundred pounds. While not usually aggressive, they are rather powerful creatures. It is also illegal to feed them. Still, camera hounds from all over the world swarm the Bay area to view these magnificent creatures.

Tonight, a shirtless man does swim with them. He does not fear them nor do they fear him. In fact, they are perfectly at home with one another. The man swims alongside the males; he knows better than to challenge their claims to females.

Besides, he has no such interest. He has developed a taste for mortal women – something so exciting exists between their legs.

The man is but half a man. His head, torso and muscular arms are human. However, from the waist down is a long scaly tail. He is a merman. He is Triton. And being in the water with these sea beasts is the happiest he has felt since his arrival on earth.

The bay is full of litter. Cans and plastic and bottles and other refuse. The garbage floats or has sunk to the ocean floor. Triton takes it upon himself to clean. No sea creature should be forced to cope with the pollution of mortals.

Triton gathers the floating pieces of plastic and paper, then swims to the shoreline and hurls the trash onto the nearby streets and sidewalks. He dives deep and even in the pitch darkness, he sees perfectly. Mountains of broken glass and intact bottles lie on the subaquatic terrain. It would take him years to clear this. Dejected, Triton surfaces for air and is hit square in the forehead by an empty bottle of cheap wine.

Triton becomes livid. He sinks beneath the waterline for a few minutes and then begins flapping his powerful tail in fury. He literally leaps from the water and onto the street above, landing not on a tail but legs.

The litterer is stunned by the sight of a naked man flying out of the water. She is very frightened but unable to scream. Quickly, Triton grabs her and drags her to the water's edge. 'Somewhere in this sea, there is a glass bottle that belongs to you. I suggest finding it and disposing of it properly.'

The woman stammers. 'But how?'

DEITIES

'By going underwater, of course.' Triton releases his grasp on the woman. 'You can go in yourself, or I can help move you along.' Triton reaches behind and picks up his three-pronged trident.

Timidly, the woman puts her foot in the water. It envelops her sandal and the water is frigid against her ankle. 'I can't do this,' she sobs. 'I'm sorry. I shouldn't have thrown it in. I wasn't thinking.'

'You only feel this way because you were caught,' Triton chastises. 'Here allow me to help.' He pushes her into the bay.

The woman treads water until Triton dives in after her. Once he's in the sea, his tail appears. 'Let's go down and look for your bottle.'

The woman struggles but Triton forces her down fifteen feet to the bottom of the shallow bay.

Triton can speak underwater but naturally, she cannot reply. 'Do you see it?' he asks rhetorically.

The woman shakes her head. She can see nothing.

'Well, we're staying down here until you find it.'

The woman is running out of air. She struggles and succeeds in freeing herself from the sea god's grasp. She kicks quickly towards the surface and is almost there.

Triton has been toying with her. He holds her ankle. She can see the surface but will never reach it. She thrashes but Triton holds her firmly in his right hand. In his left, he holds the bottle she threw. The woman loses consciousness and he drags her back to the ocean floor and buries her beneath a pile of garbage.

Satisfied with his achievement for the ecological

movement, he swims back to the shore. He stands naked below the streetlights; although, at this time of night, there will be no one to see him. He slowly dresses. First, he puts on jeans, followed by his sandals. Finally, he pulls on a sweatshirt and flips the hood up.

****

'This is an amazing bridge!' Kyrene exclaims as the cross the Golden Gate.

'That it is,' Coyote answers. Kyrene's enthusiasm is wearing a bit thin.

'Look how tall it is! Do you know how big it is?'

'No.'

Kyrene asks several questions without taking a breath. 'Are we going to that big city in the distance? Is Apollo there? How will we find him? How?'

Coyote sighs. 'I have an idea. It's a game. Do you like games?'

'Yes! How did you know?'

'Just a hunch. It's called The Quiet Game.'

Kyrene is excited. 'How do we play?'

Coyote really hopes this works. 'Well, we all stay really quiet and the first one to make noise loses. You ready?'

Kyrene nods. She seals her lips and mimics locking them and throwing away the key.

They drive in the joyous sound of silence for several miles. Then, just as Coyote is finally getting comfortable, Bacchus farts.

Kyrene bounces up and down. 'Coyote! We win! We win!'

'Actually, I think we all lose,' Coyote gripes.

DEITIES

'Sorry about that,' Bacchus says. 'Must have been that spicy food at the winery.'

'Or something crawled inside you and died. I mean, the windows are fogging up.'

Coyote and Bacchus roll down the old-fashioned crank windows while Kyrene holds her breath. The truck finally airs out. 'Try not to do that again,' Coyote warns.

They drive a little further before Coyote pulls over by the water's edge. 'This is where we get out.'

Coyote leads Bacchus and Kyrene to the docks. There, the hooded figure stands, almost as if he's been waiting.

'Coyote, you have been away for far too long. Have you accomplished your task?'

'Not as of yet,' Coyote answers.

The hooded figure peers past Coyote and for the first time, he realises they are not alone. And he recognises Bacchus and Kyrene immediately. 'Why have you brought them here?'

'They seek Apollo as well.'

Kyrene approaches the hooded figure. 'Do you know where we can find Apollo? We'd be most grateful for any help.' Because of her short stature, Kyrene can see under the hood. 'Triton!' she shrieks. 'What are you doing here? Bacchus, it's Triton! He's going to help us find our friend!'

Bacchus isn't so sure. 'Triton, you were never exactly a friend to Apollo. What makes you want to find him now?'

Triton pulls the hood down. No sense in masking his true identity any longer. 'My father sent me here to find Apollo,' he explains. 'As gods on earth, we are all friends now.'

Coyote knows this not to be true but lets it slide. It doesn't really concern him but still, he smirks.

'Something funny, shaman?' Triton demands of Coyote.

'To the contrary. I was just wondering about your cloak-and-dagger persona. I'm pretty sure no one from here would have recognised you.'

'Merely a precaution. Bacchus and Kyrene, you should know that if a god dies on this new earth, he or she, stays dead. There is no coming back from death here. I would advise you both to return to the safety of your realms.'

'We're not going anywhere without Apollo!' Kyrene exclaims.

Bacchus tries to soothe her but his previous conversation with Coyote still plays in his mind. 'Perhaps, Triton is correct. We're not warriors. If Apollo is in danger, then we may be as well. Triton, can you prepare a portal for us? I fear we will be of little help.'

'We will absolutely be able to help! Anything that is needed!'

'The most important thing,' Triton explains, 'is keeping you all alive. I shouldn't tell you this but there is a great demon that feeds on the souls of fallen gods.'

This concerns Bacchus even more. He assumed they would simply find Apollo and return to the safety of Heaven's Hotel lounge. 'Listen, Kyrene. I want to find Apollo as much as you do but I don't want to die in the process.'

Kyrene nearly explodes. 'We're not going to die! We shall find Apollo! He'd do it for us!' She says this as though she believes it to be true.

'My best advice to you,' Triton says, 'is to stay somewhere

DEITIES

safe. Do not put yourselves in harm's way. Let Coyote and myself handle the dangerous work.'

'No,' Kyrene says adamantly. 'Bacchus and I shall accompany you wherever you go. It is our friend we are concerned with.'

Bacchus shrugs. In for a penny; in for a pound. 'Yes, that is what Kyrene and I shall do. Tell me, though, can humans kill gods in this realm.'

Triton explains the best he can. 'They can. And given the opportunity, they will. Our innate powers are still intact. I can swim, Apollo can play music and Kyrene can still…'

'Control animals,' she interrupts.

'Perhaps. But Bacchus, I am thirsty. Can you create a bottle of wine from thin air?'

Bacchus nods. Of course, he can. However, he waves his hand and nothing happens. He concentrates and the result is the same – absolutely nothing appears. 'What is wrong? I have performed this parlor trick many thousands of times.'

'Not on this new earth. You are limited to your basic qualities. You, I suspect, can make and drink wine. But neither you nor Kyrene will be of use in fighting, were that to become necessary.'

'Why would that become necessary?' Kyrene asks in earnest.

Triton comes up with the best answer he can. 'Because there are others here who wish all gods harm. Earth is a very different place than we remember it. We are no longer worshipped. We are despised. Something to be feared. Something to destroy.'

36

Gold Futures

Jackson Tate had spent the morning at home, dreading the sound of the phone. He has been focused on his computer, desperately moving his finances into his off-shore accounts. If he was going to jail, there was no way his assets would be frozen. His lawyers would see to that. Of course, they would take a hefty share for their greedy selves.

Around noon, he sighs. Could it be he wasn't a wanted man? He knew he'd done an excellent job of hiding the pot and the coke. The pills were prescription. He decides to call the Calistoga Resort front desk. Six rings in, someone finally answers.

'Calistoga Resort, finest in Napa, how can I direct your call?' the operator answers.

'William Belmont, please,' Jackson says curtly.

'I'm afraid that's impossible. Mr. Belmont is only available Monday through Thursday and by appointment only.'

'Tell him it's Jackson Tate.'

DEITIES

There is silence on the line. 'Oh, Mr. Tate. I'm certain that Mr. Belmont will want to speak with you. I'll patch you through to his cell.'

Jackson is forced to wait through several minutes of instrumental hold music before Belmont is on the line. Finally, they are connected but Belmont wants to make small talk. 'Jackson, my boy, how are things with you?'

'I'm not sure. You tell me.'

'Well, it appears there has been a break-in at your cottage. Damage is mostly superficial. Except for the front door. You're going to want to get that replaced as soon as you can.'

'Is the installation something that can be handled by the Resort? I'm swamped down here in the city. Not sure when I'll be able to drive up north.' In truth, Jackson isn't sure how he'd get to Calistoga. The Range Rover is still parked in the garage.

'That shouldn't be a problem. But don't you want to pick a door yourself.' Belmont asks.

'I'll call my decorator. She can handle that part.'

'We can get to that in a few days.'

Jackson is guarded. 'Why a few days? Why not right now?'

'Jackson, your tile has blood on it. Napa's Finest are treating this like a crime scene.'

Jackson, of course, is well aware of the blood, having witnessed it firsthand. What with Coyote being cold-cocked by Diana, he knows what to expect. 'Any idea when it may be possible?'

'You know full well our officers are primarily in the DUI business. They'll clear out in a couple of days. What happened? You fall or something?'

STUART CLARKE

'Something like that.'

Belmont ignores the vague answer. 'Your Range Rover is still up here. You want us to tow it down for you?'

'What'll that run me?'

'It would be my pleasure. Just invite me to some of those legendary parties you throw. I'll hold security at bay if the noise gets out of hand.'

Jackson grins. 'That, my friend, is not a problem.' Jackson hangs up the phone knowing he's not off to prison anytime soon. He glances at the time on his iPhone. It's afternoon, he might as well pull it together and head to the office.

Jackson has little trouble ordering an Uber stretch limousine. He always tips the drivers well, so they come fighting over him. Upon reaching his office, he props his feet on the desk and reads the Chronicle. No mention of anything happening in Napa. This is good.

He has about a dozen messages sticky-noted to his desk. He reads them and immediately drops them in the circular file. They are mostly from bands he promised to get back to. He admires them for trying but frankly, if they had real talent, he would be the one tracking them down.

He breezes through the headlines but nothing catches his eye. He folds the paper and disposes of it in the wastebasket. Jackson Tate might well be the only man in the Bay area who does not recycle.

His office phone rings. He wishes Julie hadn't been at her desk when he whizzed by. He could let it ring to his voice mail but she'd know he was dodging. He could replace her with the snap of a finger – everyone wants to be in the music business.

DEITIES

But he liked her. She gave good head.

'What's going on, Julie?' he barks into the speakerphone.

'Um, the entire lobby is here to see you.'

Jackson pulls up Outlook. 'I don't see any appointments on my schedule. Send them away.'

'Well, it's that Apollo guy you like so much. And it looks like he brought an entourage,' Julie says.

Fuck. 'Is that crazy redhead and lady cop with him?'

'Yeah. And three other guys. They look like a scruffy low-end band,' Julie replies.

Jackson is weighing the big money Apollo could, potentially, bring to the table versus the psycho-bitches that Apollo definitely brings to the table. But, as usual, money wins. 'Send them up.'

'All of them?'

What the hell? 'Sure. Why not?'

Soon, Jackson has six people standing in his office, not counting himself. Diana quickly apologises and takes a seat in the corner. He's glad she's not there to arrest and lead him away in handcuffs, so he readily accepts her apology. The three strangers sit on the far sofa, leaning forward. Jackson notices two of them have brought guitar cases. Did they really think they were going to audition in his office? The short one carried drumsticks and eyes the drum set in the corner.

Apollo stands with Freya draped over him in front of Jackson's desk. 'This is my band,' Apollo announces.

Jackson shakes his head. 'Who are these people? Did you meet them on the street? I have huge plans for your career. I'm not linking you up with nobodies.'

Matt pipes up. 'We're working musicians. We play Joe's Dive Bar a few nights a week. We even sent you a demo. Do you recall it? We were called The Coverboys then.'

One thing Jackson did was to listen to every demo ever sent to him – he never knew when he'd find a diamond in the rough. He took copious notes on the 'Yeses' and the 'Maybes'. He digs through his files and finds nothing. Then, he looks in the slush file.

'The Coverboys,' he reads aloud. 'Bad tribute songs. Singer has little vocal range. Guitar and bass are adequate. Drums are drums – nothing special. Overall thoughts – this band goes nowhere fast.'

Matt shrugs off the assessment. 'Yeah but that was before Apollo joined us. We're a different group now. We've even changed our name to Delphi. We'll be writing our own music and I've never heard a singer or guitar player like Apollo. Come see us tonight at Joe's.'

'I've written a new song,' Apollo offers. 'It's a broken heart song.'

Jackson considers this. 'I do love a good break up tune. Okay, this is against my better judgment but plug into the amps. And you,' he points to the drummer. 'You will not damage my equipment.'

Freya steals a kiss while Apollo is strapping the guitar over his shoulder. 'Are you going to do my song?' she asks.

'No,' he whispers. 'This one is new. I just hope the mortals can keep up.'

Apollo lays down a punk riff, something between the Replacements and Violent Femmes. His voice changes from its

DEITIES

usual spot-on key to something more nasal. The drummer and bass player see where he's going and Matt tries to follow along. And the drummer tries to follow along.

Jackson Tate is floored by what he's just heard. 'Apollo, when did you write this song?' he asks.

Apollo lays the guitar down. 'Pretty much, just now. I was thinking about a break-up I went through with this water nymph, Daphne. She broke my heart and I turned her into a Laurel tree. I thought the song might both honour her and show her I've moved on.'

'I've got to get you boys into a studio ASAP. I can arrange something later today. Apollo, you claim to have written thirty-seven songs. How many does your new band know?'

'Two.'

'Well, it's time they start learning them. I want to fast track this. I need you all there.'

Matt interrupts. 'We're supposed to play at Joe's Dive Bar tonight. Can't miss it. It's a regular paying gig.'

'Remind me of who you are again,' Jackson fires.

'Matt Sawyer. I'm the leader of this band.'

'How cute that you think that, Matt Sawyer. One phone call and I have much better studio musicians taking your place. You rather play Joe's for the rest of your career?'

'No, sir,' Matt answers quickly.

'Fine. You're still in the band. Play your live gig at a filthy watering hole. Tomorrow, the real work begins.'

Apollo doesn't really know what this means; however, the rest of Delphi seem very excited. 'Sounds like an excellent plan.'

The Yoko Ono of the group speaks up. 'Maybe Delphi isn't the right name for the band,' Freya says. 'Perhaps, Apollo and the Oracles is better suited.'

Jackson thinks about this. 'You know, I kind of like it. Puts Apollo's name front and center. If he's lead singer and lead guitarist, he should receive top billing.'

The rest of the band grumbles. They don't like the idea of being a glorified backup band. But when would they ever get a chance like this again? They could keep playing covers or hitch their wagons to Apollo's star. 'We like it,' Matt says.

'Good.' Jackson scrawls an address on a Post-It note. 'Be here at four but if you're not early, you're late. You've got a lot of work to do. Especially, you Matt Sawyer.'

Matt is mystified but not dumb. 'Certainly, there is some contract we should sign.'

'Produce and then we'll see. You'll need to prove your worth to me.'

Matt sighs. He hopes he's up to the task.

37

Berserker

Athena is sore after the orgy and still piss drunk. Dionysus certainly knows how to show a goddess a good time. In fact, if this is the way the war was to end, she wasted thousands of years wasting her time. She wonders if she could really embrace Dionysus' Epicurean lifestyle. Probably not. But, the idea seems worth trying.

She deems her final task in this battle as going to Odin to explain the circumstances involving Poseidon's rise and the portal's fall. She allows her horse to guide her through the forest because she does not trust her inebriated self with the reins. The mare knows where she is going. Athena would only lead her off the path.

Athena is an unanticipated guest. There is no fanfare devoted to her appearance as there were on her previous visits. Odin, himself, may not even be expecting her. But still, this is a mission she must complete.

In fact, Odin is completely ignorant to her appearance.

STUART CLARKE

He amuses himself by playing a round of Kubb, a Norse game combining the class of bowling and the excitement of horseshoes. He plays against Njord, a very good player, who he seldom defeats. But today, Odin has the upper hand. He is but one baton toss away from toppling the King and winning the game. As he lines up his final toss, Athena catches his eye. He misses badly to the right.

'Can't account for everything, old man,' Njord says and rolls his baton directing into the wooden king block; thereby, securing the game for himself.

Odin sighs. So close. So close.

'Again?' Njord asks, gesturing to the game field.

'Let's see what Athena requires.'

Njord follows Odin to Athena.

'Sorry for coming unannounced,' Athena says. 'But some things have come to pass that I wanted to discuss with you face-to-face.'

'Of course, Athena,' Odin says.

Njord can detect the concern in Odin's voice. 'Perhaps, it is best that I stay for this conversation.'

Athena agrees. 'I need all the friends I can muster at this minute.'

Odin notices how Athena sweats. 'Come,' Odin invites, 'let us sit indoors away from the sun.'

Athena feels a little lightheaded. 'Yes. That would be best.'

She follows Odin and Njord through a glass door of Valhalla. Various gods and goddesses are mingling inside but their conversations come to a halt when they note Odin's serious demeanour. These gods and goddesses decide to take

DEITIES

social discussions to other parts of the hall.

Njord chooses a table for the three of them. 'Can I get you anything?' he asks Athena. 'Some mead perhaps?'

Athena makes a face, both because she hates mead and feels any more alcohol might kill her.

But Njord is being serious. 'Actually, it might help you. A reparere always does the body good.'

'A reparere?'

'Yes, based on the ancient theory of 'like cures like' by your very own Greek philosopher, Hippocrates. Besides, mead is good for what ails you. You do want to feel better, right?'

Athena groans. 'Does it have to be mead?'

Odin is annoyed with her behaviour but intervenes. 'Njord, do not tease our guest. No, Athena, you don't need to drink mead. I can offer you nectar or wine if you prefer. Or fresh water. Your body is likely dehydrated.'

'I'd like the water,' Athena says.

Odin nods to a servant, who quickly returns with two steins of mead and a pitiful glass of water. The servant is about to leave but Athena downs the glass in one large gulp and requests another.

Odin is worried. 'Athena, I must say I have never seen you in this condition. I must say it causes me grave concern. What is the matter with you?'

Athena is midway through her second glass of water. She sets it on the table. 'It's over,' she says.

'What is over?'

'The war. The Egyptians are back.'

A smile creeps across Odin's bearded face; however, Njord

hears her words differently. 'Whatever do you mean?'

Athena takes another long draw of water. 'We've lost the portal.'

Odin is shocked. 'Why am I hearing this from you? Why has Tyr not reported this to me?'

Athena exhales. 'I believe Isis turned Tyr into a marble statue.'

'Marble statue?'

Athena shakes her head. 'Possibly, iron. Not that it matters. He's adorning the halls of Heliopolis now. But I'm here because I was deemed as 'less of a threat'.'

Odin nods and then realises something. 'Heliopolis would be Horus' territory. Why would Tyr be a prisoner there?'

Athena is feeling herself again. But she doesn't wish to feel like herself. 'I think I'll have that wine now.' A Norse servant overhears her and quickly produces a goblet of red wine. It's pretty terrible wine, compared to what Bacchus and Dionysus produce but it'll do in a pinch. 'Horus turned on us. He let us thin our ranks by fighting The Darkness and then his army attacked us from behind.' She takes a sip of wine. 'Quite ingenious, really.'

Odin is stunned. 'Did The Darkness then overrun you?'

'You would have thought that would be the case. But Set's army attacked the Frost Giants. Horus and Set celebrated the victory together.'

Odin looks to Njord and demands, 'How did you not see this coming?'

'I do not know. All appeared clear. The only thing I can think of is that Isis placed a spell over their actions so as not to

DEITIES

be seen.'

Odin turns his fury to Athena. 'Is this why you're so inebriated? You've given up?'

'Oh, it gets better.' She regales the story of Poseidon taking control of Mount Olympus. Odin and Njord are appalled. Athena raises her glass in mock toast. 'To the end of the world.'

Odin needs help. He calls upon a servant. 'Please, bring me Mimir. I shall require his advice.'

The three sit silently as Mimir is summoned. After a few short minutes, his disembodied head is presented on a cart with wheels. 'I assume this is of utmost importance,' Mimir says. 'I was readying myself for bed.'

Njord explains all that has transpired, with the drunken Greek goddess, filling in the blanks. Mimir's facial expressions turn from shock to despair the more he hears. 'Odin,' he says. 'I am at a loss. Is Poseidon a trustworthy ally?'

Odin considers this thoroughly. 'I do not believe that he is.'

'That may actually work to our favour,' Mimir suggests. 'It is likely that he will be looking to the other kings to validate his claim. You hold a great deal of sway with the Celts. He will most certainly need their blessings before displacing Zeus. This means that you and Ahura Mazda are the two most important gods representing The Light.'

Athena sneers. 'What Light? There are now two sides – Egypt and everyone else. Unfortunately, they have an army and we have none. Those troops we have are scattered. I do not relish attempting to side with Hades. I am sure you would show similar concerns reaching out to Skrymir, the great Frost Giant. Our forces are entrenched in the traditional good versus evil theory of war. Now is a time, we must all work together. Njord, stare into the future. Tell me how that will play out.'

Njord doesn't have to answer as a furious Odin intercepts the conversation. 'Athena! Under what authority do you question the judgment of my advisors? It is clear to me that your people have little use for you. Why should I endure your presence?'

'I am truly sorry, Odin. I meant no disrespect.'

Odin is primed to continue his tongue-lashing but Mimir speaks. 'The Greek goddess of Wisdom is correct. We have been battling the Frost Giants for thousands of years. Now, we must seek their allegiance. It is problematic, at best.'

Athena, buffered by Mimir, stands her ground with Odin. 'It is exactly the type of diplomacy that I will be forced to engage with the Titans. The Greek gods have punished them for millennia but now we shall require their aid. I cannot think that they will be very compassionate to the cause.'

'Excuse me for a moment,' Njord says. 'Did you say that you will be engaging in diplomacy with the Titans?'

'I did,' Athena answers.

'It seems to me that it would be Poseidon who would perform that act. He is, after all, your new democratically-elected leader.'

Athena realises her mistake but verbally digs in. 'I accept neither his leadership nor his resolve. He wants to wait and see how Horus reacts with his newfound power.'

'I do not necessarily disagree with that assessment,' Odin says.

Mimir, however, does. 'Permission to speak freely, my Lord?'

DEITIES

Odin senses something dwelling. 'Granted, as always.'

'Horus may well deal fairly with his new throne but we are not accounting for Set. If the two are in liege with one another, my assumption would be that Set the Elder is the lord whilst Horus is the vassal. If this is the case, we find ourselves in a state of war already. The Underworld must be full of souls under Set's control. It only makes sense that he would desire to expand his territories. Valhalla and Olympus must never fall under Egyptian control.'

Athena says, 'And Set and Horus control the portal. They could drop an army right on Olympus or, I daresay, Valhalla and the slaughter would begin anew. Drastic steps must be taken to ensure this does not occur.'

Odin is still not convinced. 'What of Anubis? I believe he may have concerns about being replaced as Lord of the Underworld. Could an old foe become an ally?'

Athena shakes her head. 'He played an integral part during the battle for the portal.'

Njord goes into a trance. When he awakens, he is surprised by what he has seen. 'Anubis is no longer in the Underworld.'

This worries Athena. 'He could be anywhere. Plotting a devious plan to unseat various gods and goddesses.'

'No,' Njord says. 'Anubis is stranded on earth until Set sees fit to bring him back. 'Hades and Hel are on earth as well.'

'A regular 'Who's Who' of The Darkness. What about those from The Light?' Athena asks impatiently.

'Apollo, Freya, Artemis – who is calling herself Diana, Triton, Bacchus and for some reason, a Forest Nymph.'

'Kyrene,' Athena says.

'Yes,' Njord responds. 'Kyrene. Why would a Forest Nymph be there?'

Athena is piecing things together at lightning speed. 'Odin, I'm sure it was you who sent Freya to earth. But what of the others?'

'I sent Freya to recover your useless brother. But I sent none of the others,' Odin answers.

Athena lets the 'useless brother' comment slide off her back. 'Who can use the portal?'

'The triad for this millennium was to be Zeus, Ra and myself. However, Zeus is missing and Ra has been dethroned.'

Athena feels like she's had an epiphany. 'Poseidon can use it. He knows how. And if Apollo and Artemis were here, Apollo would have been anointed king of the Greek gods in Zeus' absence. Who else from The Darkness is missing?'

'Pluto,' Njord answers. 'But I no longer detect him.'

'This means…' Athena speaks so quickly she can barely keep up with her thoughts. 'This means that Poseidon has been dealing with Anubis for some time. And he is likely the one who captured my father. Njord, can you see Zeus?'

'I cannot,' Njord answers. 'But I do not detect him in the Underworld. He is likely still alive.'

'We have got to find a way to bring back those gods trapped on earth. We need Apollo, Artemis, Freya, Hel and Hades,' Athena says. 'Triton would be a useful bargaining chip against Poseidon.'

'I hate to ruin your thought but without the control of Spheri Eternus, we cannot rescue our allies or, our soon-to-be allies, from earth,' Mimir says.

DEITIES

'That's not exactly true,' Odin says. 'It is written that deep in Jotenheim, the Frost Giants guard the second portal. The fact that it has never been used, leads me to believe they lack the knowledge. But it is always ferociously defended.'

'So, we just need to convince them that we need to use it. For all our benefits,' Athena says.

'That will not be easy. They have hated us for thousands of years. And with good reason. Like your Titans, our gods supplanted them,' Odin explains.

Mimir has an idea. 'Perhaps, if they are convinced that they need us more than we need them, they will help.'

'I should be the one to deliver the message,' Athena volunteers. 'I have the most to gain and the least to lose.'

'You shall have company. These giants are not to be trifled with. Perhaps, they shall listen to me.'

38

Hell Reunited

In the afternoon sun, Anubis walks aimlessly down the street. He has been walking all night, making random right and left turns. He is hungry. He is thirsty. But most of all, he is tired. He staggers along the windy sidewalks as if he were drunk. He stops by an alleyway and sees dozens of mortals sleeping in the street. It seems as good a place as any, so he finds an empty portion of the wall and sits down. Before he knows it, he is fast asleep.

And how he dreams. Dreams of power and victory and the goddesses he once controlled. Then, he dreams of Set and Horus and how they now own all that was his. It is a troubled slumber, to be sure.

Hours may have passed – of this, he cannot be sure. But he is awakened by a repetitive kicking on his sandal. At first, he considered this merely part of his dream but eventually, he opens his eyes. He doesn't quite recognise the female. She looks familiar but his vision is still fading in and out. When he

DEITIES

looks to the male, he comprehends that it is Hades. He looks back to the female and determines that it is Hel. She is whole. No longer does she bear the resemblance of a skull on half her face. She is beautiful. He notices her clothing is native as is those belonging to Hades. He feels he is amongst friends.

Anubis sits up straight. Mentally, he questions why they have not bowed before him as they would usually do. However, in this instance, he feels glad not to be alone.

'On your feet,' Hades barks.

Anubis isn't sure he heard this correctly. He does not follow orders from anyone. Well, except maybe Set.

'He said, on your feet!' Hel reminds and kicks him in the calf.

Anubis scrambles to stand. 'Who are you to cast orders in my direction? Need I remind you who your leader is?'

Hades stares him down. 'Not on earth. Here we are all outcast and here we are all equals.'

Anubis scoffs. 'Equals? Surely you must be joking.'

'He does joke,' Hel says, keeping an eye on Hades. 'Here on earth, Hades and I are equals, superior really. You may be our follower if you choose. Or you may continue alone.'

'And this new earth is not a place where you want to be alone,' Hades adds.

Hel smiles. 'So, Anubis, what's it going to be? You want to adhere to our new earth rules or sleep with the vermin?'

Anubis realises he doesn't have many options. He does not wish to lie in the gutter with the rats. But he certainly does not appreciate the tone in which is being spoken. 'I'll come with you,' he concedes.

Hades smirks. 'Of course you will.'

'Where will we be going?' Anubis asks.

'To finish what you started,' Hades replies. 'To finish where you failed.'

****

Bacchus and Kyrene sit on a park bench watching a very animated discussion between Coyote and Triton. It is unclear what exactly it is about. Every time Kyrene tiptoes close enough to catch a word, they send her scurrying away. Bacchus wonders when Happy Hour will begin. He's in danger of sobering up.

Just out of earshot, Coyote lectures Triton. 'You're the son of some big deal god. Why did you need to involve me in your wicked little plan?'

Triton sighs. 'I needed someone who knew the lay of the land. Someone morally ambiguous. Someone like you.'

No one likes to have their scruples questioned. Coyote, however, is immune to these jabs. He lives to a code – it's just not the typical code. He learned long ago when his people were driven to reservations that right and wrong mattered little if you lived like a slave. Coyote wouldn't have it. Thus, the Creator begat the Trickster who, in turn, begat the Thief. 'I expect my payment whether or not the Prince passes or not. Frankly, I have grown tired of this entire situation. Give me my money, or I shall take it from you.'

'Nice try, Western Spirit. You think I am fool enough to keep your reward on my person? I know your type, Coyote. You have many names throughout different regions and beliefs. You are the Greek Hermes. You are the Roman Mercury. And

DEITIES

perhaps, most aptly, you are the Norse Loki.'

'I know not those of whom you speak. I am Coyote – nothing more; nothing less.'

'You are an opportunist. Nothing more and nothing less. Do you care about anything other than yourself?'

'That is none of your business,' Coyote responds quite loudly. Bacchus and Kyrene take notice.

Kyrene dashes over to the conversation. 'Is there something we can do? Perhaps, we can all be satisfied. I mean, we all want to find Apollo, correct?'

Coyote nods sadly but Triton takes control. 'Finding Apollo is of the utmost importance. All else pales in comparison.'

'Excellent. Do either of you know where he might be?'

Coyote says, 'The last time he was in the City, things did not go well for him. There are but a few places of which he is familiar. My guess is he would go to one of those.'

'Is it the rat hole, I'm thinking of?'

'It is. They have live music. It's Apollo's kind of place.'

****

Matt Sawyer finished up an uncomfortable phone call with the band's previous lead singer. As expected, the singer was most distraught about being replaced. Matt explained that The Coverboys' had split and the remainder of the band was backing up someone named Apollo. The lead singer was livid. Does he know the tunes, he asked. Can he play lead guitar and sing at the same time? When Matt answered both of these questions in the affirmative, the lead singer declared he wanted his equipment, including his amps back.

This presented a problem.

STUART CLARKE

Matt neither had the cash nor the credit to replace the gear on short notice. But their utter livelihood rests on being able to perform at peak performance during a show that Jackson Tate might well make an appearance. There is only one person to ask. That is his father.

The phone rings five times before Dad picked up. 'What do you want?'

This exchange could have started better. Matt thought better of making small talk and drove straight to the point. 'I need money.'

'You always need money. You presently owe me over twenty-thousand dollars. Why would I extend you yet another loan?'

'Well, it's actually great news. A major agent is interested in the band. He's coming to see us tonight.'

Dad is dubious. 'I've heard this story before. You're getting long in the tooth for this music hobby. I'd tell you to deliver pizzas but with those DUIs, I can't think anyone would hire you. Do you remember the times I bailed you out of jail? Paid your legal fees? You think that was free?'

Matt is playing defense. 'Of course not. And you know I appreciate it. But I could be on the brink of something big here. We have a new singer. He also writes incredible original songs.'

'What sort of songs?'

'Pop, punk, ballads, anything really. We could go far. All I need is a little to tide me over. We need some equipment, Dad. The entire night depends on it.'

Matt's father sighs. 'I'm not well-off anymore. Your mother

DEITIES

took me to the cleaners.'

'I know, Pop. And I haven't spoken to her since.'

This statement softens Matt's father. 'How much?'

'Couple grand. I need a sound system and amplifiers for tonight's show. If we impress this booking agent, the sky's the limit.'

'I'll write you a cheque. You can come by and get it this morning. But I am going to come to your show tonight. I want to see firsthand if you have any real talent.'

Matt is giddy. 'Dad, that sounds great. We'll throw in a Zeppelin song or two for you. But we're trying out some new songs as well.'

'Don't disappoint me. Again.'

****

Anubis walks three paces behind Hel and Hades. He wonders where they are going but dares not ask. He also wonders what's inside the large duffel bag that Hades carries over his shoulder. His hunger and exhaustion get the best of him. 'Where are we going?' he asks weakly.

'We assume you are hungry,' Hel says. 'We know a place a few minutes from here. We'll get you something to eat and drink. You'd like that, my pet, wouldn't you?'

It's a little after six o'clock when they reach Joe's Dive Bar. Hel requests to be seated in the far corner. The hostess isn't sure what to make of Anubis' jackal mask or odd choice in clothing but seats them all the same.

Anubis craves water more than he craves beer but he follows suit, ordering the lightest draught on tap. Hel smirks. 'Never could handle anything heavy, could you?'

STUART CLARKE

The beers arrive on the table. 'Do you know how Egyptian beer is like a Viking ship?' Hel quips.

Anubis shakes his head. 'No.'

'They're both close to water.'

Hades laughs a little too loudly for Anubis' taste. He is unaccustomed to being the butt of jokes and it does not feel good. He laughs politely as if he's trying to fit in but wonders if this is how he treated Pluto. Karma, he's been told, can be a bitch.

'How long have you been on earth?' Hades asks.

'Almost two days,' Anubis replies.

'You must be hungry. From the way your hands are shaking, I'd guess you haven't eaten.'

'No. I find myself lacking the necessary currency.'

Hades smiles. 'Don't you worry about that. Hel and I have accumulated quite the stockpile. We'll feed you, of course. Provided you're willing to make a trade.'

Anubis stares. 'What sort of trade did you have in mind?'

'Food and protection in exchange for your jackal helmet.'

'Seems like a fair trade to me,' Hel says. 'You don't exactly have anything else we want.'

Anubis is adamant. 'This mask is not for sale.'

Hades shrugs. 'It will be mine. But you may hold onto it for now. I'll collect it when I'm ready. You see, I have weapons from this new earth that can kill a god. Now, I could easily murder you but it would be much more satisfying for you to simply give it to me.'

Anubis glares at Hades which only causes the Greek god to laugh again. 'You know, Hel and I were enjoying quite the

DEITIES

meal yesterday. On earth, they now serve something called a 'cheeseburger.' I suggest we request more of those.'

'An outstanding idea,' Hel agrees. 'Perhaps, we should allow Anubis to dine with us as well. Just looking at him is making my appetite surge.'

'Just this once. And then the true negotiation for the helmet begins.'

The cheeseburgers and another round of drinks are brought to the table. Anubis samples the burger and immediately falls in love. It is the best food he has ever tasted. That is until he tries the culinary masterpiece that is the French fry. He momentarily forgets that he was shunned and exiled to earth.

But Hades snaps him back into reality. 'You're slowing down on your beer, my Egyptian friend. Is it possible that you cannot keep up with your new surroundings?'

Anubis takes this as a chance to brag. 'This is but a temporary place for me. Now that the portal is under Egyptian control, Set can bring me back anytime he wishes.'

Hel laughs and then becomes serious. 'Wait, what? The Darkness controls the portal?'

'You misunderstood. I did not mean The Darkness. I meant the Egyptians. It was such a glorious battle. Horus defeated The Light while Set and I attacked The Darkness. Now, there is only Egypt.'

'So, explain this to me,' Hades says. 'If it's an Egyptian plane, why are you on earth?'

Anubis doesn't quite have an answer for that. 'It was an agreement that Set and I reached,' he lies. 'He thought it best I oversee the final destruction of Apollo.'

STUART CLARKE

Hades doesn't believe it for a second. 'You were working with Poseidon. That became more than obvious when Hel and I were transported. What I want to know is, when did you start betraying The Darkness and working for The Light?'

'You have it backward,' Anubis explains. 'Poseidon approached me. He wanted to rid the Olympian ranks of Apollo and Artemis. He confided in me that he was planning a coup.'

'He wants to dethrone Zeus? That's a laugh. Poseidon may be ambitious but he's no match for my brother.'

'He didn't go into details but it seemed like he worked that out.'

'So, let me ask you this. Why were you so ready to sacrifice Pluto to earth?'

'He was sent here to destroy Apollo. Gods, Poseidon explained, are not immortal here. We felt Pluto would be the perfect god to eliminate Apollo once and for all.'

Hel is furious. 'You arranged with the enemy to send our friend to earth? Did it occur to you that Poseidon might not bring him back?'

'You're missing the point. Apollo's demise would bring the Greeks and the Underworld closer together. Poseidon said that once he gained control of Olympus, we would work as one.'

'And you believed him? You are so fucking naïve!'

Anubis isn't sure he heard right. 'What's "fucking"?'

Hades interjects. 'It's her new word. We tussled with a tribe called "bikers" that said it a lot. However, the fact remains that you essentially killed our friend. You think Poseidon is crying tears right now for Pluto?'

DEITIES

'No. But I'm certain that he worries about his own son, Triton. Now only Set or Horus can utilise the portal. I am the only one here who is safe. The rest of you could find yourselves trapped on earth for all eternity.'

****

It is well after eight when Coyote leads Triton, Kyrene and Bacchus to Joe's Dive Bar. Triton immediately recognises the three gods sitting in the far left corner but the others do not take notice. 'Please seat us as far away from them as possible.'

'A little bad blood?' the hostess asks.

'You have no idea.'

She leads them to a booth on the opposite corner. They follow her but Coyote feels a sudden jerk on his arm. It is Joe. He's not even pretending to be happy to see Coyote.

'What's the matter with you?' Coyote asks. 'I'm bringing you customers. Paying ones, at that.'

'I want my money,' Joe says. 'You're into me for nearly three large. You got an ETA on that?'

'The money's in my reach but I just don't quite have it yet,' Coyote says and reaches into his wallet. 'I've got close to two hundred here. That can cover whatever we drink tonight and the rest is for my tab. Sound fair?'

'Not really,' Joe grumbles. 'But I suppose it's better than nothing.'

Coyote pats Joe on the shoulder. 'That's the spirit. Now send us a pretty waitress.'

At the table, Bacchus attempts to order about forty wines, including the Sciandri Family Cab, which Joe's does not offer. He eventually settles on ale. Kyrene gets talked into something called 'Sex on the Beach.' She giggles when it appears on the table – all red and pretty, like an alcoholic flower. Coyote dares Triton into drinking whiskey. Triton handles it about as well as Apollo did.

While Bacchus and Kyrene make merry, Coyote slides his chair closer to Triton. 'You know, I usually sit at the bar. Why were you concerned about those others seeing us?'

Triton sighs. 'They are gods from what we call The Darkness. If they see me or Bacchus or Kyrene, then they might try to kill us.'

'And you're worried about your immortal souls coming to an untimely end.'

'I believe I mentioned a monster that ingests souls. If he were to be released, devastation would rampage your fair city.'

Coyote is blasé. 'Your monster does not frighten me.'

'Well, it should. This demon would cause destruction of epic proportions. Thousands of innocent mortals would be slaughtered. And that would just be the beginning. Once it is free, it could move anywhere. But I suspect it would come to San Francisco first.'

'And why is that?'

'Look around you. There is no shortage of gods here and the more it ingests, the stronger it becomes.'

'Then, why kill Apollo?' Coyote wonders aloud. 'If what you tell me is true, this demon will become free.'

'One more death shouldn't be enough. Any more than that, there will be a problem.'

'Why are you so invested in killing Apollo, anyhow?' Coyote asks. 'He seems decent enough. A little dense, perhaps.

DEITIES

But harmless.'

'It has to do with my father,' Triton explains. 'This request came from Poseidon himself.'

'You act like I have a clue who that is.'

Triton is taken aback. 'Poseidon. The great god of the Sea.'

'Never heard of him. But then, apparently, there are a lot of you gods with which I am unfamiliar. Tell me, if you are truly gods, why did you let my people be overrun by this new society? The Pomo are a peaceful tribe. We wished no ill will on anyone.'

'That must have happened after we fell from favour. The mortals are a fickle group. They change their gods every thousand years or so,' Triton rationalises.

'I agree with you on the fickle sentiment. My people have lost their way. They worship technology now. They live in squalor but have flat screen televisions and mobile phones. A slave's wage is now a day's wage in Indian reservations. That's why I'm willing to help you but it seems to me that a good, old-fashioned demon might hit a celestial reset button. We could be through with this desire for the all-mighty dollar and focus instead on hunting and growing crops.'

Triton sees something in Coyote he hasn't seen before. Coyote isn't exactly amoral. He has an endgame and is willing to do anything, including murder, to achieve it. However, Triton is not about to let Coyote's goals conflict with his. 'No demons or no deal. Triton gestures towards the far corner. 'Those three have to leave. Do what you must to get rid of them.'

Coyote peaks across the bar at Hades, Hel and Anubis. 'I

think I can handle that but Joe's not going to like it.'

'He won't like a monster destroying his place of business either.'

Coyote strolls to their table and produces a deck of red Bicycle playing cards. 'Do you three like magic?'

All three shudder, especially Anubis. When you've seen magic up close, it isn't always pretty. But Hel seems enthused. 'Sure, mortal. Show us what you got.'

Coyote shuffles the deck and fans out the cards, face down. 'Now, little lady. Think of a card and I will draw it.'

Hel makes her selection and then Coyote pretends to concentrate. He pulls a card from the deck and flips over the Ace of Spades. 'So, how did I do?'

'I was thinking of the Death card,' she answers.

Coyote is momentarily confused but then understands. 'Oh. You were expecting a Tarot deck. Sorry, these are standard regulation cards from the USA. However, this is typically accepted as a death card in modern decks. In fact, two black aces and two black eights are commonly referred to as 'Dead Man's Hand."

Hades is dubious but Hel seems impressed. She picks up the Ace of Spades and studies it. 'I rather like it,' she declares.

'I have another game you may like,' Coyote says. 'It's called Follow the Lady. I place three cards face down and all you have to do is find the Queen of Hearts. It's a pretty easy game, really. He turns up the Ace of Spades, the one-eyed Jack of Spades and the Queen of Hearts. Then, he flips them over and begins shuffling them on the table.

Hel immediately spots the Queen when Coyote is finished

DEITIES

moving the cards. 'What do I win?' she asks.

'Well, nothing but a good feeling. This game generally requires a wager.'

Hades reaches into his pocket and pulls out a twenty. 'How's this?'

'It's a good start.'

Coyote goes through the motions and Hel finds the Lady again. 'You sure you haven't played this before?' Coyote says and matches Hades' money.

Hel insists they up the wager. Coyote grimaces. 'That's a lot of money,' he says. 'Okay, one last time. Follow the Lady.' Coyote mixes the cards more rapidly but Hel is focused on each twist and turn the cards make. As Coyote, finishes his shuffling, he employs sleight of hand. The Lady turns up where Hel least expects it.

Coyote reaches for the money pile but his hand is held fast in Hades' grip. 'You are a charlatan, are you not?'

'Honestly, I've been called worst,' Coyote answers. 'But she only missed by one card. Do you think you could do better?'

'I know I could.' Hades reaches into his pocket and pulls out a C-Note.

'Big spender,' Coyote says. He turns the cards face down and prepares to shuffle. 'And away we go!'

Hades loses track of the Queen pretty quickly as Coyote manipulates the cards several times. When he stops, he's not exactly sure where the Lady is. Fortunately, neither is Hades. He selects the one-eyed Jack.

'We can keep playing,' Coyote offers.

'I'm not wasting any more currency on this foolishness,'

Hades says.

'I understand not wanting to gamble any more of your hard-earned dollars,' Coyote says. 'How about we gamble what's in your bag?'

'Not a chance,' Hades says a bit too loudly.

'Got something special in there I take it? Mind if I take a look.'

Hades nods to Anubis. Anubis unzips the bag of guns.

Coyote cannot believe his eyes. 'You've got a regular artillery in there. If you're criminals; perhaps, we should consider working together.'

'Not a chance, mortal,' Hades says.

'Come now. Surely, we can reach an agreement. Nobody has that many weapons unless they're planning on using them. So, what is it? Robbery? Don't tell me it's murder.'

Anubis speaks out of turn. 'We're going to kill somebody who has done us wrong.'

'Anyone in particular?'

Anubis feels the weight of the stares coming from Hades and Hel but doesn't care. 'His name is Apollo. He will be here tonight.'

'Apollo, you say. I know him. Turns out I need him dead as well. But unfortunately, unless I'm the one who pulls the trigger, I don't get my reward. Why don't you let me have one of those guns?'

Hades smirks. 'How about you buy one from us using the money you stole. Sounds like a fair trade to me.'

Coyote is ever the negotiator. 'I get to pick the weapon.'

'No, you don't,' Hel says.

DEITIES

'Fine.' He passes his winnings back to Hades.

Hel opens the bag and pulls out the smallest gun they possess.

This works well for Coyote. It is exactly the one he would have chosen. 'I assume it's loaded.'

'I would assume so,' Hel answers.

****

Coyote ducks back over to Triton's table and whispers, 'They're here to kill Apollo.'

'I gathered. What do you plan to do about it?' Triton responds.

'The band usually comes in through the back. I can handle this before they even know it happened.'

Kyrene heard only the part of the conversation where the word 'Apollo' came up but she couldn't make out the rest. 'What's going on?'

'Nothing you need to be concerned with,' Triton assures.

'I heard Apollo's name! Is he here yet?'

'No. But it shouldn't be too much longer.'

'I'm grabbing a smoke,' Coyote announces. 'Be right back.'

Coyote walks through the front door and ducks around to the back of Joe's. He notices a van and peers inside. It's full of music equipment. The band has started unloading the amplifiers and drums. Won't be much longer now. He lights up a cigarette and takes a long drag.

39
Spirits of Ancient Egypt

For Horus, being king is a dream come true. After a thousand years of fighting with his uncle, Set, finally, the two finally reached an accord. His mother, Isis, stands by his side, along with his wife, Hathor. The festivities in Heliopolis are still occurring. Good? Evil? It no longer matters. All for one and all for Egypt.

Horus wasn't sure about Set's battle plan. He had concerns that someone, namely Athena, would see through it. However, she gleefully played it out exactly as Isis said she would. As for Set, his plan was flawless. The forces of The Light and those of The Darkness battled like they always did. They fought and slew one another before being attacked from the rear. Now, Set had the fallen trapped in the Underworld. There would be no more battles on the Ethereal Plane. And if any outside gods attempted to invade Heliopolis, they would be destroyed and captured. Fates would be sealed. Mighty Egypt has risen again.

Horus, however, finds himself a bit bored. He is a warrior

DEITIES

god with no enemy. He looks across his throne room at the golden statue of Tyr. Oh, what a moment that was defeating him. Isis asked him what type of stone she should transform him into – as if there was any other choice. Tyr, in many respects, symbolised the fortitude of The Light. He was an excellent field general and warrior. Too bad, he was in the wrong place at the wrong time. He could have been a powerful ally. But he was Norse and now was Egypt's day in the sun.

When Set elected to allow Athena her freedom, Horus had shown apprehension. In his opinion, she was the bigger threat. However, Set and Isis overruled his concerns. She is but a girl, Set reminded him. And her own house was in shambles.

Isis enters the throne room and sees a thoughtful Horus. 'Is something awry, your majesty?' She took special care to emphasise his new title.

'Mother, does it occur to you that this was too easy?'

'Let's see,' Isis says. 'First, we ended a lifelong struggle with your uncle. Then, we seized a portal those gods have been fighting over for thousands of years. Perhaps, it seems simple but I would argue that it is the Greeks, the Norse and the Romans who made this all possible.'

'Why was it so easy to turn our backs on The Light?'

'Light. Darkness. What does it matter? Control is what is important. We have it and they do not.'

'Surely, they will attack,' Horus surmises.

'They have no army.'

'The Persians and the Celts are still intact.'

Isis laughs. 'The Persians carry nothing but spears. And I expect Ahura Mazda would seek a truce with us before attacking. And the Celts? They are a drunken lot. They are leaderless, unreliable soldiers. Trust me. Your uncle and I thought this through.'

'The Romans still have much of their army,' Horus says

'Don't worry your head about them. Without Greek leadership, they are not a threat. That reminds me. I have the most interesting news about the Greeks.'

'Tell me, mother.'

'Well, it appears that Poseidon has seized control of Olympus.'

'How do you know this?' Horus wonders.

'Our spies are everywhere. And it seems the transfer of power was a very heated one. The Greeks no longer act as one.'

'Athena,' Horus says.

'And she is angry.'

'So, Zeus is no longer a threat and Odin's best warrior is encased in gold?'

Isis smiles. 'Better yet. His other best warrior is trapped on earth. She cannot return to our realm without your or Set's permission.'

'What should we do then? Sit on our hands and celebrate?'

'There is no reason not to.'

Horus isn't so sure. 'You do not think they will rally their forces? I've always believed the best defense is a good offense.'

'Well, it is time to change your mindset. Our armies may well be invincible. If we are attacked, Set's forces will come to our aid. And when our enemies are defeated, Set will imprison their bodies so that they cannot regenerate. That is if anyone dares to tamper with our supremacy.'

DEITIES

'We will soon outnumber them,' Horus says.

'Yes and I have plans for reinforcements as well. The Mayans and Aztecs owe us greatly. They shall fight on our front lines.'

Set appears through the portal. He embraces his sister and his nephew. 'Have there been any repercussions from our rebellion?'

'None whatsoever,' Isis reports. 'In fact, the Greeks squabble amongst themselves. They pose no threat.' Isis explains Poseidon's coup in Olympus.

'Excellent. Any word from the Norse?'

'Nothing. They are without their two best generals. Freya is trapped on earth.' Isis gestures towards the statue of Tyr. 'And he is encased for our amusement. So, tell me brother, how are things in the Underworld?'

Set laughs. 'The Underworld is getting full. I may need to expand it soon. So many souls, so little ice. Those Frost Giants take up a lot of space.'

'You would think they'd like the ice,' Horus says.

'Not when they cannot move. Trust me, eternal damnation with me is not a pleasant experience.'

'Is this purely a social visit?' Isis asks. 'Or is there more to it?'

'To be honest, the Underworld is a lonely place right now. I have no underlings to torment. I wish that Pluto, Hades and Hel were there.'

'You would only encapsulate them in ice,' Horus says.

Set sighs. 'You're probably right. But I also come to deliver a warning. It is likely that Odin will send a messenger to you.

He will request that you use the portal to bring his gods back to his realm. It is very important that you do not allow him to sway you.'

'I would never engage the portal for such an action without your prior approval,' Horus says. 'Besides, it would only fortify Odin's position.'

'I'm glad you see things as I, nephew. Now, if you do not mind, I should love a beer. The three of us should drink to thousands of years of Egyptian dominance.'

40

Alley Cat

Frankly, Diana is getting a little sick of Freya. The two fought together many times on the Ethereal Plane but never really spent any time together otherwise. Now, Freya acts like a lovesick schoolgirl around the would-be rock star, Apollo. They hold hands and she sneaks kisses when he's not looking. Diana's eyes are frequently mid-roll.

The smitten new lovers walk around the corner following Diana. It's difficult to walk and French-kiss at the same time but certainly not impossible. While Diana keeps marching forward, Freya comes up for air. She sees a familiar face. She sees Coyote.

Coyote lurks behind the dumpster, smoking an American Spirit. It's his third one in fifteen minutes. He is growing antsy.

Freya shakes loose of Apollo's loving grip and charges. Unfortunately, Coyote spies her before she can reach him. She halts about six feet before she arrives as Coyote pulls his firearm.

'You might consider taking a few steps back there, Gorgeous,' Coyote says. 'You have firsthand knowledge of how these weapons perform at long distances. Care to see what happens at point-blank range?'

Freya freezes and slowly walks backward.

'Let me tell you how this is going down,' Coyote explains. 'This can be easy, or it can be difficult. Apollo will die by my hand today. The only question remaining is will there be three dead gods or only one?'

'There will only be one,' Apollo answers. 'For reasons unknown to me, you want me to die. This I can accept. But there is no reason to harm Freya or Diana in the process.'

'I am glad you feel that way, Apollo. I've felt that if circumstances were different; perhaps, we could have been friends.'

'I would hope that my friends would not attempt to have me killed. So, perhaps not.'

Coyote sighs. He addresses Diana and Freya, 'You ladies might want to turn your backs for this. Apollo, I want you on your knees.'

'I think I'll stand,' Apollo replies.

The back door swings open. It is Bacchus. 'Hey Coyote,' he says. 'I was looking for the loo and think I must have gotten turned around.' Then, he sees Apollo and dashes towards him. Coyote realises it's way too crowded and makes a split-second decision to fire upon the god of Music. His bullet lodges firmly in Bacchus' side and passes through into Apollo's torso. Bacchus falls to the ground. The bullet pierced his lung and he is fighting for breath. Apollo bleeds through his hands from his abdomen.

Coyote raises the gun again, this time taking square aim at Apollo's head. He pulls the trigger. A clicking sound occurs.

DEITIES

Coyote's gun, though loaded, as Hades assured him, had but the one bullet in the chamber and none in the clip. Those bastards. Coyote thinks for the briefest of seconds how he's been exploited. But the free-for-all he was hoping to avoid just leaped on his chest in the person of Freya.

Freya is a wildcat. She barrages Coyote with right and left hands. She grabs him by his hair and slams his head to the concrete. Utterly defenseless against the wrath of Freya, Coyote simply curls himself into a ball and withstands the beating the best he can.

Diana focuses on the injuries suffered by Apollo and Bacchus. She is no healing goddess, by any stretch but her police training included some basic first aid training. She hastily removes her blouse, hands it to Apollo and orders him to apply pressure on his wound. From there, she addresses Bacchus. The Wine god's situation is far direr. The bullet essentially exploded when it passed through his body. Diana rolls Bacchus onto his back and engages in mouth-to-mouth but he leaks blood from his chest. She can't keep him breathing and covered at the same time.

Apollo crawls over; removing Diana' blouse from his own wound and covers that of Bacchus. 'Hey, Bacchus,' Apollo says. 'Wake up. My sister is topless.'

Bacchus strains an eye open and coughs. 'Always wanted to see them before I died. You'd never let anyone near her.'

'Well, a god's got to protect his twin. For all I know, you'd try and get her drunk and have sex with her.'

Bacchus smiles. 'You know me well, brother.' He goes sullen. 'Apollo, am I going to die?'

Apollo looks across the injured Bacchus at Diana. She frowns and stares back. Apollo nods. 'I think so, my friend.'

'I had a good life,' Bacchus reflects. 'But not a great one. I was always a merrymaker. Never engaged in wars or celestial politics. Never really did anything of note.'

'Bacchus, you just saved my life. You shall never be forgotten. A truer friend, there never was.'

Bacchus turns to Diana. 'Please reach under my toga. There is something I want you to have.'

Diana flashes a quick glance to Apollo but Apollo nods. She places her hand on Bacchus' leg and slowly moves up. She is in danger of reaching his testicles and hesitates.

'There is a package I need delivered to Olympus. It's just a little higher up my leg near my hip,' Bacchus explains.

Diana finds a small bundle of vine clippings.

'Careful,' Bacchus says. 'Do not damage the grape seeds. When you return to the Heavenly realms, I want you to give these clippings to Dionysus. Tell him they're a gift from his archrival. Tell him to plant them and it will be like no wine he's ever experienced.'

****

The gunshot and ensuing melee draw the attention of Joe's patrons. Most flee out the front door away from the violence. But those from celestial dominions dash toward the sound. Triton and Kyrene reach the back door at the same time as Hades, Hel and Anubis.

As the five of them reach the exit, Triton attempts to block the doorway. 'We cannot go out there,' he insists.

Hades isn't sure he heard this son of Poseidon correctly. 'I

DEITIES

sincerely doubt you are attempting to tell me what I can and cannot do.'

Triton quickly explains Asag and the death of gods. 'When the demon is released, it is our souls he shall seek to further energise himself. He will inhale our essence and grow more and more powerful.'

Hel loves this. 'He sounds exactly like the type of monster the Underworld needs. We shall gladly set him free.'

'No! That would be suicide. He will not recognise you as from The Darkness. He understands only power. He will devour us all.'

'Perhaps, we could train him,' Hel wonders aloud.

While Triton is attempting to engage Hades in desperate conversation, the petite Kyrene slips beneath his arms and forces open the door. In a flash, she dashes through the emergency exit and into the alley. The alarm on the door blares.

****

The first thing Kyrene sees is Freya beating the hell out of Coyote. Freya is now standing over him, kicking him in the stomach and stomping on his ribs. Kyrene hasn't witnessed this level of violence in over a thousand years. She doesn't know Freya personally but certainly knows her by reputation. She thought Coyote was a friend but obviously, Freya feels differently. One thing is clear; Kyrene is not going to intervene.

Diana kneels over a body. At first, Kyrene is distracted because of Diana topless. It's all too much for her, like information overload. Then, she sees the object of her affection – Apollo. He's sitting cross-legged next to the body. She finally recognises the god lying on his back. It's Bacchus and he's barely moving.

Kyrene bypasses Apollo and goes straight to Bacchus' side. Tears stream down her face. Despite her romantic interest in Apollo, she recognises that Bacchus is her best friend. The two had so many wonderful times together and she took him for granted. She falls to the ground and crawls to his side. 'Bacchus?' she asks. 'Bacchus, can you hear me?'

Bacchus slips in and out of consciousness. 'Kyrene,' he mumbles. 'Sorry, you have to see me this way.'

'You're going to be all right,' Kyrene promises. 'We'll go back to the realms and get you put back together.' She cradles his head in her arms. 'Please hang on. A portal will open and we'll celebrate at Heaven's bar.'

Bacchus smiles sadly. 'I may have to take a rain check,' he says.

Kyrene glances at Diana. Diana looks grim.

'You can't die,' Kyrene insists. 'I won't allow it.' She looks at Apollo and begins beating his chest. 'You're a healing god. Heal!'

Apollo shakes his head. 'Kyrene, I'm powerless here. There is nothing I can do.'

'But he's suffering. Surely, someone can do something! Anything!'

A bullet breezes by Apollo's head and lodges squarely in Bacchus' skull. Bacchus dies instantly.

All turn and see Hel standing with a smoking gun. She shrugs. 'He was going to die in agony. I just sped up the process. You should really thank me. He was suffering.'

By now, Coyote is unconscious. Freya, in a combination

DEITIES

of anger and shock, leaps to confront Hel. 'What did you do?' Freya asks.

'I put him down. I know a bit more about death than you,' Hel replies.

'I am going to kill you!' Freya blurts.

Having given up on sealing the exit, Triton steps between the angry Norse goddesses. 'No one else can die or the consequences will be catastrophic.'

Freya grabs Triton by his collar and throws him aside. She stands about an inch away from Hel. 'You know death? Who fought with our warriors? Who led them to Sessrúmnir when they fell in battle?'

'And who took pity on the sick and aged? Bacchus was no warrior. His demise is clearly my domain,' Hel asserts.

'I do not think you realise what is about to happen to you. I will beat you until you beg to die.'

'Let's not forget who holds the weapon, Freya. One move and you join that Wine god in a pool of blood.'

Triton struggles to his feet. 'Goddesses,' he pleads, 'we no longer have the luxury to kill one another. We need to wait until a portal opens. Once we safely return to the Heavenly realms, you can fight to your heart's content.'

Anubis doubles over with laughter. All eyes now focus on him.

'What's so damned funny?' Apollo demands.

'There is but one portal and it is now controlled by Set. The only one of us returning from earth is me.'

'How cute that you think that,' Hades says before driving his switchblade into Anubis' ear.

41

The Beast Unleashed

Far beneath the earth's surface, the great demon, Asag, inhales deeply. The first soul he intakes has a distinct alcoholic quality about it. A few moments later, a rather rancid soul follows. He tugs with all his might at the chains, roaring as he pulls. They snap into pieces. Asag kicks off his leg cuffs as well. For the first time in ten thousand years, he is free.

Asag steps off his throne and stretches his legs. His children, the Rock Demons, hurry to gather around their father. What does this mean? And more importantly, what's next?

Asag paces the great hall and catches the scent of something most delicious. Gods and goddesses on an earthly realm. Their deaths will only serve to increase his strength. He will dominate this new earth as he once did the Sumerian landscape. With his children by his side, he will be unstoppable.

Asag looks to the tremendous ceiling and notices the

DEITIES

slightest of cracks. He begins stamping his foot and the crack grows in size. Soon, the cave crumbles. Boulders come crashing down on Asag and his offspring. These are but a minor inconvenience. The fallen stones rapidly create a mountain. Asag and the Rock Demons scale to its peak.

****

The earth shakes in San Francisco. To its residents, it starts like a minor quake but before long, people are speaking of the Richter scale and taking cover. The mountain crests above the street and the great monster emerges in the Financial District.

Asag emerges from the rubble and looks around. Earth has changed in ten thousand years. But mortals are still mortals and can be consumed in mass quantities. He is confused, yet not shaken, by the cars barreling at him. These horseless chariots stop suddenly in front of him, screeching their brakes and slamming into one another. Asag marvels at the destruction he is causing without even trying to.

The Rock Demons dash through the street ahead of Asag. Finally free, they romp about, smashing glass and terrorising people. Though no more than four feet in height, the Rock Demons are as panic-inducing as their father. The six of them split into groups of twos. They climb the buildings, paying close attention to the gargoyles as if they are long-lost brothers and sisters. The Rock Demons attempt to communicate with these statues but when the gargoyles fail to respond, the Rock Demons topple them from their perches. The sculptures come crashing to the ground, destroying cars and crushing pedestrians in the process.

Petrified citizens place emergency calls from their cell

STUART CLARKE

phones. The 911 operators are swamped. So many calls are placed, cellular towers are overloaded. All circuits are, in fact, busy. Those calls that do get through are initially ignored. Reports of a monster destroying the city seem too derivative of a Godzilla rampage. But the calls keep flooding in with similar descriptions. Authorities are notified.

The first responders shoot first and ask questions later. They fire their assault rifles into the giant beast but this only serves to enrage him. The police conceal themselves behind the open doors of their vehicles and continue to fire their weapons. But soon the beast is coming right for them. Asag lifts one of the cars above his head and hurls it at another one. The officers are brave but it is clear they are not stupid. They retreat from the monster, shooting as they run for cover.

Asag roars, making the buildings shake. There are too many mortals to worry about. He senses the existence of other gods and must find them. He craves their power. He detects them nearby and directs himself in their direction. With each giant step, he crushes an automobile or a civilian. And with each giant step, their scent becomes stronger.

****

The sounds of crumbling buildings are not lost on the gods. Neither is the fact that the reverberations are growing closer.

Diana turns to Triton. 'I take it this is the monster you warned us about.'

Triton doesn't answer. He doesn't have to.

Kyrene is very upset. 'What are we going to do? Should we flee?'

All are silent until Apollo speaks. 'We do not flee,' he says.

DEITIES

'We fight.'

These words seem strange stemming from Apollo's mouth. 'I don't think you understand the gravity of the situation,' Triton says. 'That monster will only grow stronger as we die. There is no way to defeat him.'

'I disagree,' Apollo says and motions towards Diana and Freya. 'We have two of the greatest warriors The Light has ever seen. Diana grew up fighting Titans while Freya was slaying Frost Giants.' He looks to Hades and Hel. 'The strongest of The Darkness are among us as well. Working together, we can defeat this demon.'

Triton looks unsure. 'I am no fighter,' he says. 'And neither are you.'

'I was and I will be again.'

Coyote is regaining consciousness. Freya sees this and goes to kick him again.

'Wait!' Apollo calls. 'We're going to need all the help we can get.'

Freya looks disappointed. She feigns another kick, causing Coyote to flinch. 'You're lucky,' she says to the Native-American trickster.

Coyote nods and struggles to his feet. 'Why do we not simply let this beast destroy the city? I have no love for the inhabitants here.

'Because he will hunt us regardless. The death toll among humans will be in the thousands while he searches for us.'

Coyote asks pointed questions. 'Since when do you, Apollo, care for humanity? Were you not the one who showed utter disdain towards them?'

'These are not the same people who cast us aside. They had nothing to do with dismissing us from their beliefs,' Apollo answers. 'And besides, they're kind of growing on me.'

Hel takes a step forward. 'We have a lot of generals in our midst and very few warriors. If we are to develop a plan of attack, we'd best do it quickly. The very ground shakes beneath our feet.'

'Triton,' Freya says. 'Where was this beast before he was set free?'

'He was chained to a throne in another realm. Far beneath the earth's crust.'

'I take that as a good sign that he's been captured before. And my assumption is if we are mortal, then so is he.'

'An ancient Sumerian deity named Ninurta once defeated him. But he was immortal. We are not,' Triton explains.

Diana stands but a few inches from Triton's face. 'This is your entire fault. I'd suggest you start coming up with solutions rather than excuses.'

Triton is shaken. 'I wouldn't have the foggiest idea on how to stop him.'

The first two Rock Demons bounce onto the scene. They are the smallest of them, barely taller than Kyrene. 'They're so cute!' she exclaims.

However, they don't act so cute. They climb Joe's Dive Bar and punch holes into the walls and rooftop. Bricks and shingles are tossed haphazardly into the air. A large piece of cinderblock lands in front of Coyote.

'Triton, who the hell are they?'

'Those,' Triton answers, 'would be the Rock Demons. They

DEITIES

are Asag's offspring.'

Freya studies them. They are essentially animated stones. How to kill a rock, she wonders. Surely, there must be a way.

Hades drops his bag of weapons and opens it. He passes firearms out to all gods, be them from The Light or The Darkness. He's one gun short, however. 'Sorry, Apollo. I've got nothing for you. Best of luck.'

Apollo nods. 'I'll take care of myself.'

The four remaining Rock Demons arrive. They are equally as destructive on the nearby buildings. But soon, they stop inflicting their might on inanimate objects and stare to the gods before them.

Freya fires first. She shoots a Rock Demon squarely in the chest. The bullet ricochets through the glass of a nearby sporting goods store. The Rock Demon looks down at its chest. There is the faintest hint of a crack. It becomes enraged and leaps in front of Freya. The Rock Demon rushes the Norse goddess but Freya sidesteps it and the demon crashes into a concrete wall. It is momentarily dazed but quickly regains its senses. The Rock Demon growls at Freya and sprints towards her. Again, Freya is able to make the demon miss but apparently, Rock Demons do not tire easily. Freya knows she will be crushed as soon as the demon makes contact with her. All she can do is continue dodging.

****

The footsteps grow closer. The streetlight bulbs burst, spattering broken glass onto the street below. Asag is now within view. The great Sumerian demon now sees the gods he craves. He roars and all take notice.

Asag's enormous head now peers over the streetlights. He's made visual contacts with his prey and his offspring. Asag doesn't really have a concept of the word 'fun' but he senses he will enjoy causing these gods' demise.

Asag moves into the alley. The gods are not fleeing like he'd expected them to. In fact, they are standing in a semi-circle waiting to engage him. Naturally, he doesn't recognise most of them – he's been trapped below the earth so long, he missed witnessing their heydays. He sniffs the air, though and picks up Triton's scent. This god helped him. Perhaps, he would be spared.

The Rock Demons move behind their father. This is his battle. They could easily crush the mortal gods before them but choose not to. One Rock Demon, however, is reluctant to part ways with Freya. She has embarrassed him repeatedly and he wants satisfaction. It charges her a final time but she leaps over it. He crashes into the wall with a thud.

Asag is clearly displeased with this Rock Demon. No one will touch the gods but him. He looks over the gods and notices that Kyrene, the Forest Nymph and Coyote, the Native-American, are of a different ilk. They will not serve his purpose well. He speaks telepathically to Triton. 'You and those two may leave.'

Triton does not need to hear it twice. 'Come Coyote. Come Kyrene. We are being set free.'

Kyrene refuses to depart. 'I shall stand and fight with my brethren,' she says.

'Have it your way. Coyote, it is time for us to depart.'

Coyote is surprised how easy it is to simply walk past Asag.

DEITIES

The Rock Demons even let them pass. It all seems too simple and frankly, too wrong. 'We need to help,' Coyote whispers to Triton.

'There is nothing we can do,' Triton responds. 'They are all going to die.'

****

Hel loves the gun she has kept for herself. It even produces a red dot when she aims. Her trigger finger is itchy and she fires the first bullet into Asag's chest. The great demon growls at her. He shoves the other gods out of the way and attacks her first. She leaps from his oncoming hands but his wings swat her to the ground. Hades fires a shot into his leg. Asag turns on him quickly and attempts to behead Hades with his massive teeth. Apollo sprints in and knocks Hades from harm's way. Asag's massive mouth closes on nothing but air.

Apollo is unarmed, so when Asag reaches for him, all he can do is retreat. Fortunately, Freya and Diana fire several bullets into Asag's side, distracting the monster. He lets Apollo go for the moment and chases after Diana, pinning her against a wall. Freya reacts quickly. She charges shoulder first into one of Asag's open wounds. Freya bounces back hard from the demon's rough skin but mission accomplished. He switches focus from Diana to her.

****

The Rock Demons mumble amongst themselves. Could it be their father could use their help? They assemble into a battle formation, intent on charging in to aid in their father's destruction of these pitiful gods.

Coyote grabs Triton by the arm. 'I have the most delicious

idea,' he says. Coyote grabs Triton's weapon and begins discharging it into the crowd of Rock Demons.

The Rock Demons take pause. Their stone skin shows the slightest of cracks. They look to each other and make an impulsive decision. They will kill Triton and Coyote. They drop to all fours and launch an attack on the two.

Triton shakes. 'Okay, so now what?'

'Oh, we run,' Coyote answers. 'And I hope I run faster than you.'

The Rock Demons nip at the heels of Coyote and Triton. 'Where are we going?'

Coyote is already panting. 'The Marina.'

The San Francisco hills take their toll on the body of Triton. Coyote is accustomed to running up mini-mountains such as these. However, the Rock Demons lose ground going up the hills but gain momentum going down. After what seems like ages, they reach the water.

'So, now we swim away?' Triton asks.

'Exactly. You're a strong swimmer from what I hear. And I'll get by.'

The Rock Demons are closing fast. 'They'll just follow us in,' Triton says.

'And they're made of rock. I suspect they'll sink.'

Coyote dives off the dock into the cold sea. Triton follows, hitting the water just before the Rock Demons grasp him. In one furious wave, the Rock Demons hurl themselves into the sea and fall straight to the bottom.

Coyote dog paddles back to the shore and calls to Triton. 'While you're out there, see how our friends are doing.'

DEITIES

Triton submerges. He can see the Rock Demons crawling on the floor of the bay. But one-by-one, they stop moving. He cautiously swims down to one of them and pokes at it. It doesn't move. He presses harder and, still, nothing. He smiles when he resurfaces. 'How did you know that would work?' he asks Coyote.

'I didn't. But it was the best idea I had at the time.'

Triton flaps his tail a few times and swims back to the coastline. 'Thank you,' he says. 'You've saved countless lives of the humans.'

Coyote smirks. 'You could repay me with the money you promised me.'

Triton considers this. 'That, Coyote, will not be a problem.'

****

Freya is pinned to the ground with Asag's claws buried deep into her shoulders. The monster's great mouth is open with saliva running down his hungry lips. Just as he is ready to bite, Apollo jumps the monster and grabs him around the throat. It causes just enough of a distraction for Freya to escape. Apollo punches Asag repeatedly in the Adam's apple but this only serves to anger Asag further. He flips Apollo off like a bug and the god of Music lands hard on his back.

Hel and Hades open fire on Asag but their bullets have little effect. Diana does the same, except she shoots for an ankle. This injures Asag. Diana shoots the other ankle and the beast falls to its knees.

Freya retrieves her firearm and empties her clip into Asag but he shows no pain as he scrambles to his feet. Hel and Hades rain bullets into him until, they too, are without ammunition.

Sensing an advantage, he turns his assault on Diana as she is the only one left with a weapon. He slaps it from her hand and prepares to devour her.

Apollo hurls a trash can lid, catching Asag in the jaw. The beast pushes Diana to the ground and begins tracking Apollo. Apollo crawls quickly atop a dumpster.

'Kyrene!' Apollo shouts. 'I need you to do something. That building behind you with the broken glass. Go fetch me a bow.'

Kyrene disappears into the building just as Asag lowers his fists on the dumpster destroying the steel in the process. However, Apollo sees this coming and leaps to the ground.

Hel and Hades hurl rocks and concrete fragments at Asag. Freya is severely injured and holds herself up against a wall. Diana does her best to protect Freya but by her count, she has one, maybe two, bullets left.

Asag booms a triumphant roar. He's a little confused, though. He doesn't know who to kill first. But he focuses on Apollo. The god who was supposed to die. He swipes at him but Apollo narrowly sidesteps him. Asag shrugs off Diana' remaining two bullets lodged in his back and continues his pursuit of Apollo. Soon, Apollo is backed into a corner. An evil grin crosses the lips of the Sumerian demon. He reaches for Apollo and holds him high above his twenty-foot frame. Asag toys with Apollo, hurling him against the wall.

Kyrene emerges from the sporting goods store with a hunting bow and a small quiver of arrows. She temporarily freezes as she watches the monster beat Apollo mercilessly.

Apollo locks eyes with the Forest Nymph. He needs that

DEITIES

bow and needs it now. Asag fists descend but Apollo darts between the demon's legs. 'Kyrene!' Apollo shouts. 'Toss me that bow!'

She flings it and he catches it with one hand. The arrows he catches with the other. He readies his aim and lets an arrow fly. It misses. And misses badly.

'Come on, Apollo! You can do this,' Diana calls.

Apollo pulls back the string again and manages to nick Asag on the shoulder.

'Some god of archery, you are,' Hades grumbles.

Apollo ignores his uncle and prepares another arrow. Now Asag is charging towards him. This arrow finds its mark, deep in the demon's chest. But now, Asag is upon him and swats the bow from his hands.

Asag roars, intending to finish Apollo off but Hel leaps upon Asag's back. She only stays on for a few seconds while Asag shakes her but her interference gives Apollo a second chance.

Apollo glances to Diana, who reads her twin's intentions. She lifts a heavy piece of concrete and tosses it to Apollo. When Asag turns back to Apollo, he slams the hardened material into the back of the arrow, driving it deeper into his skin and into his heart. The earth shakes when Asag falls to his knees. It shakes again when he lands face forward on the ground. The arrow's tip has pierced through his entire body and is visible through his back.

'Nothing like making sure,' Hades says. He retrieves the bow and remaining arrow and hands it to Apollo. 'Now, nephew, put one in his brain.'

Apollo does as instructed. He stands upon Asag's neck and fires the last arrow through the back of the monster's head.

Asag cannot reach the arrow. He flaps his wings and the wind he creates knocks the gods down. But black bile seeps from his head wound.

Freya climbs the dumpster and leaps on Asag. She drives her foot into the arrow, lodging it deeper into the demon's brain.

Gingerly, Hel and Diana approach the monster. They kick him and he does not respond.

Apollo smirks. 'The Light and The Darkness make quite the formidable team.'

Triton and Coyote come rushing back to the scene.

'Bravo, Apollo,' Coyote says. 'I always liked you.'

'And I, you. Except when you killed Bacchus. You lost some points there.'

Coyote sweats.

Hel speaks up. 'But he came through in the end.' She pauses. 'Freya, when we return to the Heavens, see that Valhalla welcomes him with open arms.'

42

The Mountain Top

Athena has never experienced a bitter wind like she's withstanding. The higher she climbs, the worse it gets. Occasionally, an animal peeks its head from beyond the scattered trees. Athena doesn't know these animals. The stag she recognises. And the massive doe. But there were others. Some kind of large ferret-looking animal. But with ferocious teeth and fierce claws.

Naturally, Athena was not afraid of any animal. She had fought beasts many times her size and always come out the victor. However, she always knew her advisories. This was a new creature. Did it have powers? Would it halt her before she reached her goal?

'That is but a wolverine,' Odin says. 'They are nasty for sure but have no qualms with gods such as we. They will lie down and we shall continue our journey.'

Athena could not help but have reservations. Monsters always guarded the gates. She was, perhaps, the least welcome goddess ever to trek this mountain. She had slain many a Frost Giant, some high in rank; some not so much. But it made little difference in her eyes. She was an enemy. She was the enemy. And she must be extinguished.

It isn't snow anymore. It's hail. Her helmet protects the top of her head, yet her face feels the icy sting of hard sleet. Athena shields her eyes and stares at the mountain's summit. It appears to be miles away. She turns back to the aged Odin. He knows this trek. His glance tells her that she has many steps she must complete until the journey is complete. She trudges on.

Odin is an old god and moves like one. He cannot maintain the pace that Athena is sustaining. Yet, he knows her pace is not a realistic one. This hike will take several days and she wants to be there as quickly as her legs will carry her. However, they would be stopping for rest soon, despite her tenacity. Her breath is that of a pant. She has little energy left inside her. He is tempted to let her power along but the larger goal is at stake.

'We shall stop here,' Odin commands. 'The Frost Giants will observe our presence within hours. They shall come to us.'

'Best we find them first,' Athena insists.

'Best not. We must neither be tired nor dizzy when they descend the mountain.'

Athena considers this. Surely, a battle would ensue. In her current state, she was not able to defend herself, much less an elderly god. Prisoners, they would become. Athena reluctantly agrees to sit.

Odin lights a fire utilising a few sticks from nearby bushes. He scrapes the sticks together and within seconds, a small flame emerges. Athena is mesmerised. 'I have seen this magic performed before but never in such wind has Hephaestus created such a blaze.'

Odin shrugs. 'It's all about climate and altitude.'

Athena looks around. She spies several caribou and deer. 'Should we eat?'

Odin shakes his head. 'These animals do not belong to us. Tomorrow, we shall ascend the peak. There, we shall be fed. Or slain. We shall see.'

Athena looks to the frosty ground. 'If we do not have nourishment, how shall we fight?'

'If we fight, we shall lose.'

Grudgingly, Athena agrees. She lies on the ground, resting her head on her battle helmet. Her stomach rumbles. She attempts to sleep but a full mind and an empty stomach make it difficult.

'Rest, Athena,' Odin advises. 'In the morning, you shall need your wits about you.'

Athena closes her eyes. But she is still alert to the sounds around her. She snaps herself to vigilance but sees nothing. It is the wind, she assures herself. Nothing but the wind.

Odin knows better. He knows they are being observed closely. He can hear their deep breaths despite the biting gusts. Yet, they are safe for the night. Tomorrow would be a different story.

****

The stronghold of the Frost Giants is Utgard and there Skrymir learns of Odin's ascent into his sacred territory. He holds no love for Odin and his strength and deceitfulness are unmatched amongst his kind. He could easily crush these trespassers but his curiosity intrigues him. Why would Odin approach him without an army? It could be a trap but still, there are only two travellers and only one is armed.

Skrymir, with Lieutenants at his side, thunder down the mountain to greet their unwanted guests. He looks directly at Athena. 'Your bow.'

Athena stares back. 'I don't think so.'

Odin nudges her. 'Pass your bow over. We come on a mission of peace.'

Reluctantly, she hands over her bow and shield to one of the Lieutenants.

Skrymir laughs. 'The quiver.'

Athena sighs. Over goes the quiver. She feels defenseless.

Skrymir towers over her. 'I won't crush you, Goddess. Not unless you give me a reason to change my mind.'

'I can assure you it will not come to that,' Odin assures. 'We come seeking wisdom and guidance. Our ranks are thin, as are yours. The Egyptians blindsided both The Darkness and The Light. Our casualties are tremendous. You, no doubt, find yourself in a similar circumstance.'

'Our seers witnessed the battle,' Skymir responds. 'My one question is, why was this little Princess spared?'

'I was spared to deliver the news to all gods and goddesses in this realm. Odin suggested we come to you. We need to form an alliance,' Athena replies.

Skymir scoffs. 'An uneasy alliance, that would be at best.'

'Perhaps. But a necessity,' Athena counters.

Skrymir looks to Odin. 'Does she ever shut up?'

Athena glares but hushes.

DEITIES

Odin smirks. 'Rarely, it seems, my giant friend. But she speaks the truth. We need you and you need us as well.'

Skrymir doesn't respond immediately. 'In what way do we need your help?'

'Imagine Horus or Set invading Utgard. You would be powerless to prevent an attack.'

'Ha! We would crush them before they got to the mountaintop.'

'No,' Odin reminds. 'They control the portal. They could have an army here within seconds. No offense but you would be totally unprepared for such an onslaught.'

Skrymir considers this. 'What is it you propose?'

'Some of the best warriors of The Darkness and The Light are trapped on Earth. We shall require them if we are to do battle with the Egyptians.'

'And you come to me why?'

'It is storied that you have a portal of your own; however, you need assistance with its functionality. I can provide that.'

'Hmm. Who do you wish to recall?'

Odin's eyes lighten. He is getting through to his once enemy. 'Hel and Hades to start.'

'I can agree to that. Allow me to show you to our portal.'

The Utgard Eternus sits high above the clouds upon frozen blocks of ice. Several of Skrymir's attendants guard it and they snap to attention when they realise Odin is in their midst. One makes a charge at the Norse god of The Light but is manhandled to the ground efficiently by Skrymir.

'There is no need to attack,' Skrymir insists. 'But that could change in an instant. Remain vigilant.'

STUART CLARKE

The Frost Giants eye Athena with suspicion. Or more accurately, with lust. They have never encountered a goddess like she. She steps behind Odin.

Skrymir shows Odin the Utgard Eternus. 'I have tried for thousands of years to activate this portal. In fairness to you, that is a good thing. Else Valhalla would be but a wasteland.'

Odin nods. He examines the portal. On the face, it looks much like the Spheri Eternus; however, Odin tries and cannot activate it. 'Skrymir, when did this come into your possession?'

'It was discovered within the bones of Ymir. You may recall him. You slew him.'

'Yes,' Odin said. 'But that was many, many centuries ago. Now we must fight as one.'

Athena peers at the portal. 'What are the scrawlings along the sides of the portal?'

Skrymir smirks. 'An ancient Norse dialect. One I suspect the Princess goddesses are not familiar with.'

'It is one I cannot read either,' Odin admits. 'This language has long past its relevance. I'm afraid I, too, am at a loss. Thank you for your time, Skrymir. We must find another way to help each other.'

'Wait,' Athena says. 'The scrawlings match on one half of the portal but not the other half.'

Skrymir is irate. 'Believe it or not, Princess, I've noticed that as well.'

'Can someone turn it over?' Athena asks.

'I don't know what you're trying to prove.'

'Please,' Athena begs.

Skrymir looks to Odin. Odin nods.

DEITIES

With his tremendous strength, Skrymir flips it. What he sees amazes him. 'The scrawlings. They are mirror images of the front side. But how can we properly align them?'

Odin shrugs. He doesn't know.

'Princess, any thoughts?'

'Just one. We break it in half.'

Murmurs surround her. That statement makes everyone nervous.

'We do what, Princess?'

'We break it. Carefully, mind you. And we align the scrawlings on the front with those on the back.'

Odin feels the need to intervene. 'Of course, we're not going to br...'

Skrymir interrupts. 'Yes, we are. This makes sense. And if it does not work, then we are no worse than we are now.'

Athena smiles as Skrymir gently cracks the portal. He sets the pieces on the ground and turns one over. It's a match.

****

Hel and Hades sit with their newfound allies, Apollo, Freya, Diana, Coyote and Kyrene. Just as Hel is about to drink another beer, she vanishes. The same happens to Hades.

'Oh, crap,' Apollo says. 'Not this again.'

****

Hel and Hades receive warm welcomes from Skrymir and the other Frost Giants. They are surprised to see Odin and Athena.

'Finally come to your senses, Athena? Joining The Darkness?' Hades asks.

'Not exactly,' she replies.

Skrymir turns to Odin. 'You mentioned other gods?'

'Yes. Apollo, then Artemis, followed by Bacchus and Kyrene.'

The portal works its magic. Apollo and Artemis are immediately on guard as they take in their surroundings. Kyrene starts ice-skating barefoot.

'Where is Bacchus?' Athena asks suddenly concerned.

Apollo looks sullen. 'He saved my life but his wounds were fatal.'

Athena cries at the news. Apollo joins her in tears.

Skrymir has little patience for the emotional outburst. He looks at Odin. 'Anybody else?'

Odin looks to Athena for guidance.

'Bring back, Freya,' Athena blurts out.

Skrymir becomes furious. 'I will do no such thing. She has killed more of my brothers and sisters than I can even fathom. She will not be joining this alliance.'

Odin soothes. 'But she'll be fighting alongside you now. You know how vicious she can be.'

'As you wish but once this so-called alliance reaches its end, her head will be mounted on my wall.'

Odin looks down at the portal. 'I detect another god on earth. Who is it?'

Athena answers. 'It's Triton. He's behind this entire debacle. He stays put. He's leverage if Poseidon tries anything malicious.

Kyrene pops her hand up. 'Ooh! Bring Coyote! He was a big help and he's kinda cute. In a sleazy sort of way.'

'So be it,' Skrymir says and up pops Coyote. He clearly isn't happy with the weather.

DEITIES

Coyote frowns. 'Hel, where the hell am I?'

'Jotunheim. Utgard, to be exact.'

'Thanks, Hel. That cleared up a lot.'

'How is it we're suddenly surrounded by Frost Giants and still alive?' Apollo asks.

Athena regales the story to the group.

'That sounds really bad and really dangerous. Best you beam me back to earth,' Coyote says.

Kyrene bounces over and kisses him.

Coyote blushes. 'I guess I could stick around a little while.'

Athena interrupts. 'We're going to need a rock-solid plan. Coyote is right. This is really dangerous.'

Apollo grins. 'We should plan this out at the hotel bar in Heaven.'

Athena stares at him in disbelief.

'Only joking, Sis.'

Still, Skrymir produces a large bottle. 'We shall drink to old enemies becoming new friends.' He stares at Freya. 'We are friends, correct?'

'It would appear that circumstances have made it so,' Freya replies.

Goblets are passed around and Apollo whispers to Freya. 'Do I really have to drink mead?'

'I'd do it. Unless you want a really angry Frost Giant on your hands.'

Apollo shrugs. He figures the quicker he drinks it, the less taste he would have to endure. He stares into the wooden cup, takes a breath and downs it in a single gulp. He winces as it goes down. 'Not bad,' he manages.

Skrymir smiles. 'It seems you like it.' He refills Apollo's cup.

Apollo forces a smile. 'Thank you.'

Skrymir turns to Odin. 'I have grave concerns. We are but a small cadre fighting a powerful Egyptian army. They have the soldiers. Mathematically, this battle is unwinnable.'

Odin nods. 'We recruit from the outer realms. They can be convinced to join our ranks.'

Skrymir stares at Odin. 'Those realms have limited resources and their gods have little battle expertise. Even their weapons are substandard.'

'Hephaestus will fashion powerful weapons,' Athena says. 'They shall be well-armed.'

Skrymir thinks. 'Again, we are vastly outnumbered.'

'I have thought of that as well. I know where we can get reinforcements. It will be a hard sell but one that I believe may be accomplished.'

'And where will you find these reinforcements?'

Athena takes a deep breath. Athena sighs. 'Tartarus.'

Hades looks at Athena like she's crazy. 'You wish to enlist the Titans? You do realise they are imprisoned in the deepest part of the Underworld? And that we are the ones that put them there?'

'One does not forget the brutality of the battles at Thessaly. Our only hope is that time has lessened their anger.'

'You'd be ripe for capture by Set. And need I remind you, the Titans absolutely hate us.'

'I do not believe that Set knows of the Utgard Eternus. I shall arrive undetected and state my case. If they are amenable, then we have twelve very powerful allies.'

DEITIES

Artemis shakes her head. 'They are guarded by the Hecatonchires, the hundred-handed monsters. How do you propose you get past them?'

Coyote pipes up, 'Leave that to me. I can guarantee passage. This Trickster spirit knows many tricks.'

Athena smiles.

'You two shall not go alone,' Apollo says. 'Freya and I will accompany you.'

'As will I,' Skrymir insists. 'The Titans are of The Darkness. Their ears would be less deaf coming from me. And you may require some muscle just incase these guards of which you speak confront you.' Skrymir looks to Odin. 'If this is a ploy, my lieutenants will ensure you and the others beg for death.'

'It is no ploy,' Odin says. 'Let us prepare the portal. And pray for the best.'

Acknowledgements

I wish to thank Lee for always believing

And Kevin and the entire Crystal Peake family for embarking on this journey with me.

Made in the USA
Columbia, SC
06 April 2022